ALL THE FEAR OF THE FAIR

ALL THE FEAR OF THE FAIR

Uncanny Tales of Circus and Sideshow

Edited by

EDWARD PARNELL

BRITISH LIBRARY

This collection first published in 2025 by
The British Library
96 Euston Road
London NW1 2DB
bl.uk

1 3 5 7 9 10 8 6 4 2

Represented in the EU by Authorised Rep Compliance Ltd., Ground Floor,
71 Lower Baggot Street, Dublin, D02 P593, Ireland. arccompliance.com

Cataloguing in Publication Data
A catalogue record for this publication is available from the British Library

ISBN 978 0 7123 5509 4
e-ISBN 978 0 7123 6205 4

Frontispiece illustration by Sandra Gómez.
Illustration on page 288 from *The Circus Book*, published by George
Routledge & Sons (1890). British Library shelfmark 12807.s.62.
Cover design by Mauricio Villamayor with illustration by Sandra Gómez.
Text design and typesetting by Tetragon, London
Printed in England by CPI Group (UK) Ltd, Croydon, CR0 4YY

MIX
Paper | Supporting
responsible forestry
FSC® C013604

CONTENTS

INTRODUCTION

Circuses, carnivals and fairgrounds are exotic, fleeting spaces. They arrive seemingly out of nowhere, occupying a strip of waste ground at the edge of a town for a few summer nights, before departing as quickly as they appeared. There's danger and a hint of violence in these garishly lit corners too—the thrill of attractions that can send you spinning to the heavens, or plunge you into darkness, all accompanied by the sickly, intoxicating taste of candyfloss. Just occasionally, we remember as we wait in line, there have been rides that have gone wrong, stranding their occupants for hours, or worse, injuring them horribly. But that can't possibly happen to us—*can it?*—we tell ourselves, doubt worming its way into our heads as we sit contemplating the death-defying drop from the rollercoaster's rickety zenith. We know, too, that the odds are loaded against us on the challenges and games we hand over our money to attempt. That the cheap giant teddy bear we hope to win with the throw of an undersized hoop is almost certainly unobtainable, or that the miracle product a silver-tongued salesman is peddling will never, in reality, live up to its promise. It doesn't matter, we're far too clever to fall for such patter, we're one step ahead of the hucksters—even though our very presence and the emptiness of our wallets at the end of the evening suggests otherwise...

For one night only, this is the world you're invited to enter. A world that transgresses societal norms, drawing on our willingness to be lured towards the novel and the sleazy, the desire to step outside our regular bounds and experience a glimpse of the *other*: those we might consider beyond "polite" society. It's a peek into a way of life that feels increasingly anachronistic when viewed through our twenty-first-century eyes.

Many of these tales, with their depictions of so-called "freaks", as well as some of the outdated attitudes on display towards other marginalised groups, are problematic, though I've favoured ones in which the underdogs—those who are being exploited—get to have the last laugh. In several of the narratives, however, no one emerges positively, the only winner being the darkness so often inherent at the heart of human nature.

Of course, as the evocative work of Ray Bradbury demonstrates, fairgrounds and circuses are especially enticing to children—and those things we're drawn to at a formative age frequently seem to exert a beguiling hold throughout our lives. Alongside fondly remembered visits to funfairs and arcades in my youth, my interest in this particular horror niche stemmed from seeing films like the trashily enjoyable *Vampire Circus* (1972) at almost certainly too young an age, before graduating to cinematic classics such as the German Expressionist silent film *The Cabinet of Dr. Caligari* (1920) and the starkly haunting *Carnival of Souls* (1962); later, while at university, I also have a vivid memory of watching "Humbug" from the second season of *The X Files* (1995), in which various performers from the Jim Rose Circus featured in the episode's exploration of otherness, something that seemed quite groundbreaking at the time.

Given this significant role carnivals and fairgrounds have played as spaces conducive to the strange, supernatural and horrific on the large and small screens, is the same true of weird and eerie works of short fiction? The answer, as this collection hopefully shows, is that a noteworthy body of shorter work does indeed exist. In addition to enjoying the inherent craft and good storytelling of these tales, by collecting them together the reader can more clearly see how they act as a mirror—albeit one of those distorted funfair ones. They reflect changing societal ways of thinking and behaviours, and give us a snapshot of the past, including various now uncomfortable-seeming attitudes that were popularly acceptable in previous, though sometimes not-so-distant, decades.

Alongside tales that spotlight sideshows and circuses, I've also included several that feature performers drawn from an adjacent, very similar world—albeit one that inhabits a more recognisably British cultural and entertainment landscape than that cinema-centric realm of travelling carnivals: a haunted Punch and Judy man, a couple of confused low-rent conjurers, a troubled ventriloquist, and a most mysterious puppet show. All, however, possess that same *Cabinet of Dr. Caligari* atmosphere in which life itself feels like an off-kilter fairground ride.

Roll up, roll up! And enter if you dare...

EDWARD PARNELL

FURTHER READING

I hope you enjoy this anthology of sixteen circus, carnival and showmen tales that I've chosen. They take us from the middle of the nineteenth century up to the end of the 1960s. And if this small selection whets your appetite for additional chills, here's a short list of similarly themed stories that can be found in other titles from the Tales of the Weird series. (There are also some suggestions included among the individual story headnotes.)

"The Story of a Disappearance and an Appearance" (1913) by M. R. James. In *Spirits of the Season: Christmas Hauntings* (2018).
Strange country goings on involving a Punch and Judy show.

"Unseen—Unfeared" (1919) by Francis Stevens. In *The Night Wire and Other Tales of Weird Media* (2022).
A classic of weird fiction, featuring the oddest of backstreet sideshows.

"The Loves of Lady Purple" (1974) by Angela Carter. In *Deadly Dolls: Midnight Tales of Uncanny Playthings* (2024).
A most deadly and desirous puppet show.

"The Companion" (1976) by Ramsey Campbell. In *The Platform Edge: Uncanny Tales of the Railways* (2019).
Terrors abound aboard the Ghost Train at an abandoned funfair.

Novels

A brief, and by no means exhaustive, list of longer twentieth-century fictional works on our theme which are also well worth reading.

The Circus of Dr. Lao (1935) by Charles G. Finney.
Nightmare Alley (1946) by William Lindsay Gresham.
Something Wicked This Way Comes (1962) by Ray Bradbury.
Nights at the Circus (1984) by Angela Carter.
It (1986) by Stephen King.
Geek Love (1989) by Katherine Dunn.

ACKNOWLEDGEMENTS

Many thanks to the following: Mike Ashley for advice on possible story sources; Richard Davy, for providing biographical and bibliographical information about his father Charles; Paul Duncan, for sharing his extremely helpful research into the connection between Gerald Kersh's short story and the film *Dead of Night*; Johnny Mains, for his generous assistance with providing facts about the life of Tod Robbins (and Tod Browning), as well as delving into the mystery of "Simplex"; Rosemary Pardoe, for an interesting conversation about the connection between Frederick Cowles and M. R. James; Ray Russell and Mark Valentine for kindly sharing contacts and material; and to Paul Willetts, for introducing me to "The Extraordinarily Horrible Dummy" way back when.

Finally, and most importantly, to the team at the British Library—with a special thanks to Jonny Davidson—for all their hard work in getting behind the idea and putting together *All the Fear of the Fair*.

A NOTE FROM THE PUBLISHER

The original short stories reprinted in the British Library Tales of the Weird series were written and published in a period ranging across the nineteenth and twentieth centuries. There are many elements of these stories which continue to entertain modern readers; however, in some cases there are also uses of language, instances of stereotyping and some attitudes expressed by narrators or characters which may not be endorsed by the publishing standards of today. We acknowledge therefore that some elements in the stories selected for reprinting may continue to make uncomfortable reading for some of our audience. With this series British Library Publishing aims to offer a new readership a chance to read some of the rare material of the British Library's collections in an affordable paperback format, to enjoy their merits and to look back into the worlds of the past two centuries as portrayed by their writers. It is not possible to separate these stories from the history of their writing and therefore the following stories are presented as they were originally published with two edits to the text and minor edits made for consistency of style and sense. We welcome feedback from our readers, which can be sent to the following address:

British Library Publishing
The British Library
96 Euston Road
London, NW1 2DB
United Kingdom

1849

HOP-FROG

Edgar Allan Poe

Little introduction is needed for the Gothic poetry and fiction of the nineteenth-century New England writer Edgar Allan Poe (1809–1849), whose unsettling, genre-defining tales of mystery and imagination such as "The Fall of the House of Usher" continue to find new audiences today through numerous film and television reworkings. "Hop-Frog" is one of Poe's lesser-known works, though readers familiar with Roger Corman's 1964 adaptation of *The Masque of the Red Death* will recognise the incorporation of elements of "Hop-Frog" into that masterful movie.

Although the events of the story do not take place in a circus, I include the tale here as a possible early model for the "killer" or "evil clown". Old short stories featuring evil clowns proved remarkably elusive when I was putting together this collection and it seems like the trope is a relatively recent literary/filmic invention, perhaps popularised by Stephen King's 1986 novel *It* (and, in particular, Tim Curry's memorable portrayal of Pennywise the Clown in the 1990 TV movie), and fuelled by the American serial killer John Wayne Gacy, who performed as Pogo the Clown in the late 1970s. And, of course, there are earlier popular culture characters, like The Joker from the Batman comics (who first appeared in 1940), as well as understandable psychological reasons why we might find the heavily disguised/made-up appearance of clowns unsettling. There are earlier similar figures too, such as here in "Hop-Frog", where instead of a clown we have a short-statured court "fool" or jester, who is waiting for the perfect moment to avenge himself (and his confidante Trippetta) after both have suffered poor treatment at the hands of the king.

"Hop-Frog" was written in February 1849, a little under eight months before Poe's death from unknown causes. It was first published a month later in a Boston weekly newspaper called *The Flag of Our Union*—"not a *very* respectable journal, perhaps, in a literary point of view, but one that pays as high prices as most of the Magazines", Poe wrote to a friend.

The theme of vengeance portrayed in the story shares parallels with a couple of dubious historical models, including an incident (the "Bal des Ardents") said to have taken place during the reign of Charles VI of France in 1393; or another, in the life of the perhaps-apocryphal, fifteenth-century English court jester, John Scoggin—a mysterious figure who takes up a ghostly residence at the heart of the Nicola Barker's 2007 novel *Darkmans*.

Other theories postulate that in "Hop-Frog", Poe is taking literary revenge against the poet Elizabeth Ellet, who was involved in a convoluted letter-writing scandal with Poe and later spread damaging gossip about him; if there is any substance to this then Ellet, presumably, is represented in the story by the unfortunate king.

I never knew any one so keenly alive to a joke as the king was. He seemed to live only for joking. To tell a good story of the joke kind, and to tell it well, was the surest road to his favour. Thus it happened that his seven ministers were all noted for their accomplishments as jokers. They all took after the king, too, in being large, corpulent, oily men, as well as inimitable jokers. Whether people grow fat by joking, or whether there is something in fat itself which predisposes to a joke, I have never been quite able to determine, but certain it is that a lean joker is a *rara avis in terris*.

About the refinements, or, as he called them, the "ghosts" of wit, the king troubled himself very little. He had an especial admiration for *breadth* in a jest, and would often put up with *length* for the sake of it. Over-niceties wearied him. He would have preferred Rabelais's "Gargantua," to the "Zadig," of Voltaire; and, upon the whole, practical jokes suited his taste far better than verbal ones.

At the date of my narrative, professing jesters had not altogether gone out of fashion at court. Several of the great Continental "powers" still retained their "fools," who wore motley, with caps and bells, and who were expected to be always ready with sharp witticisms at a moment's notice, in consideration of the crumbs that fell from the royal table.

Our king, as a matter of course, retained his "fool." The fact is, he *required* something in the way of folly—if only to counterbalance the heavy wisdom of the seven wise men who were his ministers—not to mention himself.

His fool, or professional jester, was not *only* a fool, however. His value was trebled in the eyes of the king by the fact of his being also a dwarf and a cripple. Dwarfs were as common at court in those days as fools; and many monarchs would have found it difficult to get through their days (days are rather longer at court than elsewhere) without both a jester to laugh *with* and a dwarf to laugh *at*. But, as I have already observed, your jesters, in ninety-nine cases out of a hundred, are fat, round, and unwieldly—so that it was no small source of self-gratulation with our king that in Hop-Frog (this was the fool's name) he possessed a triplicate treasure in one person.

I believe the name "Hop-Frog" was *not* that given to the dwarf by his sponsors at baptism, but it was conferred upon him by general consent of the seven ministers on account of his inability to walk as other men do. In fact, Hop-Frog could only get along by a sort of interjectional gait—something between a leap and a wriggle—a movement that afforded illimitable amusement, and of course consolation to the king, for (notwithstanding the protuberance of his stomach and a constitutional swelling of the head) the king, by his whole court, was accounted a capital figure.

But although Hop-Frog, through the distortion of his legs, could move only with great pain and difficulty along a road or floor, the prodigious muscular power which nature seemed to have bestowed upon his arms, by way of compensation for deficiency in the lower limbs, enabled him to perform many feats of wonderful dexterity where trees or ropes were in question, or anything else to climb. At such exercises he certainly much more resembled a squirrel, or a small monkey, than a frog.

I am not able to say with precision from what country Hop-Frog originally came. It was from some barbarous region, however, that no person ever heard of—a vast distance from the court of our king. Hop-Frog, and a young girl very little less dwarfish than himself (although of exquisite proportions and a marvellous dancer), had been forcibly carried off from their respective homes in adjoining provinces, and sent as presents to the king by one of his ever-victorious generals.

Under these circumstances, it is not to be wondered at that a close intimacy arose between the two little captives. Indeed, they soon became sworn friends. Hop-Frog, who, although he made a great deal of sport, was by no means popular, had it not in his power to render Trippetta many services; but *she*, on account of her grace and exquisite beauty (although a dwarf) was universally admired and petted, so she possessed much influence, and never failed to use it whenever she could for the benefit of Hop-Frog.

On some grand state occasion—I forget what—the king determined to have a masquerade; and whenever a masquerade or anything of that kind occurred at our court, then the talents both of Hop-Frog and Trippetta were sure to be called in play. Hop-Frog, in especial, was so inventive in the way of getting up pageants, suggesting novel characters, and arranging costume for masked balls, that nothing could be done, it seems, without his assistance.

The night appointed for the *fête* had arrived. A gorgeous hall had been fitted up, under Trippetta's eye, with every kind of device which could possibly give *éclat* to a masquerade. The whole court was in a fever of expectation. As for costumes and characters, it might well be supposed that everybody had come to a decision on such points. Many had made up their minds (as to what *rôles* they should assume) a week, or even a month, in advance; and, in fact, there was not a particle of indecision anywhere—except in the case of the king and his seven ministers. Why *they* hesitated I never could tell, unless they did it by way of a joke. More probably they found it difficult, on account of being so fat, to make up their minds. At all events, time flew; and as a last resource, they sent for Trippetta and Hop-Frog.

When the two little friends obeyed the summons of the king, they found him sitting at his wine with the seven members of his cabinet council; but the monarch appeared to be in a very ill humour. He knew that Hop-Frog was not fond of wine; for it excited the poor cripple almost to madness, and madness is no comfortable feeling. But the king loved his practical jokes, and took pleasure in forcing Hop-Frog to drink and (as the king called it) "to be merry."

"Come here, Hop-Frog," said he, as the jester and his friend entered the room: "swallow this bumper to the health of your absent friends [here Hop-Frog sighed], and then let us have the benefit of your invention. We want characters—*characters*, man—something novel—out of the way. We are wearied with this everlasting sameness. Come, drink! the wine will brighten your wits."

Hop-Frog endeavoured as usual to get up a jest in reply to these advances from the king, but the effort was too much. It happened to be the poor dwarf's birthday, and the command to drink to his "absent friends" forced the tears to his eyes. Many large, bitter drops fell into the goblet as he took it, humbly, from the hand of the tyrant.

"Ah! ha! ha! ha!" roared the latter, as the dwarf reluctantly drained the beaker. "See what a glass of good wine can do! Why, your eyes are shining already!"

Poor fellow! His large eyes *gleamed* rather than shone; for the effect of wine on his excitable brain was not more powerful than instantaneous. He placed the goblet nervously on the table, and looked round upon the company with a half-insane stare. They all seemed highly amused at the success of the king's "*joke.*"

"And now to business," said the prime minister, a *very* fat man.

"Yes" said the king; "come, Hop-Frog, lend us your assistance. Characters, my fine fellow; we stand in need of characters—all of us—ha! ha! ha!" and as this was seriously meant for a joke, his laugh was chorused by the seven.

Hop-Frog also laughed, although feebly and somewhat vacantly.

"Come, come," said the king, impatiently, "have you nothing to suggest?"

"I am endeavouring to think of something *novel*," replied the dwarf, abstractedly, for he was quite bewildered by the wine.

"Endeavouring!" cried the tyrant, fiercely; what do you mean by *that*? Ah, I perceive. You are sulky, and want more wine. Here, drink this!" and he poured out another goblet full and offered it to the cripple, who merely gazed at it, gasping for breath.

"Drink, I say!" shouted the monster, "or by the fiends—"

The dwarf hesitated. The king grew purple with rage. The courtiers smirked. Trippetta, pale as a corpse, advanced to the monarch's seat, and, falling on her knees before him, implored him to spare her friend.

The tyrant regarded her for some moments in evident wonder at her audacity. He seemed quite at a loss what to do or say—how most becomingly to express his indignation. At last, without uttering a syllable, he pushed her violently from him, and threw the contents of the brimming goblet in her face.

The poor girl got up as best she could, and, not daring even to sigh, resumed her position at the foot of the table.

There was a dead silence for about a half-a-minute, during which the falling of a leaf or of a feather might have been heard. It was interrupted by a low, but harsh and protracted *grating* sound which seemed to come at once from every corner of the room.

"What—what—*what* are you making that noise for?" demanded the king, turning furiously to the dwarf.

The latter seemed to have recovered in great measure from his intoxication, and looking fixedly but quietly into the tyrant's face merely ejaculated:

"I—I? How could it have been me?"

"The sound appeared to come from without," observed one of the courtiers. "I fancy it was the parrot at the window, whetting his bill upon his cage-wires."

"True," replied the monarch, as if much relieved by the suggestion, "but on the honour of a knight I could have sworn that it was the grinding of this vagabond's teeth."

Hereupon the dwarf laughed (the king was too confirmed a joker to object to any one's laughing), and displayed a set of large, powerful, and very repulsive teeth. Moreover, he avowed his perfect willingness to swallow as much wine as desired. The monarch was pacified; and having drained another bumper with no very perceptible ill effect, Hop-Frog entered at once and with spirit into the plans for the masquerade.

"I cannot tell what was the association of idea," observed he, very tranquilly, and as if he had never tasted wine in his life, "but *just after* your majesty had struck the girl and thrown the wine in her face—*just after* your majesty had done this, and while the parrot was making that odd noise outside the window, there came into my mind a capital diversion—one of my own country frolics—often enacted among us at our masquerades, but here it will be new altogether. Unfortunately, however, it requires a company of eight persons, and—"

"Here we *are*!" cried the king, laughing at his acute discovery of the coincidence: "eight to a fraction—I and my seven ministers. Come! what is the diversion!"

"We call it," replied the cripple, "the Eight Chained Ourang-Outangs, and it really is excellent sport if well enacted."

"*We* will enact it," remarked the king, drawing himself up, and lowering his eyelids.

"The beauty of the game," continued Hop-Frog, "lies in the fright it occasions among the women."

"Capital!" roared in chorus the monarch and his ministry.

"*I* will equip you as ourang-outangs," proceeded the dwarf; "leave all that to me. The resemblance shall be so striking, that the company of masqueraders will take you for real beasts—and of course they will be as much terrified as astonished."

"O, this is exquisite!" exclaimed the king. "Hop-Frog! I will make a man of you."

"The chains are for the purpose of increasing the confusion by their jangling. You are supposed to have escaped, *en masse*, from your keepers. Your majesty cannot conceive the *effect* produced at a masquerade by eight chained ourang-outangs, imagined to be real ones by most of the company; and rushing in with savage cries among the crowd of delicately and gorgeously habited men and women. The *contrast* is inimitable."

"It *must* be," said the king: and the council arose hurriedly (as it was growing late) to put in execution the scheme of Hop-Frog.

His mode of equipping the party as ourang-outangs was very simple, but effective enough for his purposes. The animals in question had, at the epoch of my story, very rarely been seen in any part of the civilised world; and as the imitations made by the dwarf were sufficiently beastlike, and more than sufficiently hideous, their truthfulness to nature was thus thought to be secured. The king and his ministers were first encased in tight fitting stockinet shirts and drawers. They were then saturated with tar. At this stage of the process some one of the party suggested feathers; but the suggestion was at once overruled by the dwarf, who soon convinced the eight, by ocular demonstration, that the hair of such a brute as the ourang-outang was much more efficiently represented by *flax*. A thick coating of the latter was accordingly plastered upon the coating of tar. A long chain was now procured. First, it was passed about the waist of the king, *and tied*; then about another of the party and also tied; then about all successively, in the same manner. When this chaining arrangement was complete, and the party stood as far apart from each other as possible, they formed a circle; and to make all things appear natural, Hop-Frog passed the residue of the chain, in two diameters, at right angles, across the circle, after the fashion adopted at the present day by those who capture chimpanzees or other large apes in Borneo.

The grand saloon in which the masquerade was to take place was a circular room, very lofty, and receiving the light of the sun only through a single window at the top. At night (the season for which the apartment was especially designed) it was illuminated principally by a large chandelier, depending by a chain from the centre of the skylight, and lowered or elevated by means of a counterbalance as usual; but (in order not to look unsightly) this latter passed outside the cupola and over the roof.

The arrangements of the room had been left to Trippetta's superintendence; but in some particulars, it seems, she had been guided by the calmer judgment of her friend the dwarf. At his suggestion it was that on this occasion the chandelier was removed. Its waxen drippings (which, in weather so warm, it was quite impossible to prevent) would have been seriously detrimental to the rich dresses of the guests, who, on account of the crowded state of the saloon, could not *all* be expected to keep from out its centre—that is to say, from under the chandelier. Additional sconces were set in various parts of the hall, out of the way; and a flambeau, emitting sweet odour, was placed in the right hand of each of the Caryatides that stood against the wall—some fifty or sixty altogether.

The eight ourang-outangs, taking Hop-Frog's advice, waited patiently until midnight (when the room was thoroughly filled with masqueraders) before making their appearance. No sooner had the clock ceased striking, however, than they rushed, or rather rolled in, all together—for the impediment of their chains caused most of the party to fall, and all to stumble as they entered.

The excitement among the masqueraders was prodigious, and filled the heart of the king with glee. As had been anticipated, there were not a few of the guests who supposed the ferocious-looking creatures to be beasts of *some* kind in reality, if not precisely ourang-outangs. Many of the women swooned with affright; and had not the king taken the precaution to exclude all weapons from the saloon, his party might soon have expiated their frolic in their blood. As it was, a general rush was made for the doors, but the king had ordered them to be locked immediately upon his entrance; and, at the dwarf's suggestion, the keys had been deposited with *him*.

While the tumult was at its height, and each masquerader attentive only to his own safety (for, in fact, there was much *real* danger from the pressure of the excited crowd), the chain by which the chandelier ordinarily hung and which had been drawn up on its removal, might have been seen very gradually to descend, until its hooked extremity came within three feet of the floor.

Soon after this, the king and his seven friends, having reeled about the hall in all directions, found themselves at length in its centre, and, of course, in immediate contact with the chain. While they were thus situated, the dwarf, who had followed closely at their heels, inciting them to keep up the commotion, took hold of their own chain at the intersection of the two portions which crossed the circle diametrically and at right angles. Here, with the rapidity of thought, he inserted the hook from which the chandelier had been wont to depend; and in an instant, by some unseen agency, the chandelier-chain was drawn so far upward as to take the hook out of reach, and as an inevitable consequence, to drag the ourang-outangs together in close connection, and face to face.

The masqueraders by this time had recovered in some measure from their alarm, and, beginning to regard the whole matter as a well-contrived pleasantry, set up a loud shout of laughter at the predicament of the apes.

"Leave them to *me*!" now screamed Hop-Frog, his shrill voice making itself easily heard through all the din. "Leave them to *me*. I fancy *I* know them. If I can only get a good look at them *I* can soon tell who they are!"

Here, scrambling over the heads of the crowd, he managed to get to the wall, when, seizing a flambeau from one of the Caryatides, he returned, as he went, to the centre of the room, leaped with the agility of a monkey upon the king's head, and thence clambered a few feet up the chain, holding down the torch to examine the group of ourang-outangs, and still screaming, "*I* shall soon find out who they are!"

And now, while the whole assembly (the apes included) were convulsed with laughter, the jester suddenly uttered a shrill whistle, when the chain flew violently up for about thirty feet, dragging with it the dismayed and struggling ourang-outangs, and leaving them suspended in mid-air between the skylight and the floor. Hop-Frog, clinging to the chain as it rose, still maintained his relative position in respect to the eight maskers, and still (as if nothing were the matter) continued to thrust his torch down towards them as though endeavouring to discover who they were.

So thoroughly astonished were the whole company at this ascent, that a dead silence of about a minute's duration ensued. It was broken by just such a low, harsh, *grating* sound, as had before attracted the attention of the king and his councillors when the former threw the wine in the face of Trippetta. But on the present occasion there could be no question as to *whence* the sound issued. It came from the fang-like teeth of the dwarf, who ground them and gnashed them as he foamed at the mouth, and glared with an expression of maniacal rage into the upturned countenances of the king and his seven companions.

"Ah, ha!" said at length the infuriated jester. "Ah, ha! I begin to see who these people *are* now!" Here, pretending to scrutinise the king more closely, he held the flambeau to the flaxen coat which enveloped him, and which instantly burst into a sheet of vivid flame. In less than half a minute the whole eight ourang-outangs were blazing fiercely, amid the shrieks of the multitude who gazed at them from below, horror-stricken, and without the power to render them the slightest assistance.

At length the flames, suddenly increasing in virulence, forced the jester to climb higher up the chain to be out of their reach, and as he made this movement the crowd again sank for a brief instant into silence. The dwarf seized his opportunity, and once more spoke:

"I now see *distinctly*," he said, "what manner of people these maskers are. They are a great king and his seven privy-councillors—a king who does not scruple to strike a defenceless girl, and his seven councillors who abet him in the outrage. As for myself, I am simply Hop-Frog, the jester, and *this is my last jest*."

Owing to the high combustibility of both the flax and the tar to which it adhered, the dwarf had scarcely made an end of his brief speech before the work of vengeance was complete. The eight corpses swung in their chains, a foetid, blackened, hideous, and indistinguishable mass. The cripple hurled his torch at them, clambered leisurely to the ceiling, and disappeared through the skylight.

It is supposed that Trippetta, stationed on the roof of the saloon, had been the accomplice of her friend in his fiery revenge, and that, together, they effected their escape to their own country, for neither was seen again.

1931

SATAN'S CIRCUS

Eleanor Smith

Lady Eleanor Furneaux Smith (1902–1945) led a dual life. The daughter of the 1st Earl of Birkenhead and a member of the "Bright Young Things", she also claimed to have Romany ancestry through her paternal great-grandmother. This was partly responsible for her lifelong interest in Gypsy and circus culture, though in her autobiography Smith credits her childhood discovery of *Lavengro*, George Borrow's mid-nineteenth-century memoir and depiction of Romany life, as the moment when she realised "beyond any doubt, that my existence would, in future, be somehow bound up with that of the Gypsy people". These two subjects would go on to feature in a number of the eleven novels she published during a successful writing career.

Smith began her employment as a Fleet Street journalist in the 1920s, producing society columns and later also becoming a film critic, before following her nomadic instincts and going on the road to write promotional material for the Great Carmo Circus. Further travels with various other circuses followed—her entertaining 1939 autobiography is, appropriately enough, entitled *Life's a Circus*.

Although a prolific novelist, the same cannot be said of Smith's shorter-length material, as she published just two collections in her lifetime. The first of these, *Satan's Circus* (1932)—the title story of which originally appeared the year before in the pulp magazine *Weird*

Tales—features her most-notable supernatural works, including "Mrs. Raeburn's Waxwork", which I contemplated including here; as a terrified teenager Smith apparently spent an elicit, torch-lit night in Madame Tussaud's Chamber of Horrors.

"Satan's Circus", however, feels like the perfect story for this anthology. And in Lady Eleanor Smith—with her extensive, lived circus experiences—we could not hope for a more authentic chronicler of eerie goings-on beneath the shadows of the Big Top.

I

I once asked a circus artist, whom I knew to have worked at one time with the Circus Brandt, whether or not he had enjoyed travelling with this well-known show. His reply was a curious one. Swiftly distorting his features into a hideous grimace, he spat violently upon the floor. Not another word would he say. My curiosity was, however, aroused, and I went next to an old Continental clown, now retired, who had the reputation of knowing every European circus as well as he knew his own pocket.

"The Circus Brandt?" he said thoughtfully. "Well, you know, the Brandts are queer people, and have an odd reputation. They are Austrian, and their own country-people call them Gypsies, by which they mean nomads, for the Brandts never pitch in their own land but wander the whole world over as though the Devil himself were at their heels. In fact, some call them Satan's Circus."

"I thought," I said, "that the Circus Brandt was supposed to be a remarkably fine show?"

"It is," he said, and lit his pipe; "it's expensive, ambitious, showy, well run. In their way these people are artists, and deserve more success than they have had. It's hard to say why they're so unpopular, but the fact remains that no one will stay with them more than a few months, and, what's more, wherever they go, India, Australia, Rumania, Spain, or Africa, they leave behind them a nasty, unpleasant sort of reputation as regards unpaid bills, which," he added, blowing smoke into the air, "is odd, for the Brandts are rich."

"How many Brandts are there?" I inquired, for I wished to know more about Europe's most elusive circus.

"You ask too many questions," said he, "but, this being my last reply to them, I don't mind telling you that there are two, and that they are man and wife. Carl and Lya. The lady is a bit of a mystery, but if you ask my opinion I would say that she is of Mexican blood, that she was at some time or other a charmer of snakes, and that of the two, she is on the whole the worse, although that is saying a good deal. However, all this is pure guess-work on my part, although, having seen her, I can tell you that she's a handsome piece, still a year or two on the right side of forty. And now," he said firmly, "I will speak no more of the Circus Brandt."

And we talked instead of Sarrasani, of Krone, of Carmo, and of Hagenbeck.

A year passed, and I forgot the Circus Brandt, which no doubt during this period of time wandered from Tokio to San Francisco and Belgrade up to Stockholm and back again as though the Devil himself were at its heels.

And then I met an old friend, a famous juggler, whom I had not seen for many months. I offered him a drink and asked him where he had been since our last meeting. He laughed and said that he had been in hell. I told him I was not much of a hand at riddles. He laughed again.

"Oh, hell," he said, "perhaps that's an exaggeration. But anyhow I've been as near to it as ever I want to. I've been touring with the Circus Brandt."

"The Circus Brandt?"

"Exactly. The Balkan states, Spain, North Africa. Then Holland

and Belgium, and finally France. I cleared out in France. If they'd doubled my salary, I'd not have stayed with them."

"Is the Circus Brandt, then," I asked, "as rough as all that?"

"Rough?" he said. "No, it's not rough. I can stick roughness. What I can't stand, however, is working with people who give me the creeps. Now you're laughing, and I'm not surprised, but I can assure you that I've lain awake at night in my wagon sweating with fear, and I'm by no means a fanciful chap."

By this time I was keenly interested.

"Please tell me," I asked, "what it was that frightened you so much."

"That I can't do," he replied, and ordered another drink, "for the fact is that I, personally, was not treated badly during the tour. The Brandts were very civil to me—too civil, in fact, for they'd ask me into their wagon sometimes for a chat between shows, and I hated going—it gave me goose-flesh down my back. Somehow—and you'll laugh again, I know—it was like sitting there talking to two big cats that were just waiting to pounce after they'd finished playing with you. I swear I believed, at the time, that Carl and Lya could see in the dark. Now, of course, that's ridiculous, and I know it, but I still get the creeps when I think about them. I must have been nervy, overtired, you know, at the time."

I asked whether any one else at the circus had been similarly affected by the Brandts, and he wrinkled his brows, trying to remember, with obvious distaste, any further details of his tour.

"There's one thing that happened so that all could see," he remarked after a pause, "and that was in a wild part of Rumania, somewhere near the Carpathian mountains. We were passing through a little village, on our way to a town a few miles distant, and the peasants came flocking out to watch us pass, which was, of course, only natural, for the show is a very fine one. Then, in the village street, a van stuck, and the Brandts came out of their big living-wagon to see what had happened."

"Well?" I asked, for he paused again.

"Well, it was funny, that's all. They scattered like rabbits—rushed into their cottages and banged the doors. The wagon was shoved out of the rut and we went on, but in the next village there was no sign of life, for everything was deserted and the doors were barred. But on each door was nailed a wreath of garlic-flowers."

"Anything else?" I asked, for he had relapsed into silence.

"Oh, one little thing I remembered noticing. The menagerie. The Brandts seldom bother to inspect that part of the show. They're too busy about the ring and the ticket-office. But one day she—Madam Brandt—had to go through the horse-tent and the menagerie to find some agent who was talking to the boys there. It really was a bit odd—the noise was blood-curdling. It was as though the lions and tigers were frightened; not angry, you know, or roaring for their food, but quite a different sort of row. And, when she had gone, the horses were sweating. I felt 'em myself, and it was a chilly day."

"Really," I said, "it's time you came back."

"Oh," he replied, "I don't expect you to believe me. Why should you? I wouldn't have talked if you hadn't asked me about the Circus Brandt. I'd just have said I was glad to be home. But as you asked me... oh, well, one day I'll tell you why I left them in France. It's not a pretty story. But I won't tell it tonight. I avoid the Brandts as a bedtime topic—I've been dreaming about them lately."

2

It took me some time to coax the juggler's tale from him. One morning, however, as we were walking along Unter den Linden in pale but radiant spring sunshine he consented to tell it. Translated into English, this is the story:

While the Circus Brandt was touring Northern Africa, when it was in fact only a few days from Tangier, a man arrived asking for work. He was, he said, an Alsatian, and had been a stoker, but his ship had abandoned him at Tangier and he had been seeking a job ever since. This man was interviewed by Carl Brandt himself, who had been accosted by him on the lot. They were a curiously contrasted pair as they stood talking together outside the steps of the Brandts' palatial living-wagon. The Alsatian was fair, a big, handsome young man with thick blond hair, a tanned skin, and honest, rather stupid, blue eyes. Carl Brandt was tall, too, but emaciated, wasted, and swarthy dark; he had a smooth darting black head like a snake's head; his long face was haggard, and yellow as old ivory; he wore a tiny dark Imperial beard; his black eyes were feverishly alive in heavy purple hollows and his teeth were sharp and broken and rotten. He was said to drug, and indeed he had very much the appearance of an addict. While the two men were talking, the door of the wagon opened and Madam Brandt appeared on the threshold asking her husband what the stranger wanted of him. She herself was incidentally a remarkably handsome woman, although no longer young. She was powerfully but gracefully made, with quantities of shining blue-black hair, delicate features, oblique, heavy-lidded eyes, and one of those opaque white skins that always look like milk. She had no colour, but was all black and white. Even her lips were pale, not being painted, and her face was heart-shaped against the shadow of her dark hair.

She wore white in hot countries and black in the North, but somehow one never noticed that she was not dressed in colours. She seldom looked at the person to whom she was talking, so that when she did it was rather a shock. Her voice was low, and she never showed her teeth, making one imagine that they must be bad, like her husband's.

Both Brandts stayed talking to the Alsatian for about ten minutes in the hot sunshine. It was impossible to eavesdrop, but once the Alsatian was heard reiterating rather warmly that he was a stoker by profession. Finally, however, Carl Brandt took the man off to the head keeper of the menagerie and said that he was to be given work. The Alsatian, for his part, said that his name was Anatole and that he was used to rough jobs. Soon afterward the circus went on toward Tunis.

The new hand, Anatole, was a good-natured, genial, simple fellow who soon became popular not only with the tent-men and grooms but also with the more democratic of the performers, who amused themselves, during the tedium of long "jumps," by making him sing to them, for he had a rich and beautiful voice. Generally he sang German lieder or long-forgotten French music-hall songs, but sometimes he favoured them with snatches of roaring, racy, impudent ballads couched in an *argot* with which they were every one unfamiliar. On one occasion, before the evening show, when Anatole was shouting one of these coarsely cheerful songs inside the Big Top, the flap was suddenly opened to reveal Madam Brandt's pale watchful face in the aperture.

Instantly, although some of the small audience had not seen her, a curious subtle discomfort fell upon the gay party. Anatole, whose back was turned toward the entrance, immediately became aware of some strain or tension among his listeners, and wheeling round, stopped abruptly in the middle of a bar. The little group scrambled awkwardly to its feet.

Madam Brandt murmured in her low voice:

"Don't let me interfere with your concert, my friends. Go on, you"—to Anatole—"that's a lively song you were singing. Where did you pick it up?"

Anatole, standing respectfully before her, was silent. Madam Brandt did not look at him or seem to concern herself with him in any way, but sent her oblique eyes roving over the empty seats of the great tent, yet somehow, in some curious way, it became obvious to her listeners that she was stubbornly determined to drag from him an answer.

Anatole at length muttered:

"I learned the song, Madam, on board a Portuguese fruit-trader many years ago."

Madam Brandt made no sign of having heard him speak.

After this incident, however, she began to employ the odd hand on various jobs about her own living-wagon with the result that he had less time to sing and not much time even for his work in the menagerie. Anatole, good-humoured and jovial as he was, soon conceived a violent dislike of the proprietress which he took no pains to hide from his friends, who were incidentally in hearty agreement with him on this point. Every one hated the Brandts—many feared them.

The circus crossed to Spain and began to tour Andalusia. Several performers left, new acts were promptly engaged. Carl Brandt had always found it easy to rid himself of artists. Ten minutes before the show was due to open he would send for some unlucky trapezist and pointing to the man's apparatus, complicated and heavy, slung up to one of the big poles, he would say casually:

"I want you to move that to the other side of the tent before the show."

The artist would perhaps laugh, thinking the director was making some obscure joke.

Brandt would then continue, gently: "You had better hurry, don't you think?"

The artist would protest indignantly. "It's impossible, sir; how can I move my apparatus in ten minutes?"

Brandt would watch him, sneeringly, for a few seconds. Then he would turn away, saying suavely:

"Discharged for insubordination," and walk off to telegraph to his agent for a new act.

Madam Brandt took a curious perverse pleasure in teasing Anatole. She knew that he feared her, and it amused her to send for him, to keep him standing in her wagon while she polished her nails or sewed or wrote letters, utterly indifferent to his presence. After about ten minutes she would look up, glancing at some point above his head, and ask him, in her soft languid voice, if he liked circus life and whether he was happy with them. She would chat for some time, casually asking him searching questions about the other performers; then suddenly she would look direct at him, with a strange brooding stare, while she said:

"Better than tramp ships, isn't it, eh? You are more comfortable here than you were as a stoker, I suppose?"

Sometimes she would add: "Tell me something about a stoker's life, Anatole. What were your duties, and your hours?"

Always, when she dismissed him, his hair was damp with sweat.

The Circus Brandt wandered gradually northward toward the Basque country, until the French border was almost in sight. They were to cut across France into Holland and Belgium, then back again. The Brandts could never stay long anywhere. Just before the circus entered French territory Anatole gave his notice to the head keeper. He was a hard worker and so popular with his mates that the keeper went grumbling to Carl Brandt, who agreed to an increase of salary. Anatole refused to stay on.

Madam Brandt was in the wagon when this news was told to her husband. She said to Carl: "If you want the Alsatian to stay, I will arrange it. Leave it to me. I think I understand the trouble, and, as you say, he is a useful man."

The next day she sent for Anatole, and after ignoring him for about five minutes she asked him listlessly what he meant by leaving them.

Anatole, standing rigid near the door, stammered some awkward apology.

"Why is it?"

"I have—I have had offered me a job."

"Better than this?" she pursued, stitching at her work.

"Yes, Madam."

"Yet," she continued idly, "you were happy with us in Africa, happy in Spain. Why not then in France?"

"Madam—"

She snapped a thread with her teeth.

"Why not in France, Anatole?"

There was no reply.

Suddenly she flung her sewing to the ground and fixed him with an unswerving glance. Something leaped into her eyes that startled him, an ugly, naked, hungry look that he had never before seen there. Her eyes burned him, like a devil's eyes. She said, speaking rapidly, scarcely moving her lips:

"I will tell you why you are afraid of France—shall I, Anatole? I have guessed your secret, my friend... You are a deserter from the Foreign Legion and you are afraid of being recaptured. That is it, isn't it? Oh, don't trouble to lie; I have known ever since Africa. It's true, isn't it, what I have said?"

He shook his head, swallowing, unable to speak.

It was a hot day and he wore only a thin shirt. In a second she sprang from her chair across the wagon and threw herself upon him, tearing at this garment with her fingers. Terrified, he struggled, but she was too quick, too violent, too relentless. The shirt ripped in two and she saw upon his white chest the seam of livid scars.

"Bullet wounds!" she laughed in his ear, "a stoker with bullet-wounds! I was right, wasn't I, Anatole?"

He was conscious, above his fear, of a strange shrinking sensation of repulsion at her proximity. God, he thought, she's after me. And he was sickened, as some people are sickened by the sight of a deadly snake. And then, surprisingly, he was saved.

She darted away from him, sank down in her chair, snatched up her sewing. Her quick ear had heard the footsteps of Carl Brandt. Anatole stood there dazed, clutching the great rent in his shirt. Carl Brandt entered the wagon softly, for he always wore rubber soles to his shoes. His wife addressed him in her low unflurried voice.

"You see Anatole there? He has just been telling me why he is afraid to come with us to France. He is a deserter from the Foreign Legion. Look at the wounds there, on his chest."

Anatole gazed helplessly at the long yellow face of Brandt, who stared at him for some moments in silence.

"A deserter?" Brandt said at length, and chuckled. "A deserter? You needn't be afraid, my lad, to come with us to France. They've something better to do than hunt for obscure escaped legionaries there. Oh, yes, you'll be safe enough. I'll protect you."

And he stood rubbing his hands and staring thoughtfully at Anatole with his gleaming black eyes. Anatole, to escape from them, promised to stay. He had the unpleasant sensation of having faced in the wagon that afternoon not one snake but two. He disliked reptiles.

He meant to bolt, but he had lied to Madam Brandt when he talked of a new job, and he was comfortable where he was. He was, too, an unimaginative creature and the horrors of the Legion now seemed very remote. Soon he was in France, utterly unable to believe that he was in any danger. To his delight his mistress ignored him after the scene in the wagon. She had obviously realised, he thought to himself, that he found her disgusting, almost obscene, in spite of her good looks. And he would have been completely happy had he not known that he had made a dangerous enemy.

3

The Circus Brandt employed as lion-tamer an ex-matador, a man named "Captain" da Silva. This individual was not best pleased with his situation. He had lost his nerve about a year before, but after working the same group of lions for ten months he had become more confident and consequently more content. Then, without any warning, Carl Brandt bought a mixed group of animals and told da Silva to start work at once. The tamer was furious. Lions, tigers, bears and leopards! He shrugged his shoulders and obeyed sulkily. Soon the mixed group was ready for the ring, and appeared for a week with great success.

Then one morning da Silva went to the cages and found his animals in a wild abnormal state. Snarling, bristling, foaming at the mouth, they seemed unable even to recognise their tamer. He stared at them in cold dismay. A comrade, coming to watch, whispered in his ear.

"*She walked last night.*"

Da Silva shuddered. There was a legend in the Circus Brandt that whenever the animals were nervous or upset Lya Brandt, the "she-devil," had walked in her sleep the night before, wandering into the menagerie and terrifying the beasts who presumably knew her for what she was.

The tiger roared, and was answered by the lioness. Da Silva listened for a minute, then turned to his companion.

"I'm off. I wouldn't work these cats tonight for a fortune. There are other circuses in the world. The Circus Brandt must find another tamer."

In twenty minutes' time he was at the railway station.

Carl Brandt heard the news in silence. Then he raised his arm and struck his head keeper savagely on the mouth. Wrapping his black cloak about his tall thin figure he left the office and sought his own wagon. His wife was engaged in drinking a cup of coffee. They eyed each other in silence for a moment.

Then she said, calmly:

"It's da Silva, I suppose?"

"Da Silva, yes. Already he has gone. Now who will work the mixed group?"

She drained her cup and answered thoughtfully:

"I know of several tamers."

"Probably. And how long will they take to get here?"

"Exactly," she said, pouring out more coffee, "that, I agree, is the great objection. Is there no one on the lot who could work the cats for a week or two?"

"What nonsense are you talking?"

She put her hand over her eyes. "You seem to forget Anatole. An escaped Legionary in French territory. Would he disobey your orders, do you think?"

There was a pause.

"I'll send for him," said Brandt at length.

They were silent as they waited for the Alsatian. When he came in Lya did not look at him, but began to polish her nails.

Carl Brandt turned his yellow wrinkled face toward Anatole. His eyes were dark and smouldering hollows. He said gently, pleasantly:

"You know that da Silva has left?"

"Yes, sir." Anatole was perplexed. He could not imagine why he had been sent for.

"There is no one, now, to work the animals until a new tamer is engaged."

"No, sir."

"It is not my custom to fail my patrons. I show always what I advertise. The new tamer should be here in a week. It is about this week that I wish to speak."

Another pause. Anatole's heart began to pump against his ribs. A monstrous suspicion was forming in his mind.

Brandt said placidly:

"I am about to promote you, my friend. For a week you shall be tamer and work the mixed group."

Anatole turned dusky red. He was furiously angry, so angry indeed that his fear of the silent woman sitting at the table vanished entirely. No longer conscious of her presence he blurted out violently:

"What, you wish me to go in the cage with those animals? Then you must find some one else; I'm not such a fool. I wouldn't do it for a fortune."

Brandt smiled, showing his black, broken teeth. His wife, utterly indifferent, continued to paint her nails bright red. Brandt said pleasantly:

"Are you perhaps in a position to dictate, my friend? I may be wrong, of course, but I am under the impression that we are now in French territory. *French territory*. Charming words, eh?"

Anatole was silent. He thought suddenly and with horror of the Legion—blistering sun, filth, and brutality. He thought, too, of the salt-mines, that ghastly living death to which he would inevitably be condemned in the event of capture. Then he remembered the animals as he had last seen them, ferocious, maddened, abnormal. He shook his head.

"That's bluff," he said shakily; "I'm no tamer. You can't force me into the cage."

Carl Brandt chuckled. The delicate yellow ivory of his skin seamed itself into a thousand crinkles. He pulled out his watch.

"Five minutes, Anatole, to come with me to the menagerie. Otherwise I telephone the police. If I may be permitted to advise you, I suggest the menagerie. Even the belly of a lion is preferable, I should imagine, to the African salt-mines. But take your choice."

Madam Brandt, snapping an orange-stick in two, now obtruded herself quietly into the conversation.

"No, Anatole," she said musingly, "it will not be possible to run away in the night. The Herr Director will take trouble, great trouble, to have you traced. The Herr Director has no wish to shelter criminals."

Once again she looked directly at him, fixing him with the burning and threatening glance that was like a sword. Then she dropped her eyes, absorbed in her manicure.

A pause.

Brandt glanced at his watch.

"I must remind you, Anatole, that you have only two minutes left," he said with an air of great courtesy. "How many years did you serve in the Legion, I wonder? And is it eight years in the salt-mines for deserters or perhaps more?"

"I'll work the animals," said Anatole shortly. He knew that Lya Brandt had read his thoughts, and he wiped the sweat from his face as he went toward the menagerie. It was not possible for the mixed group to appear at the matinee, but it was announced to the circus in general that the cats would work that night without fail. Anatole was to spend the afternoon rehearsing them.

His face was grey as he shut himself in the cage armed only with a tamer's switch. Outside the bars stood two keepers with loaded revolvers. They, too, were nervous. The animals stood motionless to stare at the stranger, hackles raised, restless yellow eyes fixed upon him. Around the cage were painted wooden pedestals, upon which the animals were trained to sit at the word of command. The Alsatian now gave that command. They took no notice. He repeated it louder, slapping the bars with his switch, and they scattered, in a sudden panic, to take up their accustomed seats. He pulled out the paper hoop through which the lions must jump. They snarled for several minutes, striking out with their savage paws; then, in the end, possibly deciding that obedience was less trouble, they bounded through the hoop with an ill grace. The two keepers, and Anatole as well, were soon streaming with perspiration as though they had been plunged into water. The Alsatian was now, however, more confident. He turned to the bears.

Twenty minutes later Carl Brandt rejoined his wife in the living-wagon. She was standing near the window with her back toward him.

"Better than I expected," said the director coolly. "I see no reason why things should not go well tonight. He has courage, this Legionary! And what good fortune that we are in France!"

Madam Brandt made no reply, nor did she turn her head. She seemed utterly indifferent to the affairs of Anatole.

That evening the Alsatian was supplied with a splendid sky-blue uniform and cherry-coloured breeches from the circus wardrobe. He dressed himself mechanically, taking no notice of the dresser's encouragements. Out on the lot his comrades glanced at him sympathetically. One or two, unconscious of his antecedents, warned him to defy Brandt and keep out of the cage. Anatole merely shook his head, incapable of giving an explanation.

"I must go; it is useless to warn me," he said at length.

And the circus folk were unanimous in their bitter abuse of the Brandts.

It was dusk. The bandsmen, splendid in their green and gold uniforms, played the overture inside the huge tent. A group of clowns, glittering in brilliant spangles, stood waiting to make their comic entry. Behind the clowns, six or seven grooms controlled twenty milk-white Arab stallions with fleecy white manes and tails. These horses were magnificent in scarlet trappings. The Chinese troupe, dark kimonos over gorgeous brocade robes, diligently practised near the bears' cage. Anatole sat on a bale of hay near the tigers, deaf to the advice muttered in his ear by various comrades. The circus proceeded.

Up in the dome of the tent two muscular young men in peach-coloured tights flung themselves from bar to bar with thrilling grace and swiftness. Down below the attendants rapidly constructed a vast cage, staggering beneath sections of heavy iron bars. Soon the cage was ready; the aerialists had swung themselves down from the dome. The band crashed out a chord, and Anatole, the Legionary, stepped into the cage, bowing modestly in response to the applause which greeted his spectacular entrance. Then an iron door was slid aside and down the narrow tunnel crept a file of tawny shapes.

Lions, tigers, leopards, bears. Gracefully they padded into the arena, stretching themselves, rubbing against the bars of the cage, yawning at the bright lights, showing their teeth, slinking with a cat-like agility about the ring.

Gripping his switch, Anatole uttered the first command. One minute later the animals were seated with a certain docility upon their wooden pedestals. Anatole produced his hoop. At first the people of the circus held their breath; then, gradually, as five minutes passed they relaxed. He was doing well. They sighed with relief. The climax of the act was a tableau during the course of which the animals grouped themselves, standing erect on their hind legs, about the trainer, who himself sprang upon a pedestal, arm upraised to give more effect to this subjugation of the beasts. The biggest tiger lay at his feet during the tableau, and while the other animals soon assumed their accustomed positions when ordered, the tiger was at first always unwilling to fling himself upon the sawdust.

Posing the lions and leopards, Anatole, one foot on the pedestal, spoke briskly, curtly, to the great beast, which stared at him sulkily, motionless save for the twitching of its tail. A second passed, seeming longer than a minute to the circus watchers. The tiger continued to stare, and Anatole, banging at the bars with his switch, pointed stubbornly at the ground at his feet.

His back was toward the ring entrance and he did not see the grooms and attendants draw back respectfully to allow some one to pass through the red velvet curtains. His comrades did, and nudged one another, for Madam Brandt seldom came near the arena during a performance. She stood for a moment near the curtains, tall and straight in her flowing white dress, her face pale against the dense blackness of her hair.

Then, suddenly, there was tumult in the peaceful cage as, snarling furiously, the animals leaped from their pedestals to dash themselves savagely against the bars. Caught by surprise, Anatole turned, slashing with his switch, shouting, oblivious of the sullen tiger behind him. A leopard, maddened with fright, collided against him and sent him stumbling to the ground. With the fierce swiftness of a mighty hawk the great tiger sprang. A thick choking growl that made the blood run cold, yells of terror from the crowd and then the crack of two revolver shots. Armed with hose-pipes the menagerie men drove the animals back. The tiger was wounded in the shoulder and clawed the ground, biting at itself in a frenzy of fear and pain.

Anatole lay doubled up on the sawdust looking like a rag-dummy, so limp and twisted was his body. On the bright blue of his uniform oozed a clotted stream of red. His face? Anatole had no longer a face; only a huge and raw and gaping wound. Opening a side door they dragged his body from the cage and swiftly wrapped it in the gorgeous coat of a Chinese acrobat standing near by. Screaming, weeping, cursing, the horrified audience fought, struggling and stampeding to leave the tent. In the noise and tumult Madam Brandt slipped through the red velvet curtains and vanished like a white shadow.

Pale-faced, haggard, the bandsmen were ordered to play their most cheerful march. Soon the tent was empty, save for a little group of brightly-clad people bending over the huddled shape that was Anatole and for a doctor, hastily summoned, who soon went away, for there was nothing for him to do.

That night the body was laid temporarily in a little canvas dressing-room belonging to the clowns. It was late before the show-people retired to bed, but by one o'clock in the morning all was still in the tent-town of Brandt's Circus. Only the night watchman, a stolid, unimaginative fellow, paced slowly up and down swinging his lantern, but from time to time a lion would whimper and growl in the silence of the night, or a horse kick impatiently against the wooden partition of its stall.

It was the watchman, however, who afterward related to his comrades what he saw during this lonely vigil... It was about an hour before dawn, and the man was lolling on a heap of hay, relieved, no doubt, to think the night would soon be over, when all at once his quick ear caught the soft sound of approaching footsteps. He turned, hiding his lantern beneath his coat. It was Madam Brandt, of course, walking slowly, like a sleepwalker, across the deserted arena toward the dressing-rooms, seeming no more tangible than a shadow, a white shadow that gleamed for a moment in the darkness and then was gone, swallowed by the gloom of the night. Now the watchman was a brave fellow, and inclined to be inquisitive. He slipped off his shoes and crept after her.

Madam Brandt glided straight to the little dressing-room wherein lay the mangled body of the Legionary. The watchman had not dared to bring his lantern, and it was therefore difficult for him to see what was happening, but at the same time he managed to observe quite enough. He glimpsed her white figure kneeling down near the dark shape on the floor; as he watched she struggled with some drapery or other, and he saw that she was trying to drag away the sheet that covered the corpse; having apparently achieved her purpose she remained still for a moment, staring at what she saw; this immobility, which lasted only for a second, was succeeded by a sudden revulsion of feeling more horrible than anything that had gone before, for with all the ferocity of a starving animal she flung herself upon the body, shaking it, gripping it tight to steady its leaden weight, while she thrust her face, her mouth, down upon that torn and bleeding throat... then in the distant menagerie the lions and tigers broke the silence of the night with sudden tumult.

"Yes," said the juggler after a long pause, "we liked Anatole. He was a good comrade, although, mind you, he had probably been a murderer and most certainly a thief. But in the Circus Brandt, you know, that means nothing at all."

"Where is the Circus Brandt now?" I asked, after another pause.

He shrugged his shoulders.

"Poland, I think; or possibly Peru. How can I tell? The Brandts are Gypsies, nomads. Here today, gone tomorrow. Possibly they travel fast because there is always something to hush up. But who can say? The Devil has an admirable habit of looking after his friends."

I was silent, for I was thinking both of Lya Brandt and Anatole. Suddenly I felt rather sick. "Look here," I said, "do you mind if we don't talk any more about the Brandt Circus for the moment?"

1959

CIRCUS CHILD

Margery Lawrence

Born in Wolverhampton,* Margery Lawrence (1889–1969) was a published poet, book illustrator, novelist, and author of non-fiction. A number of these latter works (in particular, 1944's spiritualist memoir *Ferry Over Jordan*) reflected her own interest in the supernatural (she was also, for instance, a member of The Ghost Club). But it is for her eerie short stories that she is best remembered today.

Nights of the Round Table (1926) is a hugely sought-after collection (with first editions almost as rare as verified ghost sightings), as is its follow-up *The Terraces of Night* (1932). In 1945, Lawrence introduced her occult detective, Dr. Miles Pennoyer—a figure in the same mould as Algernon Blackwood's Dr. John Silence and William Hope Hodgson's Carnacki—in *Number Seven Queer Street*. The character appeared again in her collection of longer tales, *Master of Shadows* (1959), from which the excellent "Circus Child" originates.

"Circus Child" was written in a post-Second-World-War Britain still scarred by the six long years of the conflict and its austerity-shrouded aftermath. Fears and suspicions about immigrants were widespread, something that Lawrence captures well in Jack's working class dialect and in the words and descriptions given to us by Latimer,

* A place that features significantly in the final tale of this anthology, Robert Aickman's "The Swords".

the story's somewhat pompous and, at times, small-minded, Watson-esque narrator; Pennoyer himself, however, looks sympathetically on Mitzi, the Jewish refugee at the heart of the tale's mystery, though the Great Markos fares less well. The Balkan conjurer—a character in the mould of George du Maurier's arch-mesmerist Svengali from his 1894 novel *Trilby*—is the epitome of the sinister and exotic Eastern European, a figure that has a long pedigree in supernatural fiction and whose dark prince is the titular count of Bram Stoker's *Dracula* (1897).

This curious adventure began one evening when I had gone down to dine with my friend Pennoyer at his flat in Blackfriars. He was still out when I arrived, but I made myself thoroughly at home, stretching my long legs out on the velvet-covered window seat and drinking a glass of the excellent sherry with which Pen's old Bavarian servant, Friedl, had immediately provided me.

It was a lovely summer evening, warm and balmy, yet with breeze enough to ruffle the surface of the Thames into dancing wavelets that curled and slapped the sides of the countless boats that ploughed the waters of the grey old river, going about their business as they had done for so many hundreds of years past. Heavy coal barges, tied nose to tail, sliding weightily past; nippy little boats of the Thames Patrol dodging in and out, lumbering freighters, so loaded that the gunwales rolled almost at water level, sleek privately-owned craft, and now and then one of the Thames "taxis", the neat double-decker boats that carry passengers from the Pool up to Hampton Court and back for a mere shilling or two. Being summer-time, these were crowded with people lining their upper decks and hanging over the rails; and from one, as it slid by, there came the faint echo of a rollicking chorus sung by the lighthearted travellers aboard.

I watched the busy scene for some time. The view from Pen's high-placed eyrie never ceased to fascinate me, and I was so absorbed that I did not hear Pen come in until an affectionate onslaught from his wolfhound Hans almost knocked me out of the window. I am one of Hans's few favourites, and a greeting from him is, to say the least, impressive!

Laughing, my friend hauled Hans away from me and shook hands warmly after I had got up and dusted myself down. I had not seen Pen for some time, having been away for a holiday in Italy, and we burst into eager talk over another glass of sherry for me—and an orange-juice for Pen, who never breaks his rule of teetotalism.

We had a great deal to discuss. Although I am no great occultist like Pen, I have been deeply interested in psychic matters for many years, and Pen has paid me the compliment of letting me work as his assistant in certain cases when he needed one. I knew he had some interesting problems on hand when I went away, and was of course eager to hear all about them. Dinner was served, and we talked nineteen to the dozen through the meal; but I knew that Pen would not start discussing his cases until we had finished and Friedl was safely out of the way in her cosy kitchen. So for once I was glad to get through dinner and settle again in the lounge—and my annoyance can be imagined when just as Friedl had brought in the Cona coffee machine and set a match to the lamp, I heard a ring at the door bell.

I had just been watching Pen, sitting with his chin on one long hand, his eyes on the little flame, dancing blue and gold below the round glass globe full of bubbling coffee, and I knew that he was in the very mood I wanted—brooding, reminiscent, full of fascinating talk as an egg of meat. Talk that, once started, would come pouring out of him as freely as the coffee, a little later, would come pouring out of the glass globe.

So I barely suppressed a bad word as the bell rang; but Pen shrugged his shoulders.

"It may not be a caller—may be a late post or a parcel or something," he said as we heard Friedl's heavy step go past. I hoped so. If it were an appeal for help, I knew my friend would never turn anyone in trouble away...

So when Friedl came into the room bearing a bit of paper with a scribbled message on it, I knew this meant an end of the cosy evening I had planned. Yet, had I known it, this was the opening of one of the most exciting adventures that I had ever known with Pen; and I had known many...

Pen read the message and nodded to Friedl.

"Tell him to come in. Sorry, Jerry, but there's trouble here—and trouble has to come first, as you know."

He rose to his feet as a young man came into the room. A stockily-built young fellow of the respectable working-class type, in a blue serge suit that fitted only where it touched, large boots that creaked, and thick red hands. But the blue eyes that looked out of his otherwise quite ordinary face were steady and honest, there was character in the turn of jaw and chin, and though when he spoke it was with the accent of Bow Bells, his voice was pleasant.

He glanced uncertainly at me, and Pennoyer spoke as they shook hands.

"This is Mr. Latimer, my friend and frequent assistant," he said easily. "You can speak before him as freely as you like—and I want you to speak freely! Sit down and tell us what the trouble is—and incidentally, how you came to hear of me?" He indicated a chair and the young man sat down. He had kept his grey tweed cap in his hand when he came in, and as he spoke he turned it round and round in his fingers after the usual fashion of men when they feel shy or awkward. But his voice was resolute enough, and I knew as I listened that here was the sterling stuff, the blunt, solid, common-sense strength that is England.

"My name's Jack Holcroft, sir, and I'm head mechanic at the 'Owl' Garridge, Hart Street, Marylebone. You won't remember me—but I've seen you before." Pen's fine brows rose slightly as the boy went on. "Last part of the war it was, when you came down to where I lived when I was a kid—Flagg Street, Camden Town. Hunting for a kid called Nicky, you were... kid whose mother got killed in the blitz down there and you was trying to find out something about her."

"Oh!" I exclaimed involuntarily. "'The Case of the White Snake!'"*

Pen frowned at me and smiled at the boy.

"Of course," he said. "How interesting! I remember meeting a lot of people in Flagg Street when I was making enquiries about Nicky's mother—but I should never have flattered myself that a boy of your age would have remembered me!" He laughed softly. "Well, that makes us in a sense old friends, doesn't it?—and it will be easier to talk. Tell me, what did you want to see me about?"

The boy drew a long breath.

"S'like this," he said bluntly. "I got a girl, and we want to get married." He paused and twirled his cap again, a flush rising to his tanned cheeks as he went doggedly on.

"I got a good job with good prospects. My boss is a grand chap and he's promised to make me foreman and give me a flat above the garridge when I get married. Mitzi an' me, we been courting about six months... but I can't say as my folks like the idea of our gettin' married, and that makes things a bit awkward." He paused again and Pennoyer spoke.

---

* This tale is told, with others, in *Number Seven Queer Street.*

"Why don't they like the idea of your getting married?"

The boy flushed again and looked embarrassed.

"Well," he said. "First of all Mitzi ain't English, she's Austrian—and she's a Jewess, and that ain't popular with my folks either! She came over with her folks when she was only a young 'un, on the run from the Nazis, and her father died over here and her mother brought her up—then her mother died and Mitzi was left alone. But she got by somehow—she's got guts, Mitzi has! She got work somehow at this and that, and finally got to working in a little caffy where I useter go for a snack sometimes, and that's where we met."

"Well," said Pennoyer, "I know, of course, the British prejudice against foreigners and Jews—but all the same, if your girl has proved herself to be as plucky and hard-working as you say, this shouldn't be impossible to get over."

There was a long pause. Pen looked at the boy in silence for a moment and then spoke gently.

"There's another reason why your folk don't want you to marry this girl, isn't there?" he said, and the boy nodded. Pennoyer went on.

"Go on, my lad, and tell me. I'm a doctor you know—a doctor of sorts at least—and you don't mind what you tell a doctor, do you?"

The boy named Jack Holcroft squared his shoulders and spoke suddenly with determination.

"No, of course—it was only—awkward-like to talk of, and sounds pretty silly really. But here goes!" He drew a long breath and started talking as though anxious to get it over—and certainly it was a very queer tale that he had to tell.

He spoke of having fallen in love with Mitzi the first moment he set eyes on her and apparently she with him, though at first she was very shy and wary, having obviously had plenty of unpleasant experiences with men in the little snack-bar-cum-café where she was employed. Jack fished out a blurred snapshot to show us how pretty she was. A little creature of about his own age with dark curly hair, great dark eyes and the prettily-rounded figure typical of the young Jewess... that figure that, alas, runs to fat all too often in middle-age but is charming in its sensuous femininity in youth.

Pennoyer handed it back with a nod of approval, and the boy went on. It seemed that Mitzi held him off for some weeks, but in the end her love defeated her and she fell into his arms... and was apparently amazed and touched to find that his intentions were strictly honourable! When she realised that she was abandoning the hand-to-mouth existence that had been hers for so long and that she was in the future actually to become a wife, honoured, loved and protected, she was touchingly grateful; and the only fly in their ointment was the fact that Jack's parents, though they had to admit they could find no fault in the girl herself—whose manners towards them, shy, humble, grateful, were impeccable—still did not at all like their only son marrying anybody of whom they knew so little.

"One thing they didn't like—and still don't," said Jack, "was that Mitzi's folk were circus folk out there." He nodded vaguely in the direction of Europe. "Father was a sword swallower and her mother did a roller-skating act with her sister, and Mitzi herself was trained as an acrobat—tumbling head over heels, tying herself in knots, and all that. Used to work with her mother and aunt, too, in their act—got throwed from one to the other and stand on the top of their heads at the end—that sort of thing. You know. But when they had to bolt to England they couldn't get no more circus work and had to do all sorts of other things to live."

"Well," said Pennoyer, "it's a tragic story, certainly, but not one that reflects any discredit on Mitzi or her people. Hundreds of poor devils from Central Europe had to fly before the Nazi menace and take refuge in England. So your people are not really being reasonable in citing that as a cause for objection to your marriage."

Jack fell once more to twisting his cap around, and his very ears were red.

"'Tisn't only that," he brought out at last. "They don't *like* it, of course—my folks are Methody and think everybody in theatres or circuses belong to the Devil—but it's not the worst. It—you see, doctor, every day at a certain time Mitzi goes to sleep!"

There was a long pause, and Pen and I looked at each other, puzzled.

"Well," Pen said at last. "What about it? At a certain time we all go to sleep! Be explicit, my boy—I see this isn't the ordinary sleep. But give me more details."

"It's so difficult," muttered Jack. "It fair stumps me, and I've known Mitzi all of six months now! I thought to start with it was only she was workin' too hard, poor kid, and simply couldn't help dropping off to sleep, but now I'm not so sure. It's *queer*." He drew a deep breath. "You see, doctor, it don't happen like it ought to—at the proper time, I mean. It happens twice a day—and always at the same times! Four o'clock in the afternoon and again at eight o'clock—and she tells me it's only started happening since we got engaged! Wherever she happens to be she'll drop off instant-like, just where she stands—she'll sleep standing up, I've seen her, if she can't find somewhere to lie down. Sleep like a dead thing for maybe twenty minutes, and then wake up again bright as a button. And she won't even know she's been to sleep."

Pennoyer frowned.

"*What* a curious business," he murmured. "When did all this start?"

"Oh," said Jack, "not until some time after we'd got together and decided to get married. I'd been talking to her about it and how we could get round my folks—it was in my room. I've got a decent room near the garridge with a good old soul who likes Mitzi and doesn't look down her nose when she comes to see me—she knows we got nowhere else to go to be together a bit. We was cooking sausages for supper, and we was ever so happy. I left Mitzi to get on with the sausages and mash some spuds to go with 'em, and nipped out for a couple of beers—and when I got back she was lying on the bed fast asleep and the sausages burning black in the frypan!" He shook his head in rueful reminiscence.

"I'd only been outa the room about five minutes, but could I wake her? Not on your life! There she lay, sound asleep, and I guessed she was tired out, poor kid, and let her lie. I rescued the sausages and did the spuds and by the time I'd finished she'd awakened—but she wouldn't believe me for ages that she'd ever been asleep! Thought I was pulling her leg."

The boy's round blue eyes, wide and troubled, roved from Pennoyer to me and back to Pennoyer again.

"Well, that was the start. I thought it was a rummy go but didn't worry much about it at first—but then it started to happen more and more often! Even when she was working it useter happen, and of course she got into awful trouble, and finally her boss sacked her when he found her asleep standing behind the counter with two or three customers bawling orders at her and her not moving a muscle to serve them!" He scowled. "I remember coming back and finding her at my place crying her eyes out, with old Mother Bunn trying to comfort her. That had happened at four o'clock in the afternoon—and dammit if she didn't go slap off to sleep that very night again at eight o'clock! Slept just twenty minutes—never sleeps more than that—and wakes up again, just like that."

He looked again from one to the other of us and meeting our attentive eyes went on, apparently comforted by our obvious interest.

"Well, I thought she was overtired and I told her I jolly well wasn't going to have her work herself to death. I wanted a nice healthy little wife, I told her, who'd give me a bunch of fine kids and run my home like I'd like to have it run—and I asked Mother Bunn if she could give Mitzi a room, if I paid for it, and let her rest a bit until we decided what to do. Old Bunn was a trump! She gave her a room and said she could do with a bit of help in the house with her lodgers, and Mitzi could work there if she liked. So there we are, and we'd be as happy as two bugs in a rug if it wasn't for this—this queer business. And that's getting us both down now."

"It got no better, then, after she left the snack-bar where she was working?" asked Pennoyer. Jack shook his head.

"No. It got worse, if anything. Useter happen only now and then, maybe a couple of times a week; but after she came to live at Ma Bunn's it's took to happening every day as regular as clockwork, and always at the same times." His hot unhappy eyes stared into ours. "It's got me beat—and she's scared to death. Can't make it out and talks about having a curse laid on her and all sorts of nonsense... but what worries me is she swears she won't marry me until she's free of it. And how do I know how long it's going to last?"

"Have you taken her to an ordinary doctor?" asked Pen. "I admit it does seem a very odd condition—but sometimes there is a physical explanation for the strangest things."

Jack nodded.

"Yes!" he said briefly. "And all the doctor said was that she was a bit run down and gave her a tonic, and that was that!" His tone was bitter. "So unless we can find out what's what about this, I don't know what we're going to do! She won't marry me while this is hanging over her, and of course my folks think she's half dotty and keep on at me to give her up... and then I remembered Flagg Street and you, sir. I looked you up in the telephone book and... well, here I am."

There was a moment's pause and then Pennoyer, rising, placed a hand on the boy's sturdy shoulder and gave it an encouraging squeeze.

"I'm glad you came, Jack," he said. "Whether I can do anything to help you and your little girl I don't know, but you can bank on it I shall try! The next step is for me to meet Mitzi. Here? No. I think if it's all right with you, I'll come one evening with Mr. Latimer up to your place at Mother Bunn's."

Mother Bunn's humble lodging-house was situated in one of the back streets lying off Marylebone Road, and humble as it was, was clean as hard work with duster, soap and scrubbing-brush could make it.

It was a tall lean house in a row, with a narrow so-called garden before it, filled with sooty grass and privet bushes, and a card stuck in the front window lettered "Bed and Brekfasts only". Behind it were close-drawn Nottingham lace curtains, darned but clean, and between them just showed the leaves of the inevitable aspidistra. This was Ma Bunn's sitting-room, spy-hole, sanctuary, retreat, whatever you liked to call it; and when Pennoyer and I came up the narrow paved path between the privet bushes we caught a glimpse of the old lady peering through the folds of the curtain to take stock of us before we rang the bell.

She opened the door to us herself—a fat old lady with three chins and a wig of preposterously unreal auburn curls, wearing an old-fashioned "hugmetight" of purple wool over her ample bosom and a black satin apron protecting her skirt. I learned afterwards that she had been housekeeper for many years in many "good houses" as she would have described them, and marrying the butler, turned to running an apartment house in London, which until the death of her husband had done very well. Now she had sunk considerably in the social scale, but still made an honest living; the aura of Mrs. Rouncewell of Bleak House clung about her and probably always would do.

She stood back and gestured us in with a wave of the hand positively royal; but as we turned to mount the narrow stairs to the first floor, where Jack's room, he had told us, was situated, she shook her head and laying a hand on Pennoyer's arms literally pushed him—gently but firmly—into her sitting-room with a conspiratorial whisper.

"Come on in here, doctor—I got something I want to tell you before you go upstairs."

Rather mystified, we followed her into the little front room and took the chairs she indicated to us. It was a typical "front parlour" of such a house, crammed with furniture far beyond its capacity to hold, mostly Victorian stuff. There was a heavy wooden overmantel above the black iron grate that bore an endless array of small shelves set against a mirrored background—shelves that were laden with scores of little ornaments of china, glass, carved ivory, enamel, and what have you. There was a sideboard laden with silver-framed photographs, conspicuous among them that of a woman in the train and feathers of Court dress—plainly the photograph of one of Ma Bunn's early employers—a central table with a red plush cloth edged with bobble fringe, a black horsehair sofa and armchair to match, both bearing antimacassars made of tatting in red and blue thread... and in the windows, as we had guessed, a little round table bearing the aspidistra. Planting herself heavily on the sofa, Ma Bunn squared her hands on her knees and spoke in the richly unctuous voice of the typical London landlady.

"Doctor, I got to tell you something I think you oughta know before you go up to them two poor kids." Her keen little black eyes bored into Pen's, her fat hands were red and worn with a lifetime of work, but suddenly I knew that I liked Ma Bunn—liked her very much. Poor and hard-working as she was, she was not too poor to exert herself to help others—witness her generous action in making a home for poor forlorn little Mitzi, her obvious eagerness now to help. Pennoyer smiled warmly at her and I knew that he was reacting towards the old lady just as I was.

"I shall be only too glad to hear whatever you can tell me, Mrs. Bunn—one never knows what may be useful," he said. "Do go on please? It's so good of you to try and help them."

"Tcha!" said Ma Bunn, "that ain't nothing! It paid me to take in the girl, s'matter of fact. I wanted help with the lodgers, and her legs is young. Them stairs don't count to her, while to *me*..." She thrust out a pair of substantial ankles and for the moment I feared that she might be deflected from her original purpose to a discussion about varicose veins, from which she was obviously suffering. But I was mistaken...

"I been watching that girl since she come here, and there's something *queer* about her, doctor? Young Jack, he's out all day and I got her here with me and I been with her often when she goes to sleep—snap, off like that, right on the dot of four and eight o'clock, wherever she may be. And doctor, lately she's got to *talking* in them sleeps—and I don't like it. It ain't right."

"Talking, eh?" Pennoyer was plainly interested. He sat forward, his hands linked loosely between his knees, the slanting light of the late afternoon sun filtering through the lace curtains upon his keen lined face. "What sort of talk, Mrs. Bunn? Talk about her early days—you know she comes of circus stock?"

Ma Bunn shook her head vigorously.

"Might be," she said, "but she don't talk in English at all—she talks her own lingo—it's German, ain't it, as they talk in Austria? In Bunn's day I could scratch up a word or two of French, because he'd travelled a lot and spoke it, and now and then we useter have a French gentleman staying with us... but I don't know a blinkin' word of German, though I know the sound of it when I hear it. But that ain't the part that worries me, Doctor. It's that when she talks she don't talk like herself at all! She talks in a voice like a man—and she don't talk in German, either. It's some queer lingo I never heard before."

There was a long pause. Pennoyer stared squarely at Mother Bunn and she stared back at him; it was plain that she was in deadly earnest. At last Pen spoke.

"You're sure of this, Mrs. Bunn? And what sort of voice has this man?"

"I'm as sure as I'm sitting here at this minute," retorted the old lady. "And as for the voice, it's a rough-like, sort of order-you-about-and-don't-talk-to-me sort of voice. It only started a week or so ago, and s'matter of fact, it was because it started that I egged Jack on to come and see you. He told me about the Flagg Street business and you, and when I went down one Sunday to see his folks, they told me some more. So I knew a bit about you."

Pen exchanged an amused glance at me. Truly, despite its immensity, London is only a little village.

"Go on," he said. "This is most interesting," and nothing loth, Ma Bunn took up her tale.

"First of all it was just muttering-like and I didn't take no notice... thought it was just the girl talking to herself in a dream, sort of. And then suddenly one day she was lying asleep here on this very sofa and I was knitting, waiting for her to wake up and make me a cup of tea, when suddenly a great loud man's voice come bursting outa that little thing, and nearly startled me outa my skin! Great rough voice it was—sounded angry too, and I'm pretty sure he was using cuss words, though I didn't understand a word..."

"Hm," Pennoyer said thoughtfully. "Pity he didn't speak English. I'd have given a lot to know just what he was saying..."

"Only one thing I'm sure of," said Mrs. Bunn, "and that is, he didn't speak the same language that Mitzi does. I got her when she woke up to say some words in her German, and it wasn't that, I'll swear. Don't know what it was."

"Did you tell her about it," asked Pennoyer. Ma Bunn shook her wise old head.

"No. I didn't want to frighten her, and God knows the poor kid's scared to death as it is. But she knows now all right—guess it happened when Jack was there, and he blurted it out. He asked her who it was and if she knew who it was and she swore she didn't... but I dunno doctor, I got a hunch somehow that she *does* know who it is, but daren't say so."

Pen rose to his feet, towering in his long lean height almost to the low ceiling of the little room. He was smiling.

"You're a wise woman, Mrs. Bunn, and what you have told me may be a very great help," he said. "I'll let you know how things go on—and meantime we'll keep this little talk to ourselves, shall we, just in case the two youngsters upstairs are sensitive about being discussed, even in the kindest way? All right! Come on, Latimer, we'll go upstairs."

*

A cheerful voice shouted "Come in" to our knock on the door that faced the stairs on the first floor, and we entered a cosy little room facing onto the street over the garden. It boasted a shallow iron balcony along which somebody—probably, I thought, Mitzi—had placed a row of pots with flowering plants, geraniums, nasturtiums and marigolds, and though there was a bed in one corner it had been carefully covered with an old blue coverlet and the pillows thrust into covers of vari-coloured cretonnes so as to give the little place the effect of a bedsitting-room. There was a worn piece of carpeting in the middle of the floor, an armchair with a faded cretonne cover, carefully washed and mended, and two upright chairs—a table in the window and a pleated pink paper "fan" filled up the little grate. On the hearth was a gas-ring on which a kettle was already boiling, and on the table a battered tin tray bore four cups and four saucers, a brown teapot, milk-jug and sugar basin plus a willow-pattern dish of fancy biscuits, a second dish bearing cheese and butter, bread and three bottles of beer. It was evident that Jack Holcroft and his future wife, humble folk as they might be, had all the true instincts of hospitality.

Jack came eagerly forward to greet us as we entered and Mitzi, rising shyly from her perch upon the bed, held out her small hand to each of us in turn as Jack introduced us.

She was fully as pretty if not prettier than the snapshot we had seen, and spoke, it was soon plain, quite good English, though with an attractive foreign accent. She wore a plain little navy blue cotton frock; but her foreign blood peeped out in the round gilt ear-rings that swung for her ears, and the triple row of twisted glass beads of many colours that ringed her neck. Pen greeted her with his usual charming courtesy and seated himself, as invited, in the large armchair while Mitzi busied herself making the tea and Jack fussed hospitably about making talk—for he was palpably nervous, though trying manfully not to show it—handing cigarettes, matches, ash-trays and so on while Pen, refusing beer, accepted a cup of tea. He and Mitzi sipped tea and munched biscuits while I companioned Jack in a glass of beer and some bread and cheese; and then without a sign or hint of warning, Mitzi, who was standing beside the table ready to pour Pen another cup of tea, stiffened suddenly and stood rigid, motionless!

Jack sprang to his feet with a muttered curse, and went over to her; guided her gently to the bed and made her lie down upon it... and Pen and I, looking at each other, glanced at the round-faced alarm clock on the mantelpiece. It was eight o'clock...

I noticed as the girl moved towards the bed that her eyes were closed, her movements mechanical as those of a sleepwalker. When Jack made her lie down she resisted faintly at first, then relaxed and lay still—and as he drew the coverlet gently over her he said bitterly.

"Well, gents both, there you are! Was I right or was I?"

Pen rose, and coming over to the bed, sat quietly down on it, studying the face of the sleeper. It was still peaceful, remote—and I was opening my mouth to ask Jack a question when with a suddenness that made us all jump, the girl's mouth opened and a voice came bursting through. A man's voice, as Ma Bunn had said. A voice loud, assertive, strong, speaking in a tongue that was strange to me but was plainly not strange to Pen, with his flair for foreign languages.

He spoke to the entity, whoever he was, that was controlling the girl, in its own tongue—spoke forcefully and at length, and the Entity replied in kind. It was plain, though I could not understand the words being used, that whoever was speaking was angry, boastful, threatening, and I listened eagerly while poor Jack, agog with anxiety and excitement, sat on the very edge of his chair hungrily watching his sweetheart as she lay unconscious on the bed while this strange and terrifying Being talked through her—watching Pennoyer as he talked with the Unknown, asking questions, pressing points, arguing, denouncing...

For a full twenty minutes the strange interview lasted, and then, with the same abruptness with which he had arrived, our unknown visitor withdrew and Mitzi sat up, pushing her hands through her ruffled hair and looking vaguely round the room. Her eyes fastened on Jack and her face fell, seeing the expression on his. Slipping off the bed, she ran to him and took his head between her hands, crooning to him, kissing him, shedding tears in the most artless and touching way. I must confess there was a smarting at the back of my throat to see them together, these two poor young things, caught up in a force strange and evil—for evil I knew well it was—of which they had never dreamed...

Johnny held her tightly in his arms for a moment until he had his emotions once more under control, but it was the girl who spoke first. She addressed Pennoyer.

"So, *mein Herr*, you have heard him—the Thing that speaks now through me." Pen nodded and she went on "Only lately has he come, and always do I know when he has been here because of the look on my poor Johnny's face."

"Do you know who he is?" Pen asked, and she shook her head vigorously.

"Nein, nein!" Yet I could have sworn that she did not speak the truth, for as he asked the question, for a split second there had been a fleeting look of fear on her eloquent little face...

Pen nodded and turned to John.

"The Entity who was speaking through Mitzi was speaking Greek," he said—and again I thought I caught that look on Mitzi's face, though it was gone in a flash, so quickly that I might have been mistaken. Though I knew that I was not...

"I suppose," said Jack gloomily, "that means my Mitzi's a medium, don't it? Can't say I cotton to the idea overmuch!"

"Well," said Pennoyer, "it certainly means that she has psychic qualities, and these are being deliberately used by this Entity for his own purposes, whatever they are. I don't know yet."

But Jack was persistent.

"Being a medium means that all sorts of dead folks can come through and talk doesn't it?" he asked. "Could anybody who wanted to come and do it?" His expression was one of strong distaste.

"Oh no, I don't think so," Pen said quickly. "I don't think that Mitzi's psychic sensitivities lie in that direction at all! But obviously this Being has somehow sensed Mitzi's psychic gifts and has forced his way through, for his own reasons. Plainly he must be got rid of and Mitzi must be freed... and I hope I shall be able to do it."

He was writing as he spoke, making notes on the small pad he always carried in his pocket, and when he had finished scribbling he slipped the pad back in to his pocket and turned to Mitzi, watching wide-eyed and troubled from the shelter of her lover's arms. Pen's voice as he spoke was warm and kindly and reassuring.

"Now Mitzi, I want you to trust me—trust me fully, and believe I am your friend and want truly to help you. But I must ask for your full co-operation over your cure? You understand? I want you to come over as soon as possible to my flat in Blackfriars—Jack will bring you, but I don't want him with us when we talk together, as there are a lot of things I must discuss with you alone. When you are there I can explain all this to you more easily so that you will understand and—I hope—give me your full confidence. You will come?"

The girl nodded, though I seemed to see something wary, guarded in her eyes even as she nodded. Pen made a date for his next free evening, and with thanks for our drinks and fresh assurance that in the end all would be well, we took our way homeward.

We drove to Blackfriars via Regent Street and Whitehall so as to go home by way of the Embankment which we both loved—the long road by the river with its lights reflected in the moving water—the long black shapes of the barges gliding by and the serried wall of lights on the further side, and as we went we discussed the events of the evening.

I told Pen what I had noticed about Mitzi's reactions to his questions about our mysterious visitor, and he nodded. He had observed them too—I might have known that nothing would have escaped my friend's keen eyes.

"It may take me some time to dig out the facts behind this possession—for possession it is," said Pennoyer as he steered the car skilfully through the traffic of Trafalgar Square into Whitehall. "It's obvious that it stems from something in Mitzi's past that she has not told Jack and doesn't want him to know. Poor kid! I hope she will trust me enough to be honest with me, otherwise my task will be a very hard one."

"Who *was* it?" I asked curiously.

"A figure from her circus days," said Pennoyer. "An old lover, I suspect. Young as she is—I should think not more than twenty-six or seven—abroad, girls mature early, and many are married and mothers by the time they are seventeen. He's a Greek—possibly partially Bulgarian; his Greek was fluent but with an ugly accent that I think was Bulgarian—and he told me quite a lot about himself, boasting and bragging and saying how great he was. Name, Gene Markos—I wrote it down here—and according to him he was the greatest conjurer, the greatest magician, the greatest hypnotist that ever lived! I must check up on him as soon as possible—and here you may be able to help me, Jerry, with your journalistic contacts. See what you can find about one Markos, who according to himself was—is—a big figure in the circus world?"

"How do you mean 'is'?" I demanded. "If he were speaking through Mitzi he must be dead, surely?"

"It doesn't follow," said Pen. "What you don't realise Jerry—and what very many people don't know and would never believe—is that under certain conditions, it is possible for a *live* person to take possession of a living medium and speak through her! When this takes place the person speaking is as a rule either in trance or asleep; but it *can* be done by somebody who possesses the knowledge and the capacity to project themselves while still awake and conscious of what they are doing—and this, I think, is what was happening tonight. It argues a considerable amount of occult knowledge and training on the part of Markos to have done it, though—which is rather disquieting. It is plain he is a good deal more than a mere circus conjurer."

I was so astonished that I had no reply, for this idea was utterly novel to me. Yet I knew that Pen's knowledge of the unknown powers of man was so great that nothing he said could be dismissed as impossible, no matter how fantastic...

"That's the most extraordinary thing I've ever heard," I said at last. "But if it's possible..."

"It *is* possible, though it's not at all common," said Pen. "But I can't say offhand whether tonight I spoke to a dead person or a live one—though I saw him standing behind poor little Mitzi quite plainly."

"You *saw* him?" I was incredulous. "What did he look like? And if you saw him, how is it you can't tell whether he was a ghost or an astral projection?"

"Because they look just the same," explained Pen. "That is one of the many traps in psychic work. Quite often a genuine and perfectly honest medium will see the astral form of a person and say it is the spirit of somebody dead, when it isn't at all, but a projection of a living person, which leads to all sorts of confusion sometimes. As to what he was like—he's a man in his late forties, I should say. Tallish, black-haired, good-looking in a flashy way, with a heavy black moustache and black eyes... wearing colourful baggy trousers and a red sash with a short gold-embroidered jacket and a cap to match with a tassel... effective circus-ground sort of dress. A bad fellow, I know—and undoubtedly dangerous, though just *how* dangerous remains to be seen. I shall be interested to find out the connection between him and Mitzi—but from her obvious anxiety to keep it from Jack's knowledge I should say it's a pretty close one."

"What if she's scared and won't talk?" I asked as we swung up from the Embankment into the quiet little square where was Pen's flat. Pen smiled.

"If she won't talk voluntarily I shall find some way of persuading her," he said. "You know my methods, Watson!"

It took quite a bit of ferreting before I could discover anything about the Great Markos—for he was, of course, nothing like as Great as he would have had Pennoyer believe!

The most astonishing part was that I found he was still alive! So the shape that Pennoyer's clairvoyant sight had seen had been not, as usual, the semblance of somebody who had left the earth behind him, but the shape of somebody who was still very much there. He was a conjurer travelling with this and that and the other circus and sometimes doing a turn on the smaller music halls as well.

His turn was a mixture of things. Sawing a woman in half, making her disappear, clairvoyance, trick-shooting—done, I've no doubt, by means of mirrors and clever sleight-of-hand—a little hypnotism and so on, all accompanied by clever patter and a showily handsome presence.

I hastened with this information to Pennoyer, who nodded his head thoughtfully.

"I rather thought it might be so," he said. "But I can't do anything more until I've seen this girl Mitzi and had a talk with her. I only hope she will be frank—but I may have difficulties with her."

"Why?" I asked curiously. "Surely she wants to be cured of this obsession? She's dying to marry Jack, but she says she won't until she is cured—so why do you think she may not be willing to play ball with you to help the cure?"

"Because she is terrified of some disgraceful secret of her past life leaking out to Jack," said Pennoyer. "It's plain she has had a tough time and had little reason to trust men, so why should she trust me not to betray her, poor little soul? She's madly in love with Jack. But if this business stems from some period in her past life of which she is ashamed, she will do all she can to hide it lest Jack grow to know of it and repudiate her—as, of course, some men would do."

I glanced at my friend's serene face, mirror as it was of the utmost honesty and sincerity.

"How she could ever dream that *you* would betray her is beyond me," I said bluntly. Pen smiled.

"Many men have let that poor little girl down," he said quietly, "and after all, she has only met me once and has no reason to trust me, any more than any other strange man. Jack is her sheet-anchor, her refuge from the storm, her haven of peace from the stresses of a cruel world... no wonder she dare not do anything that might make a breach between them!"

"I don't believe that anything would do that," I said. "I think Jack's the type that even if there were some scandal and disgrace in her past life he would say it belonged to the past, and marry her all the same."

"I think so too," said Pennoyer. "But I doubt if Mitzi would. She is a foreigner and knows the jealously-possessive attitude of her own menfolk towards their women and how, if they found a girl they had meant to marry wasn't all she should be, they would refuse to marry her at once... and so, of course, would quite a number of Englishmen. But not, I think, in the case of Jack. However, I hope we shall not need to put him to the test. I hope to be able to release her from this without betraying anything of her past life! That after all, is her own business and should remain her own. We shall see."

When the date arrived on which Mitzi was to visit us, Jack brought her, but excused himself from staying while the interview with Pen took place. He would, he said, call for her in about two hours time—he was quite frank about his reason for not waiting, though Pen offered him papers and cigarettes and a drink in the cosy dining-room, if he chose to wait. He would be, he said, "too tee'd up." It was better to kill time in a movie and come back later...

With a final hug and kiss to the girl, he left, and she sat down between us in a deep chair, looking very pretty in a red-flowered frock and red sandals, trying her best to appear at ease but plainly both nervous and over-excited. However, Pennoyer was an expert at dealing with nervous people. He made coffee, produced a box of chocolates that made her eyes bulge with appreciation, told stories, joked and laughed, and showed her various little curios from his well-stocked cabinet until her initial wariness began to relax, and she seemed willing to answer the tactful questions that after a while he began to put to her. But it soon became plain that she would not really "open out"—not as Pen had hoped, at least.

Did she know anybody called Markos? Yes, she had known him, but never very well. He had worked in the same circus in which her father and mother were engaged, but he was a star turn and they were only minor turns, so they didn't see much of him. Had she liked him? How could you say if you liked anybody, if you didn't know them? He was a big man in the circus world, and she had been only a young girl. She really didn't remember much about him, or when she had seen him last, or anything...

It was plain she was stalling, refusing to play, and after a while Pen abandoned any attempts to draw information out of her directly, and proceeded to go about it in a different way, while I watched, amused and interested. I rarely knew my friend to be defeated!

He dropped the subject of Markos and drew her on to talk of other things while he made coffee and produced a bottle of cherry brandy and some tiny green glasses that fascinated Mitzi; and while she was cautiously sipping her liqueur he steered the talk in the direction of glass and the wonderful glass makers he had visited in Italy, Murano, the Volveri works, the Salviati glass factories and so on. At first I was puzzled as to why he had chosen this particular topic, as offhand one would have thought it rather above the head of a little café waitress; but when he produced, among a group of round Victorian glass paper-weights with flowers and little scenes embedded in them, the crystal ball that I knew he occasionally used in his work, I began to understand the direction in which his talk was tending.

By this time Mitzi was completely at her ease. She had concluded that the examination she had dreaded was safely over, her wariness had vanished, and she was thoroughly interested in the lovely things that were being shown her. She had eaten plenty of chocolates and drunk two glasses of the cherry brandy, which despite its sweetness, was stronger than she realised, and, now as she stared into the depths of the crystal ball trying to see the coloured pattern that Pen assured her she would see of she looked long enough, I could see her relaxing more and more, going limp and sleepy as the hypnotic glaze filmed her dark eyes. As she relaxed Pen's voice went on, soothing, coaxing, low, an enchantment in itself...

"It's curiously made, that glass ball. You never see the pattern in it until you've looked into it for some time, but go on looking. It's a far prettier pattern than any of the others... worth taking a little trouble to see... that's right! Go on looking, but relax all you can while you look, and don't worry if you don't see it right away... it will come in time..."

Mitzi's hands dropped limply into her lap and her head fell back. The glass ball rolled downwards towards the floor, but Pen caught it before it fell and nodded, satisfied. It had worked. Mitzi was well and truly hypnotised...

With a soft little sigh she settled down into her chair. I rose and put the glass things back in their respective places and when I was once more installed in my seat, Pen began.

"Hullo Mitzi! You know me, don't you, and know that I'm your friend?"

She sighed again, but it was a sigh of relief, of confidence. She answered in her native German, which fortunately both Pen and I spoke fluently.

"Yes, I know now—but I wasn't sure at first."

"Well," said Pen. "You're sure now—and I want you to help me cure you by telling me the truth about yourself and this man Markos. You didn't tell Jack the truth, did you?"

Mitzi shook her head.

"No. I was frightened that if he knew all he might leave me, and that I could not bear."

"But you *must* tell *me* the truth, or I can't release you from this man," said Pen. She nodded.

"I know. I will tell now, because I have no fear that you will tell *mein leibling*, my Johnny." The curly dark head turned in his direction with a touching confidence.

"It was true what I told Johnny, but only up to a point. I and my father and mother were in the same circus with Markos. He was one of the big turns and they were only one of the smaller. It was true that when Hitler invaded Austria we all had to fly from Europe to England—but it was with my mother and Markos. My father had died some months before and Markos had become my mother's lover. She was a pretty woman, and he had been after her for some time—and when my father died she gave in to him and became his assistant in his act. She broke with her sister over this—they had been a skating turn together—and my aunt left the circus; I think she married somebody, but I forget. I never saw her again." She sighed faintly and settled still deeper into the embrace of the deep velvet-covered chair.

"I was only very young then, about fourteen, but as I was pretty and could do a little dancing and tumbling and all that, Markos used to use me in his act to amuse the audience while he prepared his next item—and then it happened that he began to notice me, and it broke my mother's heart. I used to hear them quarrelling over me and cower in my bed—I hated Markos and feared him, but I dared not disobey him, for he meant bread to my mother and to me, and where could we go if we left him? Also he used to try experiments in hypnotism on me, and vowed I was the best subject he ever had—he was gifted that way. The circus folk whispered that he knew black magic, and maybe he did. He could do many strange things, I do know that. Well, the time came when he told my mother he wanted me as his assistant and she could go—and that night she took poison. She must have loved him, brutal as he often was to her..."

After that there was a long pause and a sigh and the girl went on.

"Well, you can guess what happened. I was only sixteen—scarcely that—and utterly alone in the world... at this man's mercy, and he had no mercy! I hated him, but at the same time he fascinated me. I know that the frequent hypnotic trances he used to induce in me had brought me so much under his influence that I could not have broken away then. I was too weak and too young. So I became his mistress, and for two or three years it went on. I was wretchedly unhappy but dared not break away—where could I run to and what could I do? We were working the music halls in England then, since there were few circuses in the war—the smaller, cheaper halls, of course—and though we made a certain success, Markos used to drink all the money he made, and when he was drunk he was a fiend. He used to knock me about and often I used to think of following my mother's example... but then I found I was to have a baby, and that was something to live for. I even hoped that Markos would be pleased... but he was furious and swore at me, as though having the baby was my fault and he had nothing to do with it.

"He tried to get me to get rid of it, because of course it meant that for several months I would be unable to appear on the stage with him, and he would have to get another assistant... but I would not do it, and that made him wilder than ever. One night he got even more drunk than usual and knocked me about so that I fell down the stairs and broke my arm and the landlady of the rooms where we were got the doctor, and she told Markos what she thought of him, and so did some of the other lodgers. I was taken to hospital unconscious and had a severe miscarriage in which I lost my baby and almost lost my life too. And Markos was hauled up before the magistrates and got a heavy sentence for ill-treating me—and when he was taken away to prison I knew this was my chance to get away. But I was faced with the question of how I was to live if I did? I knew nothing but circus life, but I was not a turn in myself—what could I do? I made up my mind to drown myself in the Thames, and I went down to Westminster Bridge to do it, one cold winter's night. But a woman who was watching me guessed what I was meaning to do, and spoke to me as I stood on Westminster Bridge and took me back with her to her little house—God bless her!—and there she fed me and comforted me and gave me courage to take up life again. I found afterwards that she was a member of a sort of Guild called 'The Friends of the Poor' who go about trying to help people in need—and truly she was a friend in need then."

Hans stirred and barked a muffled bark in his sleep where he lay in his accustomed corner and the sound, slight as it was, seemed to disturb the speaker. Pen laid one hand softly on her head and after a moment she resumed.

"She used to work in a big office in the City and there was a cafeteria nearby where they wanted a girl. She spoke for me and said she had known me for a long time, and they knew her well and took me on her recommendation. So from that day onwards I was able to keep myself and knew I need never again go back to Markos—and I was thankful!" She shifted her position a little in her chair and went on.

"Well, I worked there for two years, and then the café changed hands and they didn't want me, so I had to find another job. But by that time I had a good reference and had no difficulty in finding another post—and then I met Johnny, and the rest you know."

"When did this daily visitation first begin?" asked Pennoyer.

"It began soon after Johnny asked me to marry him," said the girl. "And I have a feeling that my great happiness and thankfulness at being free of Markos, or even the shadow of him, and looking forward to a life of peace where I could have a home of my own and perhaps another baby, and my darling Johnny coming home to me every evening... I don't know, but I have a feeling that a sort of wave of that might have reached Markos, who was out of prison and groping and fumbling to find me, and told him where I was. Could that happen, do you think?"

"Certainly it could," said Pennoyer, "after all, for several years you were constantly hypnotised by this man, besides being his mistress, and without doubt that establishes a strong link. But I fancy there must have been something more substantial that led him to you—something that has acted as a magnet, so to speak. Were you foolish enough to keep anything belonging to him? Anything, no matter how small—a handkerchief, an old glove, a bit of writing..."

The girl frowned and then nodded.

"Yes, I did keep something. Now I remember—I don't know why, but I kept the note he sent me after he was sent to prison. It is in my bag still, tucked down inside the fining..."

Pen reached down and picked up the shabby little black leather handbag that stood beside the girl's chair. He fumbled for a moment in its interior and fished out a crumpled scrap of paper covered with writing in a flamboyantly-arrogant hand.

I bent over his shoulder, and together we read the note.

Mitzi,

I know that when I am away you will try and run away—but I warn you that wherever you go you will never escape me! When I come back I shall remake my act and concentrate entirely on hypnotism, and I shall need you more than ever. I have imposed my will upon you too often for you ever to be able to break loose. Wherever you go, I shall find you and make you mine again. Do not think this is an idle threat.

Your Master, Gene Markos.

"Hm!" said Pennoyer folding the note carefully and placing it in his breast-pocket. "It's a great pity you kept that, my child, as it gave him a 'psychic scent' to follow so he was able to track you down on the Inner Planes. However, I think I may be able to make use of it, so forget about it now. But tell me—when did you begin to suspect that this sleeping trouble was due to Markos?"

"I guessed because of the times," whispered the girl. "You see, in a circus—in these smaller travelling circuses at least—they have to give two shows a day so as to make as much money as they can while they can—and four o'clock in the afternoon and eight o'clock at night were the times when Markos's act was on—when we used to appear. I fell asleep at the precise moment when he used to hypnotise me, and wake up twenty minutes later, just as I used to do in his act. So after it happened a few times I knew who must be behind it all—and I was terrified! He had found me! He had been hunting me ever since he came out of prison and found me gone—he was tracking me down, as he said he would..."

Even in her tranced state she shuddered, and Pennoyer laid a soothing hand on her fingers twisting together feverishly in her lap.

"Don't panic child," he said. "I can help you and I will—you will be safe, I promise you. But what is his purpose? It cannot be that he is in love with you, for I am sure that he knows nothing of love!"

The girl laughed a bitter laugh.

"Love?" she said. "The only thing Markos loves is himself. But he *needs* me. His act was first of all clever conjuring tricks with a little hypnotism and clairvoyance thrown in—but as time went on he found that that was always the most popular part of the act. But he could not always find an assistant who was a good hypnotic subject—my mother, for instance, was little use to him, and with her he always had to fake—but I was the best subject he ever had; he always said so... and he wants me back! He means to force me into breaking with Johnny and come crawling back to him... to become the tool in his hands he always meant to make me..."

"Don't be afraid," said Pennoyer again. "Luckily, though he has managed to make contact with you on the Inner Planes, he does not know where you live on the physical plane, and it is to be hoped he never does. For plainly his power over you was very strong, and you might not be able to resist it did you meet him again."

"I think that I could," said the girl softly. "Because now I love Johnny with all my heart and soul, and love makes strong, does it not?"

"It does indeed," Pen said gently, "yet I hope we will not have to test your love in this way. Now I am going to tell you that when you wake you will have no memory of having been to sleep like this—and no memory of the scrap of writing that I have taken. You will remember only that you spent a pleasant evening with us here and answered various questions that revealed nothing you did not wish revealed—and you will go home happily with your Johnny and wait until I get in touch with you both again. And now I am going to wake you up..."

After the two young people had left us with many expressions of goodwill and eager promises to come again, Pen said to me.

"Sorry I can't let you go home tonight, Jerry. We've got some work to do!"

"Okay," I said. "Lucky I keep the odd pair of pyjamas here in case of emergencies. What are we going to do?"

Pen tapped his breast pocket.

"See if I can run this chap to earth via his writing," he said. "I'm going into the Silence! We'll make some tea ready for when I wake up. Come on! There are biscuits and cake and cheese in the sideboard, and you can make yourself some sandwiches if you like while I get ready. There's ham and smoked salmon, I think, in the fridge."

Smoked salmon being a weakness of mine, I duly made myself some sandwiches while the kettle was boiling, set biscuits and cheese and butter and a slab of the fruit cake Pen loved ready on a dish, and carried them with a thermos full of tea into Pen's bedroom. It was an austere little room, sparsely furnished, with a narrow divan bed in one corner, an old carved press for clothes in another, and a Queen Anne tallboy that served as dressing-table as well as chest-of-drawers in another. The single armchair stood beside the window, where I knew Pen sat each morning in his dawn meditation facing the sunrise; and on the polished floor was spread the lovely old silken Persian rug that Pen always used in these experiments of his that we called "going into the Silence"—when he left his tranced body and went travelling on God-knew-what strange journeys.

I fetched the carved ivory Chinese headrest that he always used, and as I was placing it in position on the rug he entered the room, freshly bathed and clothed in the long brown hooded woollen robe that was the only garment he wore on these occasions. He smiled and nodded his thanks as he saw my preparations, the thermos, the cake and the rest.

"Good for you, Jerry!" he said heartily. "Now, you can make yourself comfortable in my big chair—you can have a shaded light, as you know, as long as it isn't on my face, and there's plenty for you to read here. The only thing I *don't* want is for you to smoke."

"Don't worry," I said, "I'm well trained by now, and it doesn't worry me to do without a cigarette for an hour or two. How long do you think you'll be gone?"

Pennoyer shrugged.

"Impossible to tell," he said. "But I have a hunch, not too long. I don't think, somehow, I shall have to go far afield to find our quarry—I believe he's somewhere in England."

"Really?" I said. "I'd have thought that when he got out of prison he'd have headed for the Continent and oblivion as fast as he could."

"It may be," said Pen equably as he lay down on his rug and composed himself, hands folded and ankles crossed for his vigil. "But I'm not at all sure! Now so long for the present, old man—I'm off."

"Do you want me to do any 'protecting' tonight?" I asked, for on occasions when my friend had to go into the Silence, I had had to go through some quite elaborate protective measures to guard his tranced body while the spirit was away from it. Pen shook his head.

"No thanks, It isn't necessary, This room—this whole flat, indeed—is permanently protected, I see to that—and believe me, it's necessary sometimes when Those of the Dark whom I've cheated of their prey are after me!" A dry smile creased his lean features, and he opened one hand to disclose the scrap of paper covered with Markos's handwriting. "This brute used his writing to hunt down that poor child, Now I'm going to use it to hunt *him!*"

His eyes closed and he composed himself to sleep, I turned the red-shaded lamp down to a glimmer just strong enough to read by, settled myself comfortably in the armchair, and buried myself in a book. Slowly the time passed, one hour, two—and then Pennoyer stirred, breathed deeply and awoke. For a moment he lay staring vaguely at the ceiling, then turning to me, smiled and curling himself into his favourite position, cross-legged on the rug, held out his hand for the cup of tea he so badly needed after these expeditions, He always looked worn and white when he returned, but soon the hot tea brought back his normal colour, and as we ate and drank he told me what had happened.

Markos was in England, as Pennoyer had thought, He was working the halls now, and called himself an "illusionist", not a conjurer—he had altered his name too to "Markandos", probably wisely. The case against him had been an ugly one; and the British have a strange prejudice against men who beat pregnant women almost to death...

"I ran him to earth in a third-rate music hall, somewhere, I think, in the North of England judging from the look of the town," said Pen. "Drab grey cobbled streets and drab grey little houses in rows—slanting rain and high smoke stacks and cranes and slag heaps outside—mining town of some sort, I'm sure. He was in his dressing-room, taking off his make-up after the show and talking to a scared-looking little woman, cursing her and swearing at her—I suppose his present assistant in his act. He's just as I saw him, but without his make-up looks older—a bad one if ever I saw one, Jerry! But I think I've found his heel of Achilles!"

The hollowed eyes in his thin face were bright with satisfaction. "Now listen to me. This is what I want you to do..."

Two days later I was travelling resignedly up to the North of England where, in one of the minor suburban halls on the outskirts of Manchester, a certain Markandos was billed to appear. It was plain that our quarry had abandoned circus life for the moment at any rate, probably from sheer necessity, since in England since the War there were few of the itinerant circuses such as he was used to on the Continent; and his act would scarcely be good enough for the few really first-class circuses such as Bertram Mills's.

However, this made it easier to run him to earth; and after a little trouble, with the help of a friend who was a theatrical agent, I had succeeded in doing so. I arrived in Manchester late in the afternoon, had a meal at the Midland, and clad in the shabby raincoat and battered felt hat that is the virtual uniform of the reporter, I made my way to the "Grafton" Music Hall. There I sent in my card to Markandos by the stage doorkeeper—or rather Pennoyer's card, as he had instructed me—though why Pennoyer should have chosen to pose through me as a talent-scout for one of the larger music hall circuits I did not yet know, and knew my friend too well to ask.

However, the hint of anybody linked with the larger halls acted like magic, as I knew it would, and the stage doorkeeper showed me up at once to a shabby little dressing-room up countless winding stone stairs, where by the light of a flaring unshaded electric bulb the Great Markandos was making up for the show.

He was facing the flyspecked mirror in the whitewashed wall behind the narrow littered table that served as a dressing-table when I was ushered in, and I caught a glimpse of his face before he saw me and swung round with all the smiling charm and urbanity at his command—and I disliked what I saw more than I can tell! Here was a bad man in every sense of the word. Raddled, lined, with heavy blue pouches under his eyes—one could see how rakishly handsome he must have been, was still in a way, but with the good looks ran coarseness, viciousness, cruelty, and my soul sickened at the thought of what that poor child Mitzi must have suffered at those ruthless hands. But there was no denying that well made-up as he was, wearing the handsome gold-embroidered jacket and cap, scarlet sash over wide trousers, all the rest that Pennoyer had described, he was a dashing and picturesque figure enough; and his gushing welcome to me was a tribute to what he felt was my importance.

"My dear sir—Mr. Penner, er—Pennoyer—I am too flattered to feel you have taken the trouble to come all the way up from London to see my act!"

I seated myself on the battered upright chair beside the dressing-table and accepted the whisky and soda he was already pouring out—I noticed that he drank his practically neat—and responded with the casualness that I felt belonged to my adopted role.

"Well, it wouldn't be strictly true to say I came up to Manchester simply to see your turn, Mr. Markandos! I had to come anyway on business for my boss Benyon." I saw the gleam in Markandos's eyes at my casual mention of the name of the head of "Benyon's," the most famous group of music halls in England—"but he had heard of your work and told me to take time off to see your act. So here I am."

"And how pleased—how delighted I am!" Between his excitement and the whisky he had drunk—for plainly the tot he was putting away was by no means his first drink that evening—Markandos's hand was palpably shaking. It was obvious that he visualised my visit as the Open Sesame, so to speak, of his entry into the world he longed to invade, the world of the London theatre. "Mr. Benyon, what a name and what a man! How joyful I should be for the chance to work under his banner. You cannot fancy Mr. Pen..." again he boggled over the name, "how weary an artist of my calibre gets of this eternal touring!"

He flung out a hand bearing a huge seal ring in a gesture of disgust; and I must say I could not but agree with him as I glanced round the grubby little room with its single light, its cracked washbasin with one dripping tap, the battered chair in which I was sitting and the high-placed shelf piled with cardboard boxes from which a dirty cretonne curtain hung that served as a wardrobe. He went on, sipping feverishly at his drink as he talked.

"Ah, what I have suffered since the war drove me out of Europe, where I was so famous and so successful! Doubtless Mr. Benyon will have heard of me from my Continental reputation?"

Knowing precisely how "famous and successful" he had been, I confined myself to a nod, and he went on.

"You have yourself seen my act, yes?"

"Some considerable time ago I saw you," I said glibly. "Somewhere abroad—it was when you were working with a circus."

A shade fell across the man's face and the hint of a frown—then he laughed bluffly.

"Ah, I remember—but I was poor and little known in those days, and forced to work as and where I could in order to become known. I was a conjurer then, but now my act is changed. I am a magician! An illusionist—I do telepathy, clairvoyance, hypnotism—you must see me tonight, sir. I am the greatest hypnotist in the world, me!"

That you certainly are *not*, I thought to myself. But you may well be a very good—or rather a very bad—one. There is something about your eyes... aloud I said carelessly:

"Do you still work with a girl assistant? I seem to remember a girl..."

Again that shade crossed his face, and his answer was evasive.

"Oh yes—always a girl or a woman. It appeals to the audience, you understand."

"Are you working with one now then?" I asked. He nodded.

"Oh yes—but she is not very good. I am training her, and she will do—until I can get back another girl, an assistant I once had. Ah!" he kissed his fingers and wafted them ecstatically to heaven.

"Ah, there was a girl—gifted in her way as I am in mine. Never had I so good a subject—I cannot wait until she returns to me, which soon she will do."

Like hell she will! I thought, and nodded, taking out my notebook as I did so.

"I should like to take down a few notes of your life story before you go if you can spare me a minute," I said, waving my fountain pen professionally. "I shall go back and make my report to Mr. Benyon, and if he makes you the offer that I feel sure he will, we shall need some preliminary puffs in the papers—news about you, you know. Your life, your adventures, your career and all that."

Markandos glanced at the cheap "Bee" clock on his dressing-table.

"There is but little time," he began—but I was prepared for that.

"Oh, that doesn't matter," I said arily. "We can start now, and then I'll come back, after seeing your act, and get the rest. Okay?"

Again he glanced dubiously at the clock which pointed to ten minutes to eight o'clock—I knew that he was due on the stage at eight, but I did not put two and two together then as I might have done, or I would have guessed why he plainly wanted to get rid of me before he went on. But I merely looked back at him blankly, and after a moment he nodded and began to talk.

If his life had been one half as dramatic and exciting as he was making it out to be, Markandos would have merited the entire front page of the *Daily Mail*. I knew he was making more than half of it up, but pretended to be busy taking notes when a tap came at the door and the voice of the call-boy, "Five minutes, Mr. Markandos!"

Markandos muttered a curse under his breath, but instantly suppressing it, turned a smiling face on me. Pushing me before him out of the room, he called the boy back and instructed him to show me the way down to the front of the house where he assured me that a seat—one of the best in the house!—would be found for me, and then disappeared in the direction of the wings, where I caught a glimpse of a pile of props and a depressed-looking little woman wearing Eastern costume waiting for him.

The manager was waiting for me at the entrance to the stalls—the news that an emissary of the great Benyon was present had evidently gone the round of the theatre like lightning!—but I refused the seat he offered me, on the pretext that I preferred to roam the theatre as I chose and see the show from various points rather than from one fixed. Actually, of course, my reason was a very different one.

I proposed to see only a few minutes of Markandos's act, and then slip back into his dressing room for purposes of my own—and if I had been seated where he could see me from the stage that purpose might well have been defeated! So I stood beside the manager at the back of the stalls for a few minutes only while I watched the man's performance—and it was a good show of its kind, there was no doubt.

Markandos was a polished and experienced showman, and though plainly much of his act was fake, it was extremely clever fake and got the audience completely puzzled. I caught his glance one or twice directed at the seat I was supposed to occupy, and knew that he was puzzled not to see me there—but I had no intention of giving him time to wonder and grow suspicious! When the manager left me, as he did after a few minutes, I slipped quietly round the back of the stalls to the door at the side of the stage that led into the wings, went through it and up the stone stairs to Markandos's dressing-room. Here I did what I had been told to do, went down the stairs to the stage door, slipped a handsome tip into the stage doorkeeper's hand, and at the same time gave him a note to Markandos to the effect that I had found myself, after all, unable to wait to the end of his excellent performance to see him again; but that I had already quite sufficient material for some preliminary "pars" about him, and that I had little doubt that Mr. Benyon, after hearing my report of his excellent work, would offer him a contract and that he would be hearing from him shortly. With that I left the theatre and managed to catch a late train to London.

I was still staying with Pennoyer, and found him sitting up for me with a tempting little supper keeping hot on the stove and some coffee, which by that time I badly needed; and as we ate I reported the happenings of the evening and gave him the object he had sent me to get from Markandos's dressing-room.

Together we examined it with interest. I had noted it where Pennoyer had said I would see it, hanging over the dressing-table from a nail driven into the wall above the mirror—a round gilt medallion affair on a chain, about the size of an old-fashioned five-shilling piece. It looked like an outsize version of one of those Victorian lockets made to hold a piece of somebody's hair, a mourning emblem, or a miniature portrait, and the front of it was an elaborate chased and embossed oval with, in the centre, the four-armed Greek cross. At the back there was a piece of glass inset, and behind it was what looked like a scrap of dark brown leather or bark or wood of some sort.

"Markandos is, like so many of his people, madly superstitious," said Pen, "and this is his mascot. He has had it for many years—it was probably in his family—and he believes that all his luck and his future depends on it. He is never without it—and now it is in my power I believe I can save Mitzi!"

"But what *is* it?" I asked.

"It's a reliquary—and that bit of brown stuff behind it is supposed to be a fragment of the true Cross," said Pennoyer. "Though, good Lord, if all the bits and pieces of wood that are going about the world enshrined in these things and in the churches and what-have-you were put together, you would have enough material for scores of crosses! It's fake, of course, but he thinks it's real, and it is the most precious thing in his life. The only thing he reveres." He weighed the shiny thing thoughtfully in his hands. "Here we have, I think, a worthy bargaining piece—and the price I shall ask for its return is Mitzi's freedom."

"Do you think he values it as much as he values regaining possession of Mitzi?" I asked doubtfully.

Pen nodded.

"I'm sure," he said confidently. "Don't forget that I watched him that night when I was out of my body and sitting in his dressing-room—thanks to that bit of his writing that made it possible for me to contact him so quickly and easily. I watched him concentrate on Mitzi—and I know how he has managed to establish such a hold on the poor child; I watched him kiss this reliquary before he went on the stage. He's never without it, and when he finds it missing he'll go raving mad and be ready to promise anything to get it back. You wait. He's cute enough to connect you with its disappearance, and within a matter of days he'll come here to me—that's why I made you use my card to introduce yourself. Then you will have a dramatic scene to watch through the peep-hole! I'd have you here in person, but I think better not—he'll be easier to handle if I have him alone."

"Thank goodness for the peep-hole," I said fervently. "I wouldn't miss the last act in this drama for worlds!"

Markandos did not wait even a few days. It was only the next evening when Pen and I were dining quietly together when a ring came at the telephone and Pen went to answer it. The conversation was plainly a short one and to the point, and Pen came back with a satisfied smile on his lean face. I looked at him as he resumed eating his *tortilla*—that delicious mixture of eggs and vegetables that he had learnt to make in Spain and taught Friedl along with many other toothsome Spanish dishes—and he nodded.

"It's Markandos, half daft with fury and coming round to murder me! Couldn't you hear him shouting down the telephone, calling me—or rather you—thief and liar and a dozen other choice names?"

"I heard a tremendous crackling and cackling," I said, "and I guessed who it was." I looked at my friend rather nervously. "But do you think it's wise for me not to be there, Pen, when he comes? He's a big chap and, as you say, mad with rage—what if he lugs out a knife or something like that? I wouldn't trust these half-breed Mittel-Europeans further than I could see 'em!"

"Don't you worry," said Pen tranquilly. "But hurry up and finish your dinner. He spoke from some hotel in Bloomsbury—I gather he's been let off appearing tonight on the plea of ill-health—but he's coming here as fast as a taxi can bring him and you don't want to miss Friedl's cheese soufflé, do you?"

"I don't indeed," I said looking hungrily at the steaming dish that Friedl was just bringing into the room. "Friedl is the queen of soufflé-makers. I'll hurry—but don't forget, at any sign of trouble I'm coming in, Pen."

"That's all right," said Pennoyer. "You'll be able to see all right via the peep-hole and a comfortable chair behind it. We'll have coffee when he's gone and a liqueur for you by way of a celebration."

"You're so sure of success then?" I asked. Pen nodded again.

"Quite sure," he said quietly. "I shall return the reliquary to Markandos—at a price—and he'll pay the price, make no doubt of that. But it will be a high one..."

Within a quarter of an hour Pennoyer was sitting quietly waiting in his comfortable lounge and I was ensconced in an armchair close to what we called "the peep-hole". This was an old food-hatch between the dining-room and the lounge through which the dishes used to be passed, and Pen had had it filled up with what seemed to be a picture, seen from the lounge side, but was actually a sheet of clear glass through which everything that happened in the lounge could be plainly seen. I don't know how this was done—I fancy it was Japanese—but the peep-hole served a very useful purpose, since through it Pennoyer could study quietly, unseen, any of the strange visitors—and believe me, some of them were more than strange!—that came to him for help. A man drops all his defences when he is alone—or thinks he is alone; and Pen often told me he could learn more about a person from watching him quietly for a few minutes through the peep-hole than he could learn from half an hour's questioning.

There I sat in the warm dusk and waited, and watched my friend turning and twisting his amber *kombologia* between his lean fingers, and marvelled afresh at the wonderful powers contained behind that keen lined face, those nervous powerful hands. It seemed ages that we sat thus, but it was really only about a quarter of an hour—and then a loud ring at the door bell announced our visitor.

Pennoyer rose to his feet and Friedl ushered in Markandos, who was dressed in an ordinary lounge suit and so lost much of his Gypsyish good looks.

It was a coarse-featured, heavy-jowled middle-aged roué that I looked at, with dyed moustache and hair that badly needed both cutting and washing, bloodshot eyes and an incipient paunch... he came striding furiously into the room, and when he saw Pennoyer he stopped short with a blank stare of surprise.

"Mr. Pen—Pen—" he scowled furiously as he stumbled over the name. "I do not know you! I want Pen..."

"My name is Pennoyer," said Pen smoothly. "Yes, I know that you are puzzled at seeing me, because I am not the man who came to see you in Manchester and sent in my card. He is a friend of mine who called on you for special reasons—and I told him to use my name."

The man looked blank still.

"Use your name? But I do not understand..."

"The reason why I sent him to you," said Pennoyer, "is twofold. First, I wanted the gilt reliquary that hung over your dressing-table. Second, I wanted you to come and see me. Having my name and address on the card my friend gave you, I knew that following on your loss you would come to me. As you have done."

This calm matter-of-fact statement plainly staggered Markandos —I shall now call him Markos—and he blinked, confounded.

"You mean you sent a man to steal from me—you admit this?" His rage was rising again. "But this is an outrage! I miss my reliquary—and it is of my family, much precious to me..." in his fury and agitation his English was getting out of hand—"and why for you do this..."

Pen held out one hand, and the authority in his gesture was such that the man fell silent, gaping, before him.

"I see that I shall have to explain myself," he said easily, "it will not take long, but perhaps you will take this chair? I would offer you a drink, but to be honest, I will neither eat nor drink with a man of your type, Markos—yes, I know your true name as I know your history. I have made you come to see me for a special purpose, and as soon as that purpose is accomplished you will leave my flat, and the quicker the better. Do you understand?"

Markos was plainly bewildered and more than a little intimidated.

"I do not understand," he snarled. "I—you admit you sent a man to steal—you wish to see me—but say quick the reason for all this?"

"I propose to tell you now," said Pennoyer. "I know of your connection with the girl Mitzi Streicher, and I know what you are doing, or rather trying to do to her. I have watched you at work... and I mean to force you to release her, to leave her alone!"

There was a silence in which you could have heard a pin drop. I peered closely through the glass of the peep-hole and saw Markos gaping at Pennoyer in utter astonishment mixed with fear—then with a palpable effort he pulled himself together and burst into a well-simulated guffaw of laughter.

"Well, well! My good friend, what nonsense are you telling me? What rubbish has the girl, this Mitzi, been trying to put over on you, eh? Certainly it is true she was at one time my assistant, but she left me... it is a long time ago."

The bluff was not a bad one. But in the gleam of light from the lamp at Pen's elbow I could see that the man's forehead was beaded with the sweat of fear.

"Certainly," said Pen, "it is some time ago. You were sentenced to quite a long spell in prison for half-killing her when she was pregnant by you. And you left her a letter when you went inside—a letter that threatened that when you came out you would hunt her down and force her to come back to you. Not because you loved her, but because she was a malleable subject that you could bend to your evil will..."

"It is a lie, an infamous lie! I am not Markos. I am Markandos," stuttered the man, but Pen swept ruthlessly on.

"Don't lie to me! When you failed to find her on your emergence from prison, you used the magic that you knew to track her down through your letter that, through your hypnotic influence, you had made her keep. Then, once you had found her and forged a link between you on the Inner Planes, you concentrated twice a day, at the hours when you used to appear together, on sending her once more into the hypnotic sleep you used to induce in her! You did this knowing that it would mystify and—you hoped—at last disgust and put off the young man she hopes to marry, and terrify her by proving to her that your power over her was still strong. And to do this you used yet another link with her that you possessed, believing that in the end you could make that link so strong that she would break with the young man who loves her and return to you and once again become your slave!"

Pen's voice rang through the room like a silver trumpet, and the wretched man before him cowered and shook in his chair... yet he would not yield as yet. His voice came as a harsh croak.

"I tell you it is a lie! I not know magic. I not know girl—I am honest conjurer..."

"And I am a magician!" said Pennoyer. "But I use *my* magic knowledge, which is far greater than yours, to try and help others, while you use yours for your own evil and selfish ends. To prove that I can work magic, I will tell you that I have seen, while out of my sleeping body, how you link up with the girl and what you use that belongs, or rather used to belong, to her."

Now terror, naked and unashamed, began to show in the wracked face of the monster in the chair. He peered up at Pennoyer, jaw fallen, eyes suffused, incredulous, yet shaken with craven fear...

"Out of your sleeping body? You can do that, and bring back the memory of what you do and where you go? By St. Spiridion, I have known it done and tried to do it..."

"But you did not know enough to succeed," cried Pennoyer. "You could project your thought-body only, not your true self—but I, *I* can project my true self in all its conscious strength! The night before my friend called on you I was sitting in your dressing-room and watched you concentrate on this girl, consciously, deliberately, holding the link in your hands." He flung out one hand in a gesture, royal, commanding. "You have that link with you now! Give it to me."

Markos moved, but it was to draw himself together as it were—to shrink into himself, his hands and arms curved inwards as though to guard or shelter something. His face was horrible to see, a squared grin of evil like that sometimes seen on the devil masks of the "No" dancers, and his voice came breathless with terror, yet still defiant.

"I will not—I will not! Without it I cannot contact her—and I will have her! She shall be mine..."

There was a flash of gold in the lamplight as Pennoyer snatched out the reliquary from his pocket and swung it by its chain before the cringing man. With a gasping cry of recognition Markos made a wild and ineffectual snatch at it, but Pennoyer backed swiftly as he spoke, holding the gleaming thing out of reach.

"Here is your treasure—the price against what you hold! Give me what I demand, and you may have it back. But refuse me—and watch me grind it into pieces now beneath my heel!"

There was a trenchant pause—and suddenly I knew the victory was ours. Springing to his feet Markos dragged from his pocket a long dark thing that looked like a snake and flung it furiously on the carpet at Pennoyer's feet... and I knew what it was. It was a length of plaited hair! Mitzi's hair, that she must have cut off, probably at his bidding when he was her lover—hair that he had hidden and guarded all the years, knowing that with his knowledge of magic he could use it to bring her back to him whether she would or no!

I looked at the two protagonists and saw that Pennoyer was holding out the gold reliquary to Markos. The Greek snatched it with something like a sob of relief and kissed it fervently before thrusting it into his breast pocket; then he swung on his heel to go—but as he did so he turned upon Pennoyer the most sinister face I think I have ever seen, and God knows I have seen a good many.

"You!" he croaked out. "You have beat me this time! But maybe there will be another time when I, *I* will beat, I Markos! I do not forget my hates—and of all the world you, you Pennoyer, I hate with all my heart and soul! And so some day..."

But I had slipped out of the dining-room and was standing in the open doorway. I had not liked the way in which his right hand was fumbling in at his hip pocket.

"I suggest you stop making threats, Markos," I said, "and clear out as fast as you can! Yes, you can stare—it was I who posed as coming from Benyon, and I who took your reliquary—so you can add me to your hates too. And now—get out, and do it quickly!"

For a split second he hesitated, eyeing me evilly. But I am a pretty stalwart sixfooter and still in my thirties, and Pennoyer lean and muscular and plainly in good condition—and two to one was more than he could face.

The front door closed with a vicious slam behind him and Pen and I looked at each other.

"Whew," said Pen wiping his forehead. "What a party for a hot night! Do you know, though I held all the aces, I had quite a fight for it mentally now and again to hold my ground? The chap has a dangerous knowledge of magic, like so many Greeks—so I'm glad I've managed to put a permanent spoke in his wheel via his reliquary!"

"How did you find out what he was using to get control over Mitzi?" I asked curiously.

"That was simple," said Pennoyer, "as I told him, I saw it all being done. I knew that Mitzi's possession of his writing had led him to her—I think she would have destroyed this, but I'm pretty certain he had told her the last time he had put her under hypnosis that he intended to send her this letter, and that she was not to destroy it. So she kept it, and it led him to her—but it was not strong enough to enable him to establish *real* power over her; and that he knew and had already provided for! I knew he must possess, and know how to use, something peculiarly personal to her—perhaps a garment she had worn, a bit of jewellery or something like that—on which he could concentrate, that would bring him into really close *rapport* with her. So when I went out to visit him, I chose the time close on eight o'clock, when I knew he would be sending out his will to her to go to sleep; and when he was all ready, made-up, for his act I saw him glance at the clock—it was ten minutes to eight. I saw him kiss the reliquary—imagine, Jerry, the blasphemy that could invoke the Blessing of the Most High upon the invoking of Evil—and then, then he brought out this pitiful rope of hair. Sitting down, he shut his eyes and held the plait firmly between his hands—and do you know, I positively *felt* the power radiating from him towards her? Fierce, brutal, determined... I managed to break the link that night, though, for by the use of my will I caused the failure of the electric circuit, and the shock and subsequent excitement of this broke the ray he was sending out, and he had no chance, before he went on, to get it going again. You will find, I'm sure, that that night, though Mitzi showed signs of falling asleep she did not actually do so, and both she and Jack were delighted, feeling sure that her cure was on the way; and the same thing must have happened the night when you were interviewing him. He had no chance to do his evil willing." (I may add here that subsequent enquiries proved my friend right in both these instances.)

"Odd how strong the power of the human hair is," I said thoughtfully. "I remember how you used two entwined locks of hair in the

'White Snake' business, when you were trying to solve the problem of the child Nicky." Pen nodded.

"*Any* part of the human body carries the radiations of that particular person," he said. "Skin, bones, hair, nail parings, even sputum and excrement—the savages who burn or bury these fragments to prevent their being used in magic against them know something, I assure you! And hair is especially powerful, since it is a growing thing, part of the actual body itself—and this hair was cut off while it was still alive; not mere dead hair, such as might be brushed or combed out of the hair." He stroked the glossy black rope. "I've not the least doubt that when she came to work for him and he found her value he got her to cut her hair short—she was probably willing enough to do it, since short hair was fashionable among the young things—and kept this, knowing what a signal hold it gave him over her."

"What are you going to do with it?" I asked. "Give it back to Mitzi?"

"Good God, no," said Pennoyer. "That would be to revive all sorts of memories in Mitzi and serve no purpose whatever!"

"You won't tell Jack even how she has been freed?"

"I don't think so," said Pennoyer. "Again, it would serve no purpose. All that either of those two need know is that Mitzi is cured—that she will no longer fall asleep except at the normal hour at the end of the day. Now as Friedl will have gone to bed I propose we make some more coffee… and I shall burn both this hair and Markos's letter in the stove while we are doing it. So the link will be well and truly broken."

A little later while we were drinking our coffee and discussing the whole amazing adventure, I suddenly remembered Pen's remark about "putting a spoke in Markos's wheel" by means of his reliquary, and asked him what he meant by it. He smiled.

"The thing's a fake," he said, "but he believed in it, and so it held power for him. If he had not been so essentially evil a soul I would have let him have it back as it came to me—untouched. But... it was not right to allow him to roam the world planning and preparing more and more evil. So... I saw to it that this time what the glass locket at the back of the thing contained was not fake, but real."

For the moment I was puzzled.

"What do you mean?" I asked.

Pennoyer looked at me gravely.

"You know that those of us who tread the Right hand Path do not take life lightly," he said. "But my Masters told me when I consulted Them about this case, that this man's time was come, and the earth would be better without him. Therefore, with the help and permission of a priest I know who is also a Master of Occultism—there are such priests, as you know, and great men they are—I inserted a tiny fragment of the Blessed Host in the back beside the bit of wood under the glass; and since evil cannot live in the presence of holiness, I think it will not be long before Markos joins his brigand forefathers."

And as so often happens with my wise friend's prophecies, it was so, as I shall tell at the end of this story.

From that moment all Mitzi's troubles cleared up like magic. Jack Holcroft's parents capitulated, since now there was nothing in the least wrong with the girl's health they could find no other reason for objecting to the marriage, and gave in with a good grace. The two young people were married, Mitzi in white satin and net, looking as pretty as a picture, and Jack stalwart and proud in blue serge, with Ma Bunn, Pennoyer and myself and a horde of friends to cheer them—a wedding breakfast with a three-tiered cake from me and a case of champagne from Pen in which to drink the bride's health. To our considerable relief, neither Jack nor his bride made any enquiries as to how her release had been effected—and some time afterwards Jack admitted to Pennoyer that he had a hunch that if too many enquiries were made something queer might come out that would upset Mitzi. Himself, he was all for letting sleeping dogs lie. As long as she got well, that was all that mattered... in which he showed himself a singularly wise young man!

We had a blissful card from them on their honeymoon in Blackpool—and it was on that same evening that we read in an evening paper of the sudden death of Mitzi's ex-lover and deadly enemy.

The great Markos had been found lying dead in his dressing-room just before the evening show with his reliquary clutched in one hand. Heart failure was the verdict at the inquest. Once again Pennoyer had been right. Evil could not live in the proximity of holiness...

1961

A HIGH DIVE

L. P. Hartley

Leslie Poles Hartley (1895–1972) was born at the end of the nineteenth century in the Fens at Whittlesey, spending his childhood in the nearby Fletton Tower, located on the edge of Peterborough. Particularly famed as a novelist, for works including *The Shrimp and the Anemone* (1944) and his most-enduring book, *The Go-Between* (1953), Hartley was also a solid teller of macabre tales. A number of these were assembled in *The Killing Bottle* (1931) and *The Travelling Grave* (1948); the latter collection was brought into print by the American publisher Arkham House, set up a decade before by August Derleth and Donald Wandrei primarily to preserve the "weird fiction" of New England writer Howard Phillips Lovecraft, himself an admirer of Hartley's "incisive and extremely ghastly tale", "A Visitor from Down Under".

"A High Dive" first appeared in Hartley's 1961 collection *Two for the River*. It's not a story that's always bracketed among his supernaturally tinged tales, but to my mind several inexplicable things are taking place here, not least the problematically shallow depth of "the old Mermaid's tank"...

The circus-manager was worried. Attendances had been falling off and such people as did come—children they were, mostly—sat about listlessly, munching sweets or sucking ices, sometimes talking to each other without so much as glancing at the show. Only the young or little girls, who came to see the ponies, betrayed any real interest. The clowns' jokes fell flat, for they were the kind of jokes that used to raise a laugh before 1939, after which critical date people's sense of humour seemed to have changed, along with many other things about them. The circus-manager had heard the word "corny" flung about and didn't like it. What did they want? Something that was, in his opinion, sillier and more pointless than the old jokes; not a bull's-eye on the target of humour, but an outer or even a near-miss—something that brought in the element of futility and that could be laughed at as well as with: an unintentional joke against the joker. The clowns were quick enough with their patter but it just didn't go down: there was too much sense in their nonsense for an up-to-date audience, too much articulateness. They would do better to talk gibberish, perhaps. Now they must change their style, and find out what really did make people laugh, if people could be made to; but he, the manager, was over fifty and never good himself at making jokes, even the old-fashioned kind. What was this word that everyone was using—"sophisticated"? The audiences were too sophisticated, even the children were: they seemed to have seen and heard all this before, even when they were too young to have seen and heard it.

"What shall we do?" he asked his wife. They were standing under the Big Top, which had just been put up, and wondering how many of the empty seats would still be empty when they gave their first performance. "We shall have to do something, or it's a bad look-out."

"I don't see what we can do about the comic side," she said. "It may come right by itself. Fashions change, all sorts of old things have returned to favour, like old-time dances. But there's something we could do."

"What's that?"

"Put on an act that's dangerous, really dangerous. Audiences are never bored by that. I know you don't like it, and no more do I, but when we had the Wall of Death—"

Her husband's big chest-muscles twitched under his thin shirt.

"You know what happened then."

"Yes, but it wasn't our fault, we were in the clear."

He shook his head.

"Those things upset everyone. I know the public came after it happened—they came in shoals, they came to see the place where someone had been killed. But our people got the needle and didn't give a good performance for I don't know how long. If you're proposing another Wall of Death I wouldn't stand for it—besides, where will you find a man to do it?—especially with a lion on his bike, which is the great attraction."

"But other turns are dangerous too, as well as dangerous-looking. It's *being* dangerous that is the draw."

"Then what do you suggest?"

Before she had time to answer a man came up to them.

"I hope I don't butt in," he said, "but there's a man outside who wants to speak to you."

"What about?"

"I think he's looking for a job."

"Bring him in," said the manager.

The man appeared, led by his escort, who then went away. He was a tall, sandy-haired fellow with tawny leonine eyes and a straggling moustache. It wasn't easy to tell his age—he might have been about thirty-five. He pulled off his old brown corduroy cap and waited.

"I hear you want to take a job with us," the manager said, while his wife tried to size up the newcomer. "We're pretty full up, you know. We don't take on strangers as a rule. Have you any references?"

"No, sir."

"Then I'm afraid we can't help you. But just for form's sake, what can you do?"

As if measuring its height the man cast up his eyes to the point where one of the two poles of the Big Top was embedded in the canvas.

"I can dive sixty feet into a tank eight foot long by four foot wide by four foot deep."

The manager stared at him.

"Can you now?" he said. "If so, you're the very man we want. Are you prepared to let us see you do it?"

"Yes," the man said.

"And would you do it with petrol burning on the water?"

"Yes."

"But have we got a tank?" the manager's wife asked.

"There's the old Mermaid's tank. It's just the thing. Get somebody to fetch it."

While the tank was being brought the stranger looked about him.

"Thinking better of it?" said the manager.

"No, sir," the man replied. "I was thinking I should want some bathing-trunks."

"We can soon fix you up with those," the manager said. "I'll show you where to change."

Leaving the stranger somewhere out of sight, he came back to his wife.

"Do you think we ought to let him do it?" she asked.

"Well, it's his funeral. You wanted us to have a dangerous act, and now we've got it."

"Yes, I know, but—" The rest was drowned by the rattle of the trolley bringing in the tank—a hollow, double cube like a sarcophagus. Mermaids in low relief sported on its leaden flanks. Grunting and muttering to each other the men slid it into position, a few feet from the pole. Then a length of hosepipe was fastened to a faucet, and soon they heard the sound of water swishing and gurgling in the tank.

"He's a long time changing," said the manager's wife.

"Perhaps he's looking for a place to hide his money," laughed her husband, and added, "I think we'll give the petrol a miss."

At length the man emerged from behind a screen, and slowly walked towards them. How tall he was, lanky and muscular. The hair on his body stuck out as if it had been combed. Hands on hips he stood beside them, his skin pimpled by goose-flesh. A fit of yawning overtook him.

"How do I get up?" he asked.

The manager was surprised, and pointed to the ladder. "Unless you'd rather climb up, or be hauled up! You'll find a platform just below the top, to give you a foot-hold."

He had started to go up the chromium-plated ladder when the manager's wife called after him: "Are you still sure you want to do it?"

"Quite sure, madam."

He was too tall to stand upright on the platform, the awning brushed his head. Crouching and swaying forty feet above them he swung his arms as though to test the air's resistance. Then he pitched forward into space, unseen by the manager's wife who looked the other way until she heard a splash and saw a thin sheet of bright water shooting up.

The man was standing breast-high in the tank. He swung himself over the edge and crossed the ring towards them, his body dripping, his wet feet caked with sawdust, his tawny eyes a little bloodshot.

"Bravo!" said the manager, taking his shiny hand. "It's a first-rate act, that, and will put money in our pockets. What do you want for it, fifteen quid a week?"

The man shook his head. The water trickled from his matted hair on to his shoulders, oozed from his borrowed bathing-suit and made runnels down his sinewy thighs. A fine figure of a man: the women would like him.

"Well, twenty then."

Still the man shook his head.

"Let's make it twenty-five. That's the most we give anyone."

Except for the slow shaking of his head the man might not have heard. The circus-manager and his wife exchanged a rapid glance.

"Look here," he said. "Taking into account the draw your act is likely to be, we're going to make you a special offer—thirty pounds a week. All right?"

Had the man understood? He put his finger in his mouth and went on shaking his head slowly, more to himself than at them, and seemingly unconscious of the bargain that was being held out to him. When he still didn't answer, the knot of tension broke, and the manager said, in his ordinary, brisk voice.

"Then I'm afraid we can't do business. But just as a matter of interest, tell us why you turned down our excellent offer."

The man drew a long breath and breaking his long silence said, "It's the first time I done it and I didn't like it."

With that he turned on his heel and straddling his long legs walked off unsteadily in the direction of the dressing-room.

The circus-manager and his wife stared at each other.

"It was the first time he'd done it," she muttered. "The first time." Not knowing what to say to him, whether to praise, blame, scold or sympathise, they waited for him to come back, but he didn't come.

"I'll go and see if he's all right," the circus-manager said. But in two minutes he was back again. "He's not there," he said. "He must have slipped out the other way, the crack-brained fellow!"

1923

SPURS

Tod Robbins

The American director Tod Browning's subversive *Freaks* (1932) is one of the most infamous movies in history—in Britain, for instance, the film was banned until 1963, three decades after its initial release. Its sympathetic (albeit knowingly voyeuristic) use of real circus performers with disabilities was groundbreaking, shocking unprepared audiences.

Freaks is loosely based on a short story by Browning's fellow countryman and namesake, Tod (born Clarence Aaron) Robbins (1888–1949). Robbins grew up and attended school in Brooklyn, going on to study at Washington and Lee University in Virginia in 1908. The first of his several novels, *Mysterious Martin*, was published in 1912, before the release of the bestselling *The Unholy Three* in 1917. This latter work—the story of a little person, a sideshow strongman and an unhinged ventriloquist who come together to commit a crime spree—was brought to the silent big screen in 1925, with Browning as director and Lon Chaney taking top billing; Robbins reportedly received $5,000 for the film rights. The picture was a box-office hit, leading Browning and MGM to raid Robbins's back-catalogue of short stories for a similar circus-themed work that was to become the inspiration for *Freaks*. This was "Spurs", which was first published in *Munsey's Magazine* in 1923 before featuring in Robbins's 1926 short-story collection, *Who Wants a Green Bottle?*

Interestingly, Tod Browning had an earlier carnival career before finding fame as a film-maker. He worked as a barker, clown, escape artist and contortionist, prior to taking on the role of the so-called "Hypnotic Living Corpse" for a sideshow act that toured the Mississippi. Robbins led a similarly incident-packed life: at college he was a famed athlete; he was the recipient of an inheritance that meant he had few money worries, later marrying and divorcing several times; and he moved from the States to France, remaining in the Riviera during the Second World War, before being held in a concentration camp near Paris during the Nazi occupation.

For me, "Spurs" struggles to reach the unsettling heights of Browning's cinematic masterpiece—an adaptation that departs significantly from Robbins's story—but it would seem remiss not to include the original inspiration behind one of the most influential and notorious popular culture renditions of American circus and sideshow life.

I

Jacques Courbé was a romanticist. He measured only twenty-eight inches from the soles of his diminutive feet to the crown of his head; but there were times, as he rode into the arena on his gallant charger, St. Eustache, when he felt himself a doughty knight of old about to do battle for his lady.

What matter that St. Eustache was not a gallant charger except in his master's imagination—not even a pony, indeed, but a large dog of a nondescript breed, with the long snout and upstanding ears of a wolf? What matter that M. Courbé's entrance was invariably greeted with shouts of derisive laughter and bombardment of banana skins and orange peels? What matter that he had no lady, and that his daring deeds were severely curtailed to a mimicry of the bareback riders who preceded him? What mattered all these things to the tiny man who lived in dreams, and who resolutely closed his shoe button eyes to the drab realities of life?

The dwarf had no friends among the other freaks in Copo's Circus. They considered him ill-tempered and egotistical, and he loathed them for their acceptance of things as they were.

Imagination was the armour that protected him from the curious glances of a cruel, gaping world, from the stinging lash of ridicule, from the bombardments of banana skins and orange peels. Without it, he must have shrivelled up and died. But these others? Ah, they had no armour except their own thick hides! The door that opened on the kingdom of imagination was closed and locked to them: and although they did not wish to open this door, although they did not miss what lay beyond it, they resented and mistrusted any one who possessed the key.

Now it came about, after many humiliating performances in the arena, made palatable only by dreams, that love entered the circus tent and beckoned commandingly to M. Jacques Courbé. In an instant the dwarf was engulfed in a sea of wild, tumultuous passion.

Mlle. Jeanne Marie was a daring bareback rider. It made M. Jacques Courbé's tiny heart stand still to see her that first night of her appearance in the arena, performing brilliantly on the broad back of her aged mare, Sappho. She was a tall, blond woman of the amazon type. She had big, round eyes of baby blue, which held no spark of her avaricious peasant's soul, carmine lips and cheeks, large white teeth, which flashed continually in a smile, and hands which, when doubled up, were nearly the size of the dwarf's head.

Her partner in the act was Simon Lafleur, the *Romeo* of the circus tent—a swarthy, herculean young man with bold black eyes and hair that glistened with grease, like the back of Solon, the trained seal.

From that first performance M. Jacques Courbé loved Mlle. Jeanne Marie. All his tiny body was shaken with longing for her. Her buxom charms, so generously revealed in tights and spangles, made him flush and cast down his eyes. The familiarities allowed to Simon Lafleur during the course of their act, the bodily acrobatic contacts of the two performers, made the dwarf's blood boil. Mounted on St. Eustache, awaiting his turn at the entrance, he would grind his teeth in impotent rage to see Simon circling round and round the ring, standing proudly on the back of Sappho and holding Mlle. Jeanne Marie in an ecstatic embrace, while she kicked one shapely bespangled leg skyward.

"Ah, the dog!" M. Jacques Courbé would mutter. "Some day I shall teach this hulking stable boy his place! *Ma foi*, I will clip his ears for him!"

St. Eustache did not share his master's admiration for Mlle. Jeanne Marie. From the first he evinced his hearty detestation for her by low growls and a ferocious display of long, sharp fangs.

It was little consolation for the dwarf to know that St. Eustache showed still more marked signs of rage when Simon Lafleur approached him. It pained M. Jacques Courbé to think that his gallant charger, his sole companion, his bedfellow, should not also love and admire the splendid giantess who each night risked life and limb before the awed populace. Often, when they were alone together, he would chide St. Eustache on his churlishness.

"Ah, you devil of a dog!" the dwarf would cry. "Why must you always growl and show your ugly teeth when the lovely Jeanne Marie condescends to notice you? Have you no feelings under your tough hide? Cur, she is an angel, and you snarl at her! Do you not remember how I found you, a starving puppy in a Paris gutter? And now you must threaten the hand of my princess! So this is your gratitude, great hairy pig!"

II

M. Jacques Courbé had one living relative—not a dwarf like himself, but a fine figure of a man, a prosperous farmer living just outside the town of Roubaix. The elder Courbé had never married; and so one day, when he was found dead from heart failure, his tiny nephew—for whom, it must be confessed, the farmer had always felt an instinctive aversion—fell heir to a comfortable property. When the tidings were brought to him, the dwarf threw both arms about the shaggy neck of St. Eustache and cried out:

"Ah, now we can retire, marry, and settle down, old friend! I am worth many times my weight in gold!"

That evening, as Mlle. Jeanne Marie was changing her gaudy costume after the performance, a light tap sounded on the door.

"Enter!" she called, believing it to be Simon Lafleur, who had promised to take her that evening to the Sign of the Wild Boar for a glass of white wine, to wash the sawdust out of her throat. "Enter, *mon chéri*!"

The door swung slowly open, and in stepped M. Jacques Courbé, very proud and upright, in the silks and laces of a courtier, with a tiny gold-hilted sword swinging at his hip. Up he came, his shoe button eyes all aglitter to see the more than partially revealed charms of his robust lady. Up he came to within a yard of where she sat, and down on one knee he went and pressed his lips to her red-slippered foot.

"Oh, most beautiful and daring lady," he cried, in a voice as shrill as a pin scratching on a window pane, "will you not take mercy on the unfortunate Jacques Courbé? He is hungry for your smiles, he is starving for your lips. All night long he tosses on his couch and dreams of Jeanne Marie!"

"What play acting is this, my brave little fellow?" she asked, bending down with the smile of an ogress. "Has Simon Lafleur sent you to tease me?"

"May the black plague have Simon!" the dwarf cried, his eyes seeming to flash blue sparks. "I am not play acting. It is only too true that I love you, *mademoiselle*; that I wish to make you my lady. And now that I have a fortune, now that—" He broke off suddenly, and his face drew up into angry wrinkles till it resembled a withered apple. "What is this, *mademoiselle*?" he said, in the low, droning tone of a hornet about to sting. "Do you laugh at my love? I warn you, *mademoiselle*—do not laugh at Jacques Courbé!"

Mlle. Jeanne Marie's large, florid face had turned purple from suppressed merriment. Her lips twitched at the corners. It was all she could do not to burst out into a roar of laughter.

Why, the ridiculous little manikin was serious in his love-making! This pocket-sized edition of a courtier was proposing marriage to her! He, this splinter of a fellow, wished to make her his wife! Why, she could carry him about on her shoulder like a trained marmoset!

What a joke this was—what a colossal, corset-creaking joke! Wait till she told Simon Lafleur! She could fairly see him throw back his sleek head, open his mouth to its widest dimensions, and shake with silent laughter; but *she* must not laugh—not now. First she must listen to everything the dwarf had to say, and draw all the sweetness out of this bonbon of humour before she crushed it under the heel of ridicule.

"I am not laughing, M. Courbé." She managed to say. "You have taken me by surprise. I never thought, I never even guessed—"

"That is well, *mademoiselle*," the dwarf broke in. "I do not tolerate laughter. In the arena I am paid to make laughter; but these others pay to laugh at *me*. I always make people pay to laugh at me!"

"But do I understand you aright, M. Courbé? Are you proposing an honourable marriage?"

The dwarf rested his hand lightly on his heart and bowed.

"Yes, *mademoiselle*, an honourable marriage, and the wherewithal to keep the wolf from the door. A week ago my uncle died and left me a large estate. We shall have a servant to wait on our wants, a horse and carriage, food and wine of the best, and leisure to amuse ourselves. And you? Why, you will be a fine lady! I will clothe that beautiful big body of yours with silks and laces. You will be as happy, *mademoiselle*, as a cherry tree in June!"

The dark blood slowly receded from Mlle. Jeanne Marie's full cheeks, her lips no longer twitched at the corners, her eyes had narrowed slightly. She had been a bareback rider for years, and she was weary of it. The life of the circus tent had lost its tinsel. She loved the dashing Simon Lafleur; but she knew well enough that this *Romeo* in tights would never espouse a dowerless girl.

The dwarf's words had woven themselves into a rich mental tapestry. She saw herself a proud lady, ruling over a country estate, and later welcoming Simon Lafleur with all the luxuries that were so near his heart. Simon would be overjoyed to marry into a country estate; and these pygmies were a puny lot. They died young! She would do nothing to hasten the end of Jacques Courbé. No, she would be kindness itself to the poor little fellow; but, on the other hand, she would not lose her beauty mourning for him.

"Nothing that you wish shall be withheld from you as long as you love me, *mademoiselle*," the dwarf continued. "Your answer?"

Mlle. Jeanne Marie bent forward, and with a single movement of her powerful arms raised M. Jacques Courbé and placed him on her knee. For an ecstatic instant she held him thus, as if he were a large French doll, with his tiny sword cocked coquettishly out behind. Then she implanted on his cheek a huge kiss that covered his entire face from chin to brow.

"I am yours!" she murmured, pressing him to her ample bosom. "From the first I loved you, M. Jacques Courbé!"

III

The wedding of Mlle. Jeanne Marie was celebrated in the town of Roubaix, where Copo's Circus had taken up its temporary quarters. Following the ceremony, a feast was served in one of the tents, which was attended by a whole galaxy of celebrities.

The bridegroom, his dark little face flushed with happiness and wine, sat at the head of the board. His chin was just above the tablecloth, so that his head looked like a large orange that had rolled off the fruit dish. Immediately beneath his dangling feet, St. Eustache, who had more than once evinced by deep growls his disapproval of the proceedings, now worried a bone with quick, sly glances from time to time at the plump legs of his new mistress.

Papa Copo was on the dwarf's right, his large round face as red and benevolent as a harvest moon. Next him sat Griffo, the giraffe boy, who was covered with spots, and whose neck was so long that he looked down on all the rest, including even M. Hercule Hippo, the giant. The rest of the company included Mlle. Lupa, who had sharp white teeth of an incredible length, and who growled when she tried to talk; the tiresome M. Jejongle, who insisted on juggling fruit, plates, and knives, although the whole company was heartily sick of his tricks; Mme. Samson, with her trained baby boa constrictors coiled about her neck and peeping out timidly, one above each ear; Simon Lafleur, and a score of others.

The bareback rider had laughed silently and almost continually ever since Jeanne Marie had told him of her engagement over a glass of white wine at the Sign of the Wild Boar. Now he sat next to her in his crimson tights, with his black hair brushed back from his forehead and so glistening with grease that it reflected the lights overhead, like a burnished helmet. From time to time he tossed off a brimming goblet of Burgundy, nudged the bride in the ribs with his elbow, and threw back his sleek head in another silent outburst of laughter.

"And you are sure that you will not forget me, Simon?" she whispered. "It may be some time before I can get the little ape's money."

"Forget you, Jeanne?" he muttered. "By all the dancing devils in champagne, never! I will wait as patiently as Job till you have fed that mouse some poisoned cheese. But what will you do with him in the meantime. Jeanne? You must allow him no liberties. I grind my teeth to think of you in his arms!"

The bride smiled, and regarded her diminutive husband with an appraising glance. What an atom of a man! And yet life might linger in his bones for a long time to come!

M. Jacques Courbé had allowed himself only one glass of wine, and yet he was far gone in intoxication. His tiny face was suffused with blood, and he stared at Simon Lafleur belligerently. Did he suspect the truth?

"Your husband is flushed with wine," the bareback rider whispered. *Ma foi, madame*, later he may knock you about! Possibly he is a dangerous fellow in his cups. Should he maltreat you, Jeanne, do not forget that you have a protector in Simon Lafleur."

"You clown!" Jeanne Marie rolled her large eyes roguishly, and laid her hand for an instant on the bareback rider's knee. "Simon, I could crack his skull between my finger and thumb, like this hickory nut!" She paused to illustrate her example, and then added reflectively: "And perhaps I shall do that very thing, if he attempts any familiarities. Ugh! The little ape turns my stomach!"

By now the wedding guests were beginning to show the effects of their potations. This was especially marked in the case of M. Jacques Courbé's associates in the sideshow.

Griffo, the giraffe boy, had closed his large brown eyes, and was swaying his small head languidly above the assembly, while a slightly supercilious expression drew his lips down at the corners. M. Hercule Hippo, swollen out by his libations to even more colossal proportions, was repeating over and over:

"I tell you I am not like other men. When I walk, the earth trembles!"

Mlle. Lupa, her hairy upper lip lifted above her long white teeth, was gnawing at a bone, growling unintelligible phrases to herself, and shooting savage, suspicious glances at her companions. M. Jejongle's hands had grown unsteady, and, as he insisted on juggling the knives and plates of each new course, broken bits of crockery littered the floor. Mme. Samson, uncoiling her necklace of baby boa constrictors, was feeding them lumps of sugar soaked in rum. M. Jacques Courbé had finished his second glass of wine, and was surveying the whispering Simon Lafleur through narrowed eyes.

There can be no genial companionship among great egotists who have drunk too much. Each one of these human oddities thought that he or she alone was responsible for the crowds that daily gathered at Copo's Circus; so now, heated with the good Burgundy, they were not slow in asserting themselves. Their separate egos rattled angrily together, like so many pebbles in a bag. Here was gunpowder which needed only a spark.

"I am a big—a very big man!" Hippo said sleepily. "Women love me. The pretty little creatures leave their pygmy husbands, so that they may come and stare at Hercule Hippo of Copo's Circus. Ha, and when they return home, they laugh at other men always! 'You may kiss me again when you grow up,' they tell their sweethearts."

"Fat bullock, here is one woman who has no love for you!" cried Mlle. Lupa, glaring sidewise at the giant over her bone. "That great carcass of yours is only so much food gone to waste. You have cheated the butcher, my friend. Fool, women do not come to see *you*! As well might they stare at the cattle being led through the street. Ah, no, they come from far and near to see one of their own sex who is not a cat!"

"Quite right," cried Papa Copo in a conciliatory tone, smiling and rubbing his hands together. "Not a cat, *mademoiselle*, but a wolf. Ah, you have a sense of humour! How droll!"

"I *have* a sense of humour," Mlle. Lupa agreed, returning to her bone, "and also sharp teeth. Let the erring hand not stray too near!"

"You, M. Hippo and Mlle. Lupa, are both wrong," said a voice which seemed to come from the roof. "Surely it is none other than me whom the people come to stare at!"

All raised their eyes to the supercilious face of Griffo, the giraffe boy, which swayed slowly from side to side on its long, pipestem neck. It was he who had spoken, although his eyes were still closed.

"Of all the colossal impudence!" cried the matronly Mme. Samson. "As if my little dears had nothing to say on the subject!" She picked up the two baby boa constrictors, which lay in drunken slumber on her lap, and shook them like whips at the wedding guests. "Papa Copo knows only too well that it is on account of these little charmers, Mark Antony and Cleopatra, that the sideshow is so well attended!"

The circus owner, thus directly appealed to, frowned in perplexity. He felt himself in a quandary. These freaks of his were difficult to handle. Why had he been fool enough to come to M. Jacques Courbé's wedding feast? Whatever he said would be used against him.

As Papa Copo hesitated, his round, red face wreathed in ingratiating smiles, the long deferred spark suddenly alighted in the powder. It all came about on account of the carelessness of M. Jejongle, who had become engrossed in the conversation, and wished to put in a word for himself. Absent-mindedly juggling two heavy plates and a spoon, he said in a petulant tone:

"You all appear to forget *me*!"

Scarcely were the words out of his mouth, when one of the heavy plates descended with a crash on the thick skull of M. Hippo; and M. Jejongle was instantly remembered. Indeed, he was more than remembered; for the giant, already irritated to the boiling point by Mlle. Lupa's insults, at this new affront, struck out savagely past her, and knocked the juggler head over heels under the table.

Mlle. Lupa, always quick-tempered, and especially so when her attention was focused on a juicy chicken bone, evidently considered her dinner companion's conduct far from decorous, and promptly inserted her sharp teeth in the offending hand that had administered the blow. M. Hippo, squealing from rage and pain like a wounded elephant, bounded to his feet, overturning the table.

Pandemonium followed. Every freak's hands, teeth, feet, were turned against the others. Above the shouts, screams, growls, and hisses of the combat, Papa Copo's voice could be heard bellowing for peace:

"Ah, my children, my children! This is no way to behave! Calm yourselves, I pray you! Mlle. Lupa, remember that you are a lady as well as a wolf!"

There is no doubt that M. Jacques Courbé would have suffered most in this undignified fracas, had it not been for St. Eustache, who had stationed himself over his Tiny master, and who now drove off all would-be assailants.

As it was, Griffo, the unfortunate giraffe boy, was the most defenceless, and therefore became the victim. His small round head swayed back and forth to blows like a punching bag. He was bitten by Mlle. Lupa, buffeted by M. Hippo, kicked by M. Jejongle, clawed by Mme.

Samson, and nearly strangled by both the baby boa constrictors, which had wound themselves about his neck like hangmen's nooses. Undoubtedly he would have fallen a victim to circumstances, and would never have left the banquet board alive, had it not been for Simon Lafleur, the bride, and half a dozen of her acrobatic friends, whom Papa Copo had implored to restore peace. Roaring with laughter, they sprang forward and tore the combatants apart.

M. Jacques Courbé was found sitting grimly under a fold of the tablecloth. He held a broken bottle of wine in one hand. The dwarf was very drunk, and in a towering rage. As Simon Lafleur approached with one of his silent laughs, M. Jacques Courbé hurled the bottle at his head.

"Ah, the little wasp!" the bareback rider cried, picking up the dwarf by his waistband. "Here is your fine husband, Jeanne! Take him away before he does me some mischief. *Parbleu*, he is a bloodthirsty fellow in his cups!"

The bride approached, her blond face crimson from wine and laughter. Now that she was safely married to a country estate, she took no more pains to conceal her true feelings.

"Oh, *la, la*!" she cried, seizing the struggling dwarf and holding him forcibly on her shoulder. "What a temper the little ape has! Well, we shall spank it out of him before long!"

"Let me down!" M. Jacques Courbé screamed in a paroxysm of fury. "You will regret this, *madame*! Let me down, I say!"

But the stalwart bride shook her head.

"No, no, my little one," she laughed. "You cannot escape your wife so easily! What, you would fly from my arms before the honeymoon!"

"Let me down!" he cried again. "Can't you see that they are laughing at me?"

"And why should they not laugh, my little ape? Let them laugh, if they will; but I will not put you down. No, I will carry you thus, perched on my shoulder, to the farm. It will set a precedent which brides of the future may find a certain difficulty in following!"

"But the farm is quite a distance from here, my Jeanne," said Simon Lafleur. "You are as strong as an ox, and he is only a marmoset. Still I will wager a bottle of Burgundy that you set him down by the roadside."

"Done, Simon!" the bride cried, with a flash of her strong white teeth. "You shall lose your wager, for I swear that I could carry my little ape from one end of France to the other!"

M. Jacques Courbé no longer struggled. He now sat bolt upright on his bride's broad shoulder. From the flaming peaks of blind passion he had fallen into an abyss of cold fury. His love was dead, but some quite alien emotion was rearing an evil head from its ashes.

"So, *madame*, you could carry me from one end of France to the other!" he droned in a monotonous undertone. "From one end of France to the other! I will remember that always, *madame*!"

"Come!" cried the bride suddenly. "I am off. Do you and the others, Simon, follow to see me win my wager."

They all trooped out of the tent. A full moon rode the heavens and showed the road, lying as white and straight through the meadows as the part in Simon Lafleur's black, oily hair.

The bride, still holding the diminutive bridegroom on her shoulder, burst out in a song as she strode forward. The wedding guests followed them. Some walked none too steadily. Griffo, the giraffe boy, staggered pitifully on his long, thin legs. Papa Copo alone remained behind.

"What a strange world!" he muttered, standing in the tent door and following them with his round blue eyes. "Ah, these children of mine are difficult at times—very difficult!"

IV

A year had rolled by since the marriage of Mlle. Jeanne Marie and M. Jacques Courbé. Copo's Circus had once more taken up its quarters in the town of Roubaix. For more than a week the country people for miles around had flocked to the sideshow to get a peep at Griffo, the giraffe boy; M. Hercule Hippo, the giant; Mlle. Lupa, the wolf lady; Mme. Samson, with her baby boa constrictors; and M. Jejongle, the famous juggler. Each was still firmly convinced that he or she alone was responsible for the popularity of the circus.

Simon Lafleur sat in his lodgings at the Sign of the Wild Boar. He wore nothing but red tights. His powerful torso, stripped to the waist, glistened with oil. He was kneading his biceps tenderly with some strong-smelling fluid.

Suddenly there came a sound of heavy, laborious footsteps on the stairs, and Simon Lafleur looked up. His rather gloomy expression lifted, giving place to the brilliant smile which had won for him the hearts of so many lady acrobats.

"Ah, this is Marcelle!" he told himself. "Or perhaps it is Rose, the English girl; or yet again little Francesca, although she walks more lightly. Well, no matter—whoever it is, I will welcome her!"

By now the lagging, heavy footfalls were in the hall, and a moment later they came to a halt outside the door. There was a timid knock.

Simon Lafleur's brilliant smile broadened.

"Perhaps some new admirer who needs encouragement," he told himself: but aloud he said: "Enter, *mademoiselle*!"

The door swung slowly open, and revealed the visitor. She was a tall, gaunt woman dressed like a peasant. The wind had blown her hair into her eyes. Now she raised a large, toil-worn hand, brushed it back across her forehead, and looked long and attentively at the bareback rider.

"You do not remember me?" she said at length.

Two lines of perplexity appeared above Simon Lafleur's Roman nose, and he slowly shook his head. He, who had known so many women in his time, was now at a loss. Was it a fair question to ask a man who was no longer a boy, and who had lived? Women change so in a brief time! Now this bag of bones, which seemed to be held together by the rags she wore, might at one time have appeared desirable to him.

Parbleu! Fate was a conjurer! She waved her wand, and beautiful women were transformed into hags, jewels into pebbles, silks and laces into hempen cords. The brave fellow who danced tonight at the prince's ball might tomorrow dance more lightly on the gallows tree. The thing was to live and die with a full belly. To digest all that one could—that was life!

"You do not remember me?" she said again.

Simon Lafleur once more shook his sleek, black head.

"I have a poor memory for faces, *madame*," he said politely. "It is my misfortune, when there are such beautiful faces."

"Ah, but you should have remembered, Simon!" the woman cried, a sob rising up in her throat. "We were very close together, you and I. Do you not remember Jeanne Marie?"

"Jeanne Marie!" the bareback rider cried. "Jeanne Marie, who married a marmoset and a country estate? Don't tell me, *madame*, that you—"

He broke off and stared at her, openmouthed. His sharp black eyes wandered from the wisps of wet, straggling hair down her gaunt person till they rested at last on her thick cowhide boots incrusted with layer on layer of mud and dust from the countryside.

"It is impossible!" he said at last.

"It is indeed Jeanne Marie," the woman answered, "or what is left of her. Ah. Simon, what a life he has led me! I have been merely a beast of burden! There are no ignominies which he has not made me suffer!"

"To whom do you refer?" Simon Lafleur demanded. "Surely you cannot mean that pocket edition husband of yours—that dwarf, Jacques Courbé?"

"Ah, but I do, Simon. Alas, he has broken me!"

"He—that toothpick of a man?" the bareback rider cried, with one of his silent laughs. "Why, it is impossible! As you once said yourself, Jeanne, you could crack his skull between finger and thumb like a hickory nut!"

"So I thought once. Ah, but I did not know him then, Simon! Because he was small, I thought I could do with him as I liked. It seemed to me that I was marrying a manikin. 'I will play Punch and Judy with this little fellow,' I said to myself. Simon, you may imagine my surprise when he began playing Punch and Judy with me!"

"But I do not understand, Jeanne. Surely at any time you could have slapped him into obedience!"

"Perhaps," she assented wearily, "had it not been for St. Eustache. From the first that wolf dog of his hated me. If I so much as answered his master back, he would show his teeth. Once, at the beginning, when I raised my hand to cuff Jacques Courbé, he sprang at my throat, and would have torn me limb from limb, had not the dwarf called him off. I was a strong woman, but even then I was no match for a wolf!"

"There was poison, was there not?" Simon Lafleur suggested.

"Ah, yes, I, too, thought of poison, but it was of no avail. St. Eustache would eat nothing that I gave him, and the dwarf forced me to taste first of all food that was placed before him and his dog. Unless I myself wished to die, there was no way of poisoning either of them."

"My poor girl!" the bareback rider said pityingly. "I begin to understand; but sit down and tell me everything. This is a revelation to me, after seeing you stalking homeward so triumphantly with your bridegroom on your shoulder. You must begin at the beginning."

"It was just because I carried him thus on my shoulder that I have had to suffer so cruelly," she said, seating herself on the only other chair the room afforded. "He has never forgiven me the insult which he says I put upon him. Do you remember how I boasted that I could carry him from one end of France to the other?"

"I remember. Well, Jeanne?"

"Well, Simon, the little demon has figured out the exact distance in leagues. Each morning, rain or shine, we sally out of the house—he on my back, the wolf dog at my heels—and I tramp along the dusty roads till my knees tremble underneath me from fatigue. If I so much as slacken my pace, if I falter, he goads me with his cruel little golden spurs, while at the same time St. Eustache nips my ankles. When we return home, he strikes so many leagues off a score which he says is the number of leagues from one end of France to the other. Not half that distance has been covered, and I am no longer a strong woman, Simon. Look at these shoes!"

She held up one of her feet for his inspection. The sole of the cowhide boot which incased it had been worn through, and Simon Lafleur caught a glimpse of bruised flesh caked with the mire of the highway.

"This is the third pair that I have had," she continued hoarsely. "Now he tells me that the price of shoe leather is too high, and that I shall have to finish my pilgrimage barefooted."

"But why do you put up with all this, Jeanne?" Simon Lafleur asked angrily. "You who have a carriage and a servant should not walk at all!"

"At first there was a carriage and a servant," she said, wiping the tears from her eyes with the back of her hand; "but they did not last a week. He sent the servant about his business and sold the carriage at a nearby fair. Now there is no one but me to wait on him and his dog."

"But the neighbours?" Lafleur persisted. "Surely you could appeal to them?"

"We have no near neighbours, for the farm is quite isolated. I would have run away many months ago. If I could have escaped unnoticed; but they keep a continual watch on me. Once I tried, but I hadn't travelled more than a league before the wolf dog was snapping at my ankles. He drove me back to the farm, and the following day I was compelled to carry the little fiend till I fell from sheer exhaustion."

"But tonight you got away?"

"Yes." she said, with a quick, frightened glance at the door. "Tonight I slipped out while they were both sleeping, and came here to you. I knew that you would protect me, Simon, because of what we have been to each other. Get Papa Copo to take me back in the circus, and I will work my fingers to the bone. Save me, Simon!"

Jeanne Marie could no longer suppress her sobs. They rose in her throat, choking her, making her incapable of further speech.

"Calm yourself, Jeanne," Simon Lafleur said soothingly. "I will do what I can for you. I shall have a talk with Papa Copo tomorrow. Of course, you are no longer the same woman that you were a year ago. You have aged since then; but perhaps our good Papa Copo could find you something to do."

He broke off and eyed her intently. She had stiffened in the chair, and her face, even under its coat of grime, had gone a sickly white.

"What troubles you, Jeanne?" he asked a trifle breathlessly.

"Hush!" she said, with a finger to her lips. "Listen!"

V

Simon Lafleur could hear nothing but the tapping of the rain on the roof and the sighing of the wind through the trees. An unusual silence seemed to pervade the Sign of the Wild Boar.

"Now don't you hear it?" she cried with an inarticulate gasp. "Simon, it is in the house—it is on the stairs!"

At last the bareback rider's less sensitive ears caught the sound his companion had heard a full minute before. It was a steady *pit-pat, pit-pat*, on the stairs, hard to dissociate from the drip of the rain from the eaves; but each instant it came nearer and grew more distinct.

"Oh, save me, Simon, save me!" Jeanne Marie cried, throwing herself at his feet and clasping him about the knees. "Save me! It is St. Eustache!"

"Nonsense, woman!" the bareback rider said angrily, but nevertheless he rose. "There are other dogs in the world. On the second landing there is a blind fellow who owns a dog. Perhaps it is he you hear."

"No, no—I know St. Eustache's step! My God, if you had lived with him a year, you would know it, too! Close the door and lock it!"

"That I will not," Simon Lafleur said contemptuously. "Do you think I am frightened so easily? If it is the wolf dog, so much the worse for him. It will not be the first cur that I have choked to death with these two hands!"

Pit-pat, pit-pat—it was on the second landing. *Pit-pat, pit-pat*—now it was in the corridor, and coming fast. *Pit-pat, pit-pat*—all at once it stopped.

There was a moment's breathless silence, and then into the room trotted St. Eustache. M. Jacques Courbé sat astride the dog's broad back, as he had so often done in the circus ring. He held a tiny drawn sword, and his shoe button eyes seemed to reflect its steely glitter.

Simon Lafleur made an involuntary step backward. He had been prepared for St. Eustache, but not for the wolf dog's master.

The dwarf brought the dog to a halt in the middle of the room, and took in at a single glance the prostrate figure of Jeanne Marie. St. Eustache, too, seemed to take silent note of it. The stiff hair on his back rose up, he showed his long white fangs hungrily, and his eyes glowed like two live coals.

"So I find you *thus, madame*!" M. Jacques Courbé said at last. "It is fortunate that I have a charger here"—he patted St. Eustache on the dog's shaggy neck—"who can scent out my enemies as well as hunt them down in the open. Without him, I might have had some difficulty in discovering you. Well, the little game is up. I find you with your lover!"

"Simon Lafleur is not my lover!" she sobbed. "I have not seen him once since I married you until tonight! I swear it!"

"Once is enough," the dwarf said grimly. "The impudent stable boy must be chastised!"

"Oh, spare him!" Jeanne Marie implored. "Do not harm him, I beg of you! It is not his fault that I came! I—"

But at this point Simon Lafleur drowned her out in a roar of laughter.

"Ho, ho!" he roared, putting his hands on his hips. "You would chastise me, eh? *Nom d'un chien!* Don't try your circus tricks on *me*! Why, hop-o'-my-thumb, you who ride on a dog's back like a flea, out of this room before I squash you! Begone, melt, fade away!" He paused, expanded his barrel-like chest, puffed out his cheeks, and blew a great breath at the dwarf. "Blow away, insect," he bellowed, "lest I put my heel on you!"

M. Jacques Courbé was unmoved by this torrent of abuse. He sat very upright on St. Eustache's back, his tiny sword resting on his tiny shoulder.

"Are you done?" he said at last, when the hareback rider had run dry of invectives. "Very well, *monsieur*! Prepare to receive cavalry!" He paused for an instant, then added in a high, clear voice: "Get him, St. Eustache!"

The dog crouched, and at almost the same moment sprang at Simon Lafleur. The bareback rider had no time to avoid him and his tiny rider. Almost instantaneously the three of them had come to death grips.

Never in the history of warfare was there a stranger combat than this at the Sign of the Wild Boar. Legend has it that the knights of King Arthur's Round Table rode out to do battle with giants; but surely never one rode such a valiant steed as St. Eustache. Here was a charger who bit and tore, and whose cruel white fangs were soon turned to crimson. It was a gory business.

Simon Lafleur, strong man as he was, was bowled over by the wolf dog's unexpected leap. St. Eustache's clashing jaws closed on his right arm and crushed it to the bone. A moment later the dwarf, still clinging to his dog's back, thrust the point of his tiny sword into the body of the prostrate bareback rider.

Simon Lafleur struggled valiantly, but all to no purpose. Now he felt the foetid breath of the dog fanning his neck, and the wasp-like sting of the dwarf's blade, which this time found a mortal spot. A convulsive tremor shook him and he rolled over on his back. The circus *Romeo* was dead.

M. Jacques Courbé cleansed his sword on a kerchief of lace, dismounted, and approached Jeanne Marie. She was still crouching on the floor, her eyes closed, her head held tightly between both hands. The dwarf touched her imperiously on the broad shoulder which had so often carried him.

"*Madame*," he said, "we now can return home. You must be more careful hereafter. *Ma foi*, it is an ungentlemanly business cutting the throats of stable boys!"

She rose to her feet, like a large trained animal at the word of command.

"You wish to be carried?" she said between livid lips.

"Ah, that is true, *madame*," be murmured. "I was forgetting our little wager. From one end of France to the other, eh? Ah, yes! Well, you are to be congratulated, *madame*—you have covered nearly half the distance."

"Nearly half the distance," she repeated in a lifeless voice.

"Yes, *madame*," M. Jacques Courbé continued. "I fancy that you will be quite a docile wife by the time you have done." He paused, and then added reflectively: "It is truly remarkable how speedily one can ride the devil out of a woman—with spurs!"

Papa Copo had been spending a convivial evening at the Sign of the Wild Boar. As he stepped out into the street, he saw three familiar figures preceding him—a tall woman, a tiny man, and a large dog with upstanding ears. The woman carried the man on her shoulder; the dog trotted at her heels.

The circus owner came to a halt and stared after them. His round eyes were full of childish astonishment.

"Can it be?" he murmured. "Yes, it is! Three old friends! And so Jeanne Marie still carries him! Ah, but she should not poke fun at M. Jacques Courbé. He is so sensitive; but, alas, they are the kind that are always henpecked!"

1927

WAXWORKS

W. L. George

Walter Lionel George (1882–1926) was born in Paris to British parents. He lived in the French capital until he was 23, when he came to England. In London he forged a journalistic career, becoming the foreign correspondent of various newspapers and writing several left-leaning political and feminist tracts. His first novel, *A Bed of Roses* (1911), is a gritty tale of a struggling widow who descends into prostitution. It became a commercial success, allowing George to turn full-time to writing, putting out more than a dozen books over the next fifteen years. Notable works include his posthumously released novel *Children of the Morning* (1926), an exploration of what might become of a group of children shipwrecked on an island off the Venezuelan coast that pre-dates William Golding's *Lord of the Flies* by a quarter of a century. George seemed to enjoy these kind of hypothetical thought experiments—in a 1922 article for the *New York Herald* he attempted to answer the question of "What the World Will be Like in a Hundred Years"; his predictions, on the whole, stand up to modern scrutiny save for a few stray suggestions, such as his forecasts that in 2022 "a complete meal may be taken in four pills", or that twenty-first-century cities would be enclosed and "roofed with glass".

Alongside his novels, George wrote many shorter fictional works that are collected in his posthumous *Selected Stories* (1927), though few are macabre or supernatural in subject. It feels fitting to include a story here that explores the waxworks/Chamber of Horrors branch of the sideshow universe, a space which has long been fertile ground for the sowing of fear. This is particularly the case on the big screen, beginning, more than a century ago, in 1924, with Paul Leni's German Expressionist *Waxworks*; before the 3D Vincent Price vehicle *House of Wax* (1953); the 1988 US horror-comedy *Waxwork*; and even, arguably, *Carry on Screaming!* (1966).

Henry Badger rapidly paced the City churchyard; his air of anxiety seemed to overweigh his small, though not unpleasing features. He was an insignificant little man, dressed in pepper-and-salt tweeds. His hair was cut very close, except where a love-lock, plastered down with jasmine-oil, trailed over his forehead from under his hard black hat. Whenever he completed the circuit of the churchyard he peered towards the gate through which must come disturbance and romance. His worry expressed itself in a nervous twisting of his watch-chain from which hung a masonic sign, a jubilee sixpence, and a swimming medal. He was a creature of small ways and minor responsibilities, of even life and restricted future, who worked between trains and between trains slept. But all the same Henry Badger was in love, and he could not escape the consequences of his share in our common delight and affliction.

Suddenly brightness overspread his sharp features. It was she! She, in a pink crêpe de Chine blouse, disconnected rather than connected with her white serge skirt by a patent-leather belt. About the pink blouse was an equally pink neck, and a rather pretty face, all soft curves. She was bright blue of eye and tumbled in pleasant fairness about the hair, under a large straw hat from which drooped upon the left a fragment of ivy that might with advantage have been placed elsewhere. But her name was Ivy, and she liked to live in harmony.

"I'm late," she said with pretty briskness, as they shook hands. "So sorry, Henry. Only the boss got dictating, and he likes to hear himself talk, even if it is only to little me. Still, better late than never," she added, with a smile indicating wit.

Henry Badger gave a desperate twist to the swimming medal and replied: "Yes." He wondered if it would be good policy to attack her for being late. Since he felt at fault, no doubt it would. Only... an argument with Ivy, one never knew what that would lead to.

"Well, you dummy," she said, "is that all you've got to say? Got the tickets?"

"Er..." said Henry Badger, "no."

"What do you mean?" said Ivy, crossly.

"What I say," replied Henry Badger, with feeble determination. "Fact is, Ivy, I'm sorry, but I forgot."

The blue eyes stared at him, incredulous. "Forgot! what you been and done that for?"

Henry Badger explained profusely. The night before he'd had an awful headache, and it had slipped his memory to go round to the Imperial Music Hall, and this morning the manager...

Ivy trampled upon these confused excuses. "All I can see," she said, "is here we are landed on a Saturday afternoon with nowhere to go except the pictures. And it's so hot in those places. Last time I was fair melted. I do think it's too bad of you."

It was then that Henry Badger expressed himself: "Fact is, Ivy, I been thinking."

"Hope you didn't break anything," said Ivy, "but since you done it, what's the ideer?"

"I been thinking that we don't know the town we live in. I was reading a book the other day, 'Strange Sights of London', it was called. And, would you believe it, Ivy, there's lots of things I got to learn."

"Ah, I do believe it," said Ivy.

"For instance," said Henry, "did you know that the church of St. Ethelburga wasn't burnt down in the Fire of London?"

"No," said Ivy, "and now I do know it, I don't seem to be much better off."

"Ah!" said Henry, "that's where you're wrong, Ivy. It improves your mind to know that sort of thing. And that's how I got my ideer. I been thinking we might go round to the docks."

"What for?"

"Oh, I dunno. Just to mooch round. Ever been to the docks? No? Well, why not try 'em? You know, Ivy, people spend a lot of money going to the Riviera, and they never see the place round the corner. See your own country first," he added with originality.

"Well," said Ivy, after a moment, "seeing you've mucked up this afternoon, and mother's gone out and there won't be any tea, I suppose we may as well."

It was a hot and heavy day, for a listless wind blew from the south. It carried a glowing pile of cloud which heightened the effect of greyness and gloom of the East End. The two little people, for neither of them was quite five foot six, wandered along the East India Dock Road, where an omnibus had deposited them. They thought the landscape queer, but not very amusing—the tall black warehouses, the shuttered shops, the railway bridges and the deep shadows they made across the street. But all the same they felt adventurous as they peered into the side streets, where life was as active and as crowded as in a pond in summer, where enormously stout women conversed loudly from door to door, and where each street had its mob of children engaged in mysterious games. They listened for a moment to a barrel organ, then hurried away, feeling that their city clothes made them noticeable in the land of shirt sleeves and curling pins. They went east, feeling rather hot, until at last they found and crossed the river that was oily and swan grey. For an hour they wandered the tragic land where none live for pleasure, and where slowly the soot falls to obliterate sooty footmarks. They were too tired to be pleased when behind a long brick wall they found the docks. They perceived the smell of the East, oil of macassar, piled logs of sandalwood, barrels of copra; at a point against the sky, where now the dark clouds were racing, they saw outlined tall spars, while a funnel striped in yellow and blue threw out a shower of sparks against the sky that was like a dun veil touched with tinsel. The heat seemed to grow. Henry tried to interest his fiancée in a parrot which sat upon the back of a chair outside a sweetshop. It was a wonderful bird, mainly bright green, with a ruffled scarlet head; it maintained upon them the stare of its unwinking golden eye. It was entirely still, thus denying the screaming excess of its colour. It embodied the impassive violence of the East, its cruelty that is not cruelty because it is indifference, its still ferocity. After staring for some time at the savage exile, the pale citizen of a peaceful land formulated: "They say parrots live over a hundred years."

They lost their direction, not liking to ask their way of the rough inhabitants, not knowing where they wanted to go. They were astray, unprotected lambs in a land of slender law. Ivy began to drag her feet as loudly as she could, to show that she was displeased. Both were secretly oppressed because that day they had not kissed.

At that moment came rain. Very slowly at first in separate warm drops that made upon the pavement spots as large as a coin.

"My!" said Henry, "it's going to come down like billy-o!"

"I don't care," said Ivy.

"Come on," said Henry, "let's see if we can get under shelter somewhere." But they were still progressing along another brick wall; opposite, the warehouses were closed. They ran, for now the rain was beginning to fall with greater determination.

"Here," gasped Henry, as he ran, "we must get in somewhere; you'll be sopped through. Let's go into a shop."

They stopped irresolutely at the corner of a side-street. As it was almost entirely occupied by warehouses no living creature could be seen. But just as they prepared to run on through the rain, Henry observed a tottering post, bearing a battered sign. The sign was in the shape of a hand pointing up the lane, and upon it were painted the words: "To the Waxworks."

"Here," he cried, dragging Ivy along, "that'll do. I didn't know they had waxworks in this part of the world, but it'll save us getting wet."

They ran up the street, expecting a verandah and a commissionaire. At the end of the lane they had found nothing, and paused irresolute, when upon the door of a three-floored house Ivy saw the word "Waxworks", with the addition: "Mrs. Groby, Proprietress." Henry seized the door handle which resisted for a moment. The door jammed, but with a great effort he forced it open. It made a great clatter as he flung it against the wall. Breathless and wiping their wet faces, the two stood giggling in the hall. Then, feeling alone, suddenly they kissed. The excitement of the run and of the caress sheltered them against an impression which the place imposed upon them only by degrees. They were in the hall of a house, of a house like any other house. The walls were the colour of dry chocolate; the floor was made of soiled boards; a window at the back was coated with whitewash and shone ghastly like a blind eye. There was no noise in the house except for a slight sound. It felt deserted. The door handle on the right was covered with dust. Nobody had gone into that room for a long time. An unaccountable emotion developed in them. The house was still except that at last they identified the slight sound: far away a tap was leaking. They found themselves listening to the drip which came regularly from the basement.

"Well," said Henry, with forced cheerfulness, "here we are." And as if to reassure himself: "Anyhow, we shan't get wet."

They stood for a moment looking out at the rain which now came faster. The effect of this falling water, soft and hot, the dusty silence of the place except for that regular drip far away, combined to cast upon them a sort of uneasiness, an almost physical oppression. Ivy began to look about her with unexplainable anxiety. The darkness of the stairs, the banisters broken in several places, the dusty door handle, stirred in her a vague fear; she looked about her like a cat in a strange place and preparing to flee. As the feeling communicated itself to Henry his manliness revolted. It would be too silly to have the jumps. So he said: "Ive, since we're here, why not go upstairs and see the show?"

After a moment's hesitation, Ivy dominated her disturbance and said: "All right."

They went up the stairs, firmly but with instinctive slowness, troubled by the sound of their feet upon the boards, followed by the fainter drip of the distant tap. The first floor was like the ground floor. Here, too, the door handles were dusty, and here, too, there came no sound from beyond the doors. They had to make an effort to go up farther. The sense that here was emptiness made emptiness frightful. But Henry was leading, and still went up. He didn't know why, but knew he must go up. Perhaps because he was a man and couldn't run away from anything, not even from nothing. The second floor comforted them, for here was a pay-box, empty, it is true, but marked: "Pay here." Henry released a great sigh. It really was a show. It had a human air.

"Come on, Ivy," he said in a loud voice which rang unpleasantly down the uncarpeted stairs. "Since there's nobody down here we can pay when we get to the top."

Ivy silently followed him up, and so they reached what seemed to be a large attic. Once again a reluctant door yielded to their hands, and Henry stepped into the doorway with a sort of jauntiness, but Ivy paused for a moment at his back. Waxworks, yes, but she didn't know why, at once she was terrified. One couldn't see very well in the attic, for the dust of years lay upon the skylight, and the avaricious light of the sullen sky hardly penetrated. The walls had been whitewashed, but now were stained black with damp, soiled by the touch of hands, the smoke of lamps. About the door hung rags of dirty red damask. And in the immense silence of the place, hearing not even the drip of the distant tap, they found themselves alone with the wax figures.

Some stood upon little thrones of red-painted wood, here a man in day clothes, staring emptily from a yellow countenance, here a woman spreading crimson nostrils to an absent scent. The two were still in the doorway, not knowing why they did not go in. They were conscious of a secret vileness in these faces. The things stood so still, but sure of themselves, as if they had always stood in the dust and twilight. But at last Henry seized Ivy's arm more firmly and they went in.

Altogether there were fourteen figures. Three of the men were labelled Charles Peace, Dr. Crippen, and Gouffé. The woman with the intense gaze was Mrs. Maybrick, and there were two other women, one with bright red hair over which a spider had built its web. But Henry and Ivy, as they stood before them, did not at once read the legends telling how Crippen had killed his wife and burnt her body in the furnace, nor did they gaze at Gouffé, the bailiff, who had been carved into pieces and packed in a trunk. A little later Ivy read that ticket to the end and shudderingly stepped away from the invitation to draw apart the figure's clothing and see indicated the lines along which the body had been cut up. At that moment she was cowering against Henry, who instinctively had laid an arm about her shoulders, for the single figures were less terrifying than two groups represented in action. One of the groups comprised a man and a woman in a pink flannelette dressing-gown. With an expression of pinched determination, the murderer was forcing the female figure down into a bath, where a sheet of mica, tinted green, represented water. In the grasp of a bony hand, the female figure held the edge of the bath, wildly raising the other arm, while into her distorted mouth floated the green edge of the water that was to drown her. It was a work of art of indescribable horror. It was as if the snakelike fingers moved, as if in another moment the head would disappear under that still green surface.

With an exclamation Henry turned aside to the other group, that stood dim within the shadow, away from the faint rays that fell through the skylight. This represented a very old woman, lying on her face, her white hair scattered and stained with blood, while kneeling over her, a sandbag still half-raised, was a short man in the clothes of the day, his face set and coated with a horrible scarlet flush.

Now a new sound made them start. It was the growing rain, pattering upon the skylight, as if goblins raced across it. In a sudden desire for union again they kissed, quickly falling apart, as if espied.

They turned away for a moment, fascinated, they did not know how, in this gallery of crime. The still things about them seemed to have a motion, a vibration of their own. They found themselves looking sharply into corners as if something were there after all, as if these were not creatures of wax, but actually poisoners, men and women experienced in violence and still capable of evil. The great horror, which always drew them back to itself, was that bath, soiled, chipped, and streaked with black rivulets of dirt, into which the murderer was endlessly pressing down the figure that endlessly strove for life.

So great was the tension that Henry tried to rejoin the ordinary world. He whispered: "We ought to have paid someone," but while he spoke he looked from side to side, as if begging some material custodian to appear with a familiar ticket and a sounding punch.

Ivy did not reply; she was holding his arm in a nervous clutch; once or twice she moved away from him, and then came back, as if her fingers grasped him independently of the processes of her brain. She was opening and closing her mouth, striving to speak and finding her tongue dry. Only at last did she find a whisper: "I don't like it. Let's go."

Henry Badger also wanted to go, but he was so unaccountably afraid that he dared not go. His virility spoke: it told him that if he went now he would be everlastingly ashamed. He was afraid to tell himself that he was afraid. So, in a voice the loudness of which half-startled him, he replied: "Oh, rot! Since we've come up we may as well see the lot of them." So, Ivy still grasping his arm, they circled the attic, stopping in turn before each figure. Ivy did not want to see, but she could not look away. It was as if she must meet material, human eyes. It was always the eyes she looked at. Those of Devereux, who murdered wife and two sons, strangely refined, with a contemptuous merriment in the pale brown cornea, which glittered against the blood-injected bluish whites. He was horrible. And horrible, too, Catherine Wilson, who almost every year poisoned a victim with colchicum. And Wainwright, dandified, with whiskers equally combed, as if oiled for the passage of his vanity in Pall Mall. Wainwright, who, after slaying her, had carried the corpse of his beloved in a parcel of oilskin.

Ivy had to see. There was a challenge in the eyes. It was the defiance of the dead which she must meet. She must again view the bath, look down through the green surface of the water upon the agonised limbs which twisted in the dimness that was to be their grave. But now there was a change. Perhaps because habit made that first seem less awful, the second group gained in horror. It was not only the sight of the blood coagulated on the white hair, it was something else, something unnamable. The art of the sculptor had gone too far; here was mere and abominable reality. Real hair, and crouching above, with drooping eyelids, the figure of the murderer, ill-shaven and flushed with health. Something twisted in Ivy's body as she thought that upon the still mask she could discern beads of sweat. They stayed staring, half-conscious that they had been here a long time, though little more than a minute had passed. The beating of their hearts deafened them, and combined with the hissing sound of the rain, as if thin ghosts shod in cloud were racing across the skylight. Her eyes still fixed upon the creature with the sandbag, Ivy whispered again: "Let's go."

Then, in the far distance, they heard the front door slam.

At that sound a confused terror seized them both. The contrast between incoming humanity and the unearthly silence here affected them like a blow. Heat and weakness rushed up their limbs, and in Ivy's ears was a sound like the distant unwinding of an endless chain. Henry was the first to recover; a compound emotion formed in him; the proprietress... of course... he wanted to get out... they really ought to pay... he'd better see. This summarised itself in an inarticulate sound. Turning, he ran to the landing and looked down the stairs. He did not know what he expected to see, but something, and after a few seconds, as he heard nothing, such a weakness overcame him that he let himself go against the balustrade, his head hanging down over the well of the stairs, where all was silence and darkness.

But almost at once he recovered, for suddenly behind him there came a long cry, a cry with a strange, torn quality, like that of a beast in pain, that jerked him to his feet as it dragged from his pores a sheet of cold sweat. As he turned, Ivy came tumbling out of the attic, her arms outstretched before her as if she fumbled for her way. She could not see, for her eyes were so retroverted that only the whites showed under the falling lids. He caught her just as she was going to throw herself down the stairs. As he touched her, she flung her arms about his neck with maniacal strength, and he could not free himself from that grasp. As they stumbled together down the stairs, he thought that it was like being held by bones. They fell together at the foot of the second landing, somehow struggled to their feet. There was a moment of incredible effort before they could pull open the outer door, which had been closed by the wind. They halted for an instant upon the steps, close-locked under the falling hot rain, and Henry did not understand what drove him then, what strange relief or exaltation, what insane excitement made him press his mouth to the lips drawn tightly into pallid lines. At the kiss, Ivy's nerves suddenly relaxed. She became a bundle in his arms, something he dragged along, staggering as he fled, he knew not from what. They shared but one idea: to get away. The pavement streamed before them as they ran with downcast eyes. Then, with a shock, they were stopped by two policemen in oilskins, with whom they nearly collided at the junction of the lane and the main road. The policemen stared at these two, instinctively holding them by the arm, not understanding that they were at the limit of terror, and already suspecting that they had committed some crime. Indeed, Henry and Ivy were struggling in their grasp, still dominated by their one desire: to get away. At last, when they grew quiet and stood breathing hard, their mouths relaxed by nervous exhaustion, the elder policeman, who was a sergeant, said: "Now then, what's all this?"

"I don't know," said Henry.

"Come on," said the sergeant, "you don't put me off like that. What you been up to, you two?" Henry did not reply. "Mark you, it'll be all the worse for you if you don't talk. What's happened?" He shook his prisoner, suggesting that he'd make him talk yet, but failing to draw a reply, he turned to the girl: "You, why were you running?"

Ivy seemed to have recovered more quickly than her companion. Though her eyelids did not cease to twitch, she managed to say: "I saw something."

"Saw something?" said the sergeant. "Saw what?"

"Oh, I couldn't," said Ivy.

"I expect they're drunk," said the constable.

"No," said the sergeant, meditatively, "I can't smell it on 'em."

"Oh, no," cried Ivy, "no, of course not, only it's the waxworks... the waxworks."

"Waxworks?" said the sergeant. "What waxworks?"

"I know, sergeant," said the constable, nodding up the lane. "Mrs. Groby's place."

"Oh, yes," said the sergeant, "I know now. Sort of chamber of 'orrors. Well, you been to the waxworks. What about it?"

"I saw something," whispered Ivy.

"Saw what?" said the constable. "Saw Mrs. Groby, I suppose. Funny old dame, sergeant. She's been living in that house all by herself for the last forty years, alone with them things. Used to make a lot of money out of them, and they say she's got a lot saved up. Between you and me and the lamp-post, I'm surprised no one's knocked her on the head yet and walked off with her money."

Ivy gave a low cry. "Yes... that's it... there's a man in there... he's killed her... blood all over her head."

"What's all this?" asked the sergeant, professionally incredulous. "What's all this story? And how do you know anything about it?"

"There was a noise," said Ivy. "The door slammed... Henry ran out. I couldn't move for a moment... she was on the floor and the man..." Her voice became shrill. "... As I turned to look after Henry I just... he raised his arm and rubbed it... just with the corner of my eye... I..." She gave a heavy sigh, and her head fell back upon the policeman's chest.

But she had not fainted, and in a moment the policemen were striding up the lane, followed by Henry and Ivy, who clung to the companionship of these tall, loud-speaking men. As they went the sergeant theorised:

"I see the dodge. He did the old woman in; then he heard this pair come up the stairs, and rigged himself up as a wax figure. Got cramp, I suppose, and took the chance to rub his arm when he thought she wasn't looking. Cheer up, missy," he added to Ivy, who was crying out of weakness. "We'll soon get him." As they reached the door of the museum he winked at her and drew his truncheon. "Better stay downstairs, missy," he added, as he led the way up.

But after a moment Ivy and Henry could not bear their loneliness, and tiptoed up the stairs behind the blue shapes that walked with such assurance, making no attempt to muffle their tread. When they reached the attic, the policeman looked in a puzzled way into the twilight.

"Which one is it?" said the policeman, and instinctively his voice fell to a whisper.

Ivy, who was just behind him, pointed at the kneeling shape carrying the sandbag. "That one," she said.

The sergeant did not understand his own feeling, but he received some dim impression from the grey place. He walked only three feet into the room. Then, in an uneasy voice he addressed the kneeling figure:

"Now then, my man. The game's up. You better go quietly."

There was no reply, and the echoes died away, repeating a quivering uncertainty in the policeman's voice.

After a moment's pause the sergeant, irritated by the silence, strode into the room; raising his truncheon, he went up to the kneeling figure and touched it on the shoulder. He drew back his hand, touched the body again. Then, suddenly, he burst into a roar of laughter, as with a derisive gesture he passed his hand up and down over the waxen face.

"Wax!" he cried. "Bert! have you ever seen such a pair of gabies as these two? Been here and got the 'orrors, the two of them, and ran out like a pair of loonies to tell us this dummy is Jack the Ripper posing for the Russian bally. Oh, my!"

"Wax!" whispered Ivy. "Oh, no. Oh, please don't touch it. It's not wax. No, it's not."

"Come on," said the sergeant, kindly, "touch it yourself."

"Oh, I couldn't," said Ivy, quivering, but with a laugh the policeman seized her wrist, and, drawing her towards the figure, forced her to lay her hand upon the waxen coldness of the cheek.

"Wax," said the policeman, "you silly kid. That's only wax. And so's this wax," he added, as he bent down and negligently laid his hand upon the blood-stained white hair. But, in the same movement almost, the policeman jumped up and recoiled, his staring eyes glaring at his hand. For less than a second did he gaze at it; then, with a cry, as if seized by ungovernable hysteria, he brought down his truncheon upon the head of the kneeling man, which, under the blow, scattered into tiny fragments of tinted wax. Then the other policeman drew back as he saw his comrade's hand stained with fresh blood.

"A waxwork," he gasped. "What... how? It isn't a waxwork. It's Mrs. Groby." He laid a single finger on the woman's head, stared at his own blood-stained hand. "Dead... still warm." His voice rose high: "Killed... by what?"

In the silence, far below, could be heard the thin drip of the leaky tap.

1932

THE HARLEM HORROR

Charles Birkin

In 1942, the aristocratic Sir Charles Lloyd Birkin (1907–1985) succeeded his uncle as the 5th Baronet Birkin. By that point he'd made a, perhaps unlikely, name for himself as the editor of (and a frequent contributor to) the "Creeps" series of fourteen anthologies of horror short stories published between 1932 and 1936, which regularly featured contributions from H. Russell Wakefield, Elliott O'Donnell and Tod Robbins.

Birkin's writing and editing career was upended by the Second World War, in which he served in the Sherwood Foresters, an infantry regiment of the British army. However, his work experienced something of a renaissance in the 1960s, after Herbert van Thal and Dennis Wheatley included a number of his tales in anthologies they curated; several more of Birkin's own new volumes followed between 1964 and 1971.

Devil's Spawn (1936) was Birkin's first sole-authored collection. Most of the stories had previously appeared in the "Creeps" books under the pseudonym Charles Lloyd, and they largely share a bloodthirsty, exploitative sensibility which would not seem out of place on the stage of Paris's Grand Guignol theatre. "The Harlem Horror" was originally published in *Shudders: A Collection of Uneasy Tales* (1932), the third in the "Creeps" series. With its garish depiction of an excursion to a Coney Island freak show, it offers no exception to the sensationalism of Birkin's other works. But, even if the horrors on display here are far from subtle, they are undoubtedly effective.

Michael Harwood walked quickly along the platform. All around him were people, pushing, jostling—making sure of getting their seats in the train. Yes—he could just do it. He ran the few steps to the sliding door, and stepped inside as they were closing. There was a moment's pause, and then the train slithered into the black hole of the tunnel. Michael looked at the rows of tired faces of the passengers opposite him. Lord! how he hated the Underground. He opened his paper, and glanced at the headlines.

MYSTERY OF SCIENTIST'S DISAPPEARANCE
SIR JOHN TROWBRIDGE NOT YET FOUND
LADY TROWBRIDGE INCONSOLABLE

and then, lower in the column in angry black letters

WHAT ARE THE POLICE DOING?

He turned over the page. He remembered the case. It had filled the newspapers for the last week. Sir John Trowbridge—perhaps the most brilliant surgeon of the day—had walked out of his house some ten days previously, and had never been seen since.

Michael pondered what could have happened to him. He turned the page...

ACTRESS ROBBED IN HYDE PARK

Michael looked up, the train was slowing down.

"Oxford Circus."

Briskly he rose to his feet and hurriedly left the train. He was late, and anxious to get home.

Six months later Michael stood on the deck of the ss. *Gigantic*. He stood spellbound, gazing at the wonder that was New York's skyline. The skyscrapers shot up in arrogant splendour as if to probe the secrets of the sky itself. The towers of the most amazing city in the world, Michael thought, a city that in the last hundred and fifty years had sprung from a humble Colonial town. Yet a city of crime and mystery. Only recently the world had been horrified at a series of inexplicable disappearances of children from the crowded suburbs of New York. During the last three weeks no fewer than eight children had vanished; vanished as completely as if the earth had opened and swallowed them, leaving no trace. In every instance they had been members of poor families—and had last been seen playing in the streets. The American police had done their best, no line of inquiry had been ignored, but nothing had been discovered. There had been a panic among the mothers of the districts, and a national outcry for some solution. Then, after a discreet interval, the matter had been dropped, and the disappearances had taken their place among the unsolved mysteries of recent years.

The morning promised great heat; for it was early July, and New York was experiencing one of its blazing summers.

And now Michael was to set foot in New York for the first time; the gangways were being put into position, the passengers were bustling to and fro in their eagerness to be the first ashore, and the liner was the scene of great activity. The docks were crowded with people meeting friends and relatives—handkerchiefs were fluttering—questions and answers were shouted eagerly by those on deck and those who waited for the moment when officialdom should permit passengers to leave the liner. Michael felt aloof, as he looked at the smiling faces and gesticulating figures of his companions. New York seemed foreign—far more so than France or Germany.

"Isn't it marvellous, darling?"

Mary, his wife, put her hand on his coat-sleeve. She smiled up into his face.

"I'm glad you like it," Michael laughed; "we're here for the next three years, you know."

"I'm going to love it, I know I shall."

"We can go now, darling, if you're ready. Shall I carry Clare?" Mary glanced at the child at her skirt.

"Yes, do, Michael. Isn't it a pity she's not old enough to remember this?"

"Well, she'll remember leaving it—she'll be nearly nine by the time we go home."

They were struggling towards the nearest gangway.

"Oh, Michael—isn't this all exciting!"

Michael squeezed his wife's arm. They were very much in love—and this America *was* just a little alarming.

Over two years had passed since that day when Michael and Mary arrived with some hesitation on the threshold of New York. There was only a week until Christmas, and all the shops were bright with special displays—great electric signs bewildered the eye with their brilliancy, and crowds battled on the sidewalks, gazing in admiration at the store windows, or thrusting their way through the parcel-impeded throng into the store itself.

Michael walked slowly. He really must think of something to give Mary, something that she would really like. Clare was no problem—children were easy to please. But Mary...

He stopped in front of a window filled with lingerie and stockings made apparently from gossamer. No, he decided, clothes weren't exactly a "holiday" present. The next shop was a jeweller's, and suddenly he saw what he wanted. A ring. It was a large aquamarine, mounted in platinum. He went in and asked the price. Two hundred dollars, the sales girl said. It was rather more than he had wanted to pay—but after all it was Christmas, and only that afternoon a letter had come from the Head Office in London, saying that the directors were very pleased with his work, and that promotion was waiting for him on his return.

And that was—in just over a year.

"Thank you, I'll take it."

He laughed as he thought of Mary's pleasure. He pulled out his watch, a heavy gold hunter that had been his grandfather's, and snapped it open. Seven o'clock. He hadn't realised it was so late... and they were dining early and going to a cinema.

Mary met him at the door of their furnished "apartment." She looked worried.

"Michael! The most terrible thing has happened. I tried to get you at the office—but you'd just left. Clare is lost—oh, what can we do?"

"Mary—what do you mean? She can't be lost."

"I don't know what to do. I came in about six o'clock, and was just going to fetch her from Sally O'Brien's, where she was having tea—as you know, it's at the end of this block—when the telephone rang. It was Sally, who told me not to bother to come, as Clare would come back by herself. There are no streets to cross, so I told myself not to coddle the child. I said I'd go and meet her. Well—I went, and I couldn't find her. It only takes two minutes from door to door, and Sally says she can't understand how I missed her. She's as upset as I am. I'll never forgive myself if anything has happened to her. Never. Never."

Michael ran his finger round the inside of his stiff white collar.

"Darling, what could have happened to her? It's not your fault, sweetest. Tell me—what did you do then?"

"I told the nearest policeman what had happened, and he telephoned to head-quarters." She was crying with choking, gulping sobs. "And he said that they'd find her in no time. And then I telephoned you."

"But, Mary, that was over an hour ago. Haven't you heard anything since?" Michael's eyes were worried, the line of his jaw very hard.

"No—nothing."

And they heard no more that night, nor the next day. In fact, Clare had disappeared just as if she had never existed.

It was a sad Christmas for the Harwoods. Mary, languid and worn with ceaseless grief and worry, refused to be comforted. Michael spent his days trying to discover some clue, however slight, to solve the mystery.

And then, as time went on, they ceased to feel tearing, rending sorrow, but a dull grief was always in their hearts. Mary refused to keep anything that reminded them of Clare. Not even a photograph was allowed to remain. But, unknown to her, Michael carried one in his pocket-book, and sometimes in his office he would look at it, and remember all the vivid frail beauty of his lost child—her fair hair, her wonderful topaz-coloured eyes fringed with dark lashes. They were so unusual that even strangers stopped to exclaim at their beauty; he thought of how, in the boat, Clare had been by far the loveliest child. He wondered if he and Mary would have more children. Nothing else, he knew, would banish that look of hopelessness from her face. She seemed frozen, in a trance. There had been a telegram of condolence from Sir James Wood, the head of his firm: "My most sincere sympathy, if there is anything I can do cable me." What could he or anyone do?

Of course, Michael realised, he was lucky. Damn lucky; he had his work, and so could forget—sometimes. But Mary... he had suggested her going home to England, but she had replied: "Does it matter where we are... any more?"

He turned to the pile of papers awaiting his attention. He was glad to see the work lying there on his desk.

Another sweltering July held New York suffering in its fiery grip. Michael had noticed at breakfast that morning that Mary looked unusually washed-out. He was thankful that they were returning to England at the end of August.

It was a Saturday morning, and the office week finished at midday.

"Where shall we go this afternoon, darling?"

"A cinema?"

"Mary, dear. In this heat?"

"They're very well cooled."

"Even so. I say, darling—what about Coney Island? We've never been there, and as we're going home so soon it seems a pity to miss seeing it."

"But think of the crowds."

"That will make it all the more fun." His face was eager. He was boyish in his enthusiasm.

"All right."

"I'll be back at one. Let's have a cold lunch—and start directly afterwards. Then we can come back early and go to a cinema this evening, if you still want to."

Three o'clock found the Harwoods climbing up into one of those gigantic motor charabancs that plied to Coney Island—the Fun Fair of the New Yorkers. They got the last two seats; sitting wedged among pretty shopgirls and typists gay in the light summer frocks, and escorted by leather-belted young men in flannel suits and straw "boaters." Laughter and talk filled the air.

"Any seats left?" a lovely young Jewess asked the conductor.

"Sorry, sister—try the next coach."

The charabanc moved off.

Coney Island beach was literally black with sweltering humanity. The myriad sideshows were doing good business. Switchbacks bearing their cargoes of shrieking passengers swooped up and down, "barkers" inveigled the passers-by into the sideshows, sellers of rock and peanut brittle were doing a brisk trade; the ice-cream soda bars were three deep in patrons.

The sun beat pitilessly down upon this scene of bustling pleasure.

Michael and Mary followed the crowd. They threw darts at playing cards, were thrilled by the dangers of "The Wall of Death," drank ice-cream sodas.

And then the rain came. At first in big slow drops, then in a quick tattoo. The holiday-makers dashed for the nearest cover. Michael put his arm round Mary, "In here, darling. Quickly, or your dress will be ruined."

They pushed their way into a large stuffy tent; peering over the shoulders of the people in front.

"Fifty cents!" a blowsy woman tapped Michael's back. "Fifty cents to see the Freaks, sir," she repeated.

Michael fumbled for the coin in his trousers' pocket.

"Oh, Michael, how horrible, don't let's," Mary turned to go out. But they were by now pushed some yards from the doorway, and could hear the rain pouring down outside.

"They won't be too bad, darling. They're mostly faked."

Slowly they made their tour of the big tent—looking at its incredible denizens. The fat lady, her face inhuman in its stupidity; the living skeleton; the two tiny dwarfs.

They were stopped by a crowd in front of a small wooden enclosure. In front of it was a placard, on which was printed: "The Missing Links: These extraordinary creatures are believed to be the only two remaining in the world today. At terrific expense we..."

Michael couldn't see how it went on.

Between the shoulders of two young men in their shirt sleeves, Mary caught a glimpse of "The Missing Links." Their skin was dark brown, and leathery in texture, their heads distorted out of all semblance to a human being's. Their tiny eyes were lashless and red rimmed, and their limbs moved constantly, aimlessly. Faint clucking noises came from their twitching mouths.

"They're ghastly—take me out. I don't mind if it *is* raining."

Michael could see the flapped entrance of the tent a little way in front of him. Only one more "exhibit" remained. But their way was blocked, for this evidently was the star attraction.

A showman stood in front of a wooden pen similar to that containing the two monstrosities. He was addressing his gaping audience. A huge coarse-looking fellow, he was standing with his thumbs tucked into the wide leather belt that encircled his mighty waist. Sweat glistened on his face and hairy arms.

"And now, ladies and gentlemen, you will see the world-famed 'What-is-it?' The only creature of its kind in the world today. The creature that has baffled the most famous scientists. Discovered in the forest of one of the upper reaches of the River Amazon it is believed to be unique. Medical men can give no explanation—they say it is a female, probably of under ten years of age. But a female of what? See if any of you ladies and gentlemen can decide. I will give fifty dollars if any of you can give an explanation of this remarkable phenomenon." He paused to wipe his arm across his streaming forehead. "She's beautiful, isn't she? Any of you young men like to marry her?" He grimaced at his audience. "She'd make a good wife."

Mary and Michael found themselves pressed close to the pen's side. On a bed of straw sat the "What-is-it?" Its hair was long and dark, its skin mottled with spots like a leopard's. Its fingers hung straight from the second joints. Ears it had none. One of its eyes was missing.

"This remarkable creature," continued the showman, "is unfortunately completely dumb. But in a woman that's an advantage, eh?" He laughed lewdly.

The creature got slowly to its feet.

"Go and shake hands with the ladies and gentlemen."

It waddled towards the side where Michael stood. Its one eye of a remarkable golden colour was without intelligence.

"And now, ladies and gentlemen—photographs of the 'What-is-it?' may be purchased at the door. Ten cents each."

The crowd surged towards the opening; and Mary found herself once more in the fresh air. The rain had almost stopped.

"It was horrible... horrible. Michael, I think I'm going to be sick." Suddenly she began to cry.

"Let's leave this place. I'm sorry, darling, I didn't know they'd be as bad as that."

Their bus back to New York was almost empty; but they passed fleets of other charabancs going to the Island. Saturday night was the best night of the week. All the sideshows were full; and hundreds of thousands of dollars changed pockets.

Mary stood in the sitting-room of the flat that had been their home for the last three years, the flat where she had known such unhappiness. Strapped trunks, and half-filled suit-cases cluttered the floor. She frowned slightly as she tried to think if anything had been forgotten—her fur coat and Michael's big woolly Teddy-bear coat lay across a chair ready for the voyage that evening.

At the thought of going back to England her heart warmed. And she had news for Michael—glorious news.

She heard his key in the lock, and the next minute he strode into the room, big and broad-shouldered; and she was in his arms.

"Excited, darling?"

"Aren't you?"

"You bet! What time is the baggage-man coming for the luggage?"

"At three o'clock."

"Oh, Mary, it's good to be going home, isn't it?"

"Michael!"

"Yes, darling?"

Mary pulled his head down to hers. "Michael, darling, I think I'm going to have another baby."

"Mary—my sweet darling Mary!"

He closed his eyes. They were leaving New York that night—and with New York he hoped that Clare's memory would gradually fade.

They were going home, and now Mary was going to have a baby, and they could make a fresh and happier start.

"Oh, Mary," he said again, and there was great joy in his voice.

Michael paid off the taxi at the docks and followed his wife. As he turned into the dark doorway of the customs shed a boy touched his sleeve. "Paper, sir? Horrible discovery in Harlem, sir."

Absent-mindedly Michael took a paper and thrust a quarter into the boy's hand.

"Thank you, sir."

On the great liner *Atlantis* all was confusion. Flashlight photographs of celebrities making the trip to Europe intermittently dazzled the eyes. He asked a steward where he could find out the number of their cabin.

Half an hour later, he and Mary stood by the rail watching New York draw away from them. Her great turrets were outlined against a sky illumined by a thousand lights, their bulk pierced by countless windows, lending them glamour.

His hand felt something in his overcoat pocket. It was the newspaper he had bought before coming on board. He unfolded it. On the front page in staring black letters he saw the following announcement sprawled across the whole sheet:

HARLEM HORROR!
GHASTLY DISCOVERY IN UNDERGROUND SURGERY!
FOUR YEARS' OLD ENGLISH MYSTERY EXPLAINED!

Fascinated he read of how the police had forced their way into a house in a low quarter of Harlem, how they had been obstructed by a maniac who was subsequently found to be Sir John Trowbridge, the famous plastic surgeon who had disappeared from his home in London four years before; of the scene of horror that had met their eyes in the Laboratory, of the bodies of children, vivisected out of all semblance to the human form, of those of mutilated animals; of how it was difficult to differentiate between those of the children and those of the animals. Of how Sir John had babbled and boasted of his remarkable achievements, and of his success in selling his "productions" to fairs and freak shows. Michael felt the world reel. He remembered Coney Island, and the "What-is-it?" with one vacant topaz eye...

Mary was reading the paper over his arm.

"Michael! Oh, God—those children!... you don't think that Clare..." Her voice rose to a shrill scream.

"No, dear, no, of course not."

"But how can we ever know, how can we ever know...?"

Michael realised that he had to make his decision quickly.

"I know. Darling—I never dared to tell you, but Clare was run over... she never suffered, poor little thing. They took me to see her body."

At all costs Mary must never never realise this supreme horror.

"But, Michael, my own child, and you never told me! You denied me the right of seeing my child for the last time." Mary's voice was cruel in its cutting quiet. "I think I hate you for this. I shall always hate you."

The great liner ploughed on towards the open sea.

Michael said nothing. There was nothing to say. Only that Mary must never know.

1957

FREAK SHOW

Robert Silverberg

Born in 1935 in Brooklyn, Robert Silverberg is a hugely prolific American science fiction and fantasy author. He started submitting stories to sci-fi magazines while still at high school, while his first novel, *Revolt on Alpha C*, was published in 1955. Throughout the rest of the decade he wrote voraciously for the pulps, branching off into crime and erotic fiction after the downturn in the science fiction market at the beginning of the 1960s.

His numerous later science fiction and fantasy novels dating from the late-1960s to the early 1980s are generally well thought of, and Silverberg holds the record for the number of times (nine) that he has been a finalist in the annual Hugo Award for Best Novel. *Nightwings* (1968) won the Hugo Best Novella award in 1969, with *A Time of Changes* (1971) winning a Nebula award, and his fantasy novel *Lord Valentine's Castle* (1981) a Locus award. Silverberg was inaugurated (alongside Ray Bradbury) in 1999 into the Science Fiction and Fantasy Hall of Fame, and in 2004 he was given the lifetime honour of a Grand Master Award by the Science Fiction and Fantasy Writers Association.

"Freak Show" first appeared in the March 1957 issue of *Fantastic* magazine, under the pseudonym Hall Thornton (a pen name was used as Silverberg had another story, "Forgotten World", included under his own). It's an entertaining tale that straddles science and weird fiction, capturing wonderfully that sense of danger and youthful excitement that lingers in our imaginations, like miasma, about those 1950s small-town travelling carnivals.

"And here's the Man from Mars," the sideshow barker said ringingly. "Brought to this planet at *fantastic* expense, kept alive only through day-and-night care by a team of skilled scientists travelling with this circus."

Davy Kilbourne felt his mouth sag open. He turned to Les Barclay. "Jeez, look at that! From *Mars*, yet!"

"You fall for that stuff, Davy?" From the vantage-point of his fourteen years, Les could play cynic well. "Why, that's just a fake suit."

"Don't believe it," Davy said vehemently. At twelve, he was anxious to appear wise, but just as hopeful of seeing a real Martian.

The creature on the platform, real or not, was certainly convincing. It was contained in a tank of some clear, viscous fluid. Green-skinned, small and wiry, with four jointed legs and a tangle of boneless tentacles in place of arms, the Martian stared forward at the crowd before it. Its eyes—it had just two—were round and lidless; deep, they seemed filled with loneliness and longing for home.

"He looks unhappy," Davy said.

Les snorted. "You'd be too, if you had to wear an outfit like that on a hot day."

The barker flourished his arms in the air for silence. "Ladies and gentlemen! You've seen our Man from Mars—now, who'll pay two bits, the fourth part of a dollar, to step inside this tent and see the rest of our interstellar menagerie? Twenty-five cents, good people, for a view at the strangest denizens of the galaxy! Step right this way, if you please."

Davy fumbled in his pockets and pulled out a quarter. He looked at it soulfully; it was all that there was left of his allowance for the week, and it was only Wednesday. Then he glanced up at the Martian again, and at the beckoning flap of the menagerie tent.

"You goin' in there?" Les asked.

Davy nodded eagerly. "Sure! Don't you want to see—"

"Yeah, yeah. Interstellar denizens." Les chuckled. "You really eat all that junk up, don't you? Look here—how come the government don't say anything, if there's Men from Mars on Earth? We can't even go to the Moon yet."

A momentary doubt flickered across Davy's face. Then he shook his head. "It's only a quarter, Les."

Something appeared at the tent flap—something tall and angular, with grainy red skin. It was visible for a second, then moved back into the shadows. Davy's eyes widened.

"Come on—I'm going in there. You?"

He stared at the older boy, who tried unsuccessfully to conceal his own curiosity. After a minute, Les dug down and produced a quarter too.

"Two tickets, please."

The tent was bigger than it seemed from the outside, and had a strange, alien smell about it. The two boys stood at the entrance, looking around.

There were a dozen exhibits, each in its own cage.

"Over here," Davy said. "Man from Jupiter."

They stared. The Man from Jupiter was a monstrous slug, round and featureless, that lay still, its vast slimy sides moving up and down slowly. Every few minutes it emitted a deep grunt and quivered.

The barker came over to them. "Straight from the Solar System's biggest planet," he said. His voice was rich and full; he was a good barker, Davy thought. "Our collecting team suffered four casualties getting him."

"He's pretty big himself," Davy said.

"Fifteen feet in circumference. He could swallow you in one gulp. His mouth's on the other side. We feed him a live cow every Sunday."

"What's that over there?" Les asked.

"He's from Saturn. A spider man."

It was the red-skinned creature that had poked its grotesque face through the tent-flaps before. It was moving around, uncaged. Tall, shambling, with four jointed arms about an inch in diameter. It wasn't pretty.

"How come you let him move around?" Davy asked.

"They're harmless, and they enjoy the company," the barker said.

Les nudged Davy and jerked his head in the direction of the spider man. The Saturnian was surreptitiously slipping one of his bony arms inside someone's pocket.

"That's why they let him walk around," Les whispered. "He's a trained pickpocket! These guys are just crooks!"

Davy blinked in surprise as the spider man extracted a wallet and deftly tucked it in the folds of his voluminous robe. "Maybe they are," he whispered back. "But they're *real*, all the same."

Les grinned and moved on. The next exhibit was a Venusian. It swam in a tank of dark green liquid, and resembled a horned octopus. It moved in slow, dignified circles, staring at the gaping sideshow customers with sedate majesty. Davy tried to picture the world from which the creature had come. Suddenly, goosepimples crept down his neck as he thought of the amazing wonderland of space and the strange planets that lay out there, waiting for Man to reach them.

Or had Man reached them? It was funny, Davy thought, that no one knew about it. Evidently these circus people had gone to the planets—why had nobody else?

He shrugged and kept moving. There was a native of Pluto, squatting malevolently on a block of ice. It was all horns and bristles, and was kept behind thick bars. There was a jellyfish-like thing from Uranus, and a strange-looking furry beast hailing from Neptune.

Finally the long summer's day came to its end.

"Suppertime," Les said matter-of-factly. "We better get going or we won't get fed."

"But—"

"You remember what happened the last time you came home late," Les reminded him. "You want to get tarred again?"

Davy didn't. Reluctantly, he left the Big Top, passed over the circus grounds, and started up the street toward home.

At supper, Davy's father remarked, "Well, we've finally got those fakers chased out of town."

"Which fakers, Dad?"

"Why, that carnival, of course. That phony circus with the Men from Mars. I suspected all along that they were just pickpockets and thieves, but we got the goods on them today. Seems Police Chief Harkins was there, and the Man from Saturn grabbed his wallet. That was all they needed. Judge Lewis issued a court order, and they're clearing out tomorrow at dawn. Today was the last day for them."

Davy was silent. He stared unhappily at his soup. So the circus was going, eh? And he'd been hoping to squeeze a quarter from his bank upstairs and go back for another look at the other-world beings.

Now he would never get the chance. The circus would move on, and they'd never come back to Hoytsville. Angrily, he kicked the leg of the kitchen table—not hard enough for his father to notice, but hard enough to express some anger.

"And where were *you* today, Davy?" his mother asked. "You and Les were out from dawn to dusk."

"Why, we were—" He stopped. Suddenly he didn't want to talk about the circus at all. "We went down to the picnic grounds. We had a swim and played ball. It was a real good day."

"That's odd—your hair's not wet at all."

"Oh—the sun was hot. We came out early and dried off playing ball."

"I see," his mother said. But she didn't seem convinced.

When bedtime came, Davy's feeling of dejection still had not left him. He made his goodnights and traipsed off to his bedroom, hating Police Chief Harkins and Judge Lewis and all the other people who had driven the circus away. He hated the whole town—the whole dull Earthbound town.

He gasped. He knew what he wanted.

He could get away—away from these tiresome people, away from this dreary town.

What of it if the circus people were just phonies and pickpockets? That was the life, Davy thought happily.

And if the men from other worlds happened to be real—

That didn't matter. He knew where he wanted to go, what he wanted to do.

Silently, he climbed out of bed and slipped back into his clothes. He made a little bundle—his baseball mitt, his toothbrush, an extra pair of socks. The night was cool, so he put a jacket on.

Then he slipped down the back way, through the silent kitchen, out into the alley. He broke into a run, moving as fast as his short legs could go.

*

The circus was chaotic. Men were everywhere, taking down the trapezes, pulling the concession booths apart, lowering the tents. An elephant stood patiently to one side; the spidery Man from Saturn was wandering around the scene, but otherwise none of the other-world creatures were to be found.

Davy moved determinedly through the busy grounds, stepping over cables and around trucks. Finally he found the man he was looking for.

The barker was busy directing the handling of a couple of animal cages. He brushed Davy away impatiently, but the boy continued to tug at his sleeve.

Finally the barker turned. "What do you want, boy?" he asked, in his rich, resonant voice.

"You leaving tonight?"

"That's right, kid. We're pulling up stakes."

"I heard about it. Too bad, mister."

"Yeah—isn't it? Why don't you go home and go to bed, now? We've got a lot of work before morning."

"That when you're leaving?" Davy asked. "Morning?"

"First thing in the morning. We'll be out of here by seven a.m. Go away now, huh?"

Davy stepped back and watched the barker in silence for a moment more. Then, deepening his voice to make it sound more impressive, he said, "You think you got room for another hand?"

"No," the barker said without turning around. "We've got plenty. Go away."

"But—you sure? Sure you can't use somebody extra? like *me*, for instance?"

The sideshow man was silent for a moment. Then he turned, frowning, and stared down at Davy. The silence seemed to last forever. Finally he said, "You know, maybe we can. Sure—we can use you."

"You mean that?"

The barker nodded. "Sure. You've got the circus way about you. You can come along with us."

Davy was too delighted to be able to say anything. He grinned nervously and gulped. Visions of big cities—Detroit, Chicago, maybe even New York—opened out before him. A lifetime with the circus!

"Gosh," he said. "Thanks, mister."

"Nothing of it, son."

"And where's the next stop? Where's the circus heading from here? Chicago? Texas, maybe?"

The barker smiled, showing bright white teeth. "Mars," he said.

Sometime later, Davy awoke.

There was a crowd around him, and he smelled the familiar smells of the circus. *I must have been asleep*, he thought. *I missed the whole trip*.

The barker had said they were going to Mars. That was silly, of course. But where were they?

He looked around—

And felt cold chills wriggle down the middle of his back.

There were the familiar other-world men. The Man from Jupiter pulsated hideously in his vat, the Man from Venus still swam with dignity. They were all there—all except the Man from Mars. Davy didn't see him, the first time around.

Then he looked through the open flap of the tent, and he did see him. He was standing just in front of the tent, on the outside. And Davy was on the inside, with the other-world creatures.

Davy peered a little further through the tent flap and looked at the audience. It was a good crowd outside, there on the sandy, windswept reddish ground. They were all small and wiry, with tangled boneless tentacles.

The one on the platform was speaking, and his voice was that of the barker's, deep and resonant. What he was saying was impossible gibberish, in a strange and alien language. But Davy knew suddenly what he was saying.

He was saying, "Step right up, ladies and gents. Put your money on the line and enter this tent. Within, you'll see the wonders of the Galaxy—including a genuine, real-live Man from Earth, the only one in captivity. Step right up, folks—step right up!"

1912

THE CONJURER

Richard Middleton

Richard Barham Middleton (1882–1911) was born in Staines, on the western fringes of London, in October 1882. After attending boarding school, in 1901 Middleton procured a job as a clerk at the Royal Exchange Assurance Corporation, distracting himself from the humdrum nature of his everyday existence by going to bookshops, immersing himself in his own writing, and making copious trips to the theatre (his 1901 diary, for instance, notes 97 such visits). However, he was clearly unhappy, quitting his job in 1907 to try his luck as a bohemian poet, writer and journalist. In early 1911, the penniless Middleton left London to live in Belgium with friends, but the tantalisingly close prospect of a successful literary career was extinguished a few months later when, aged 29, he committed suicide in Brussels after taking poison. His first collection of, largely, supernatural tales, *The Ghost Ship & Other Stories*, came out in the year following his death. No less an authority than Arthur Machen composed the preface: "I have just been reading in proof a volume of short stories by an author named Richard Middleton. He is dead. It is an extraordinary book, and all the work in it is full of a quite curious and distinctive quality. In my opinion it is a very fine work indeed."

A volume of melancholy childhood reminiscences, *The Day Before Yesterday*, was also published in 1912, before the poet and anthologist John Gawsworth—a committed champion of Middleton's writing—edited *The Pantomime Man* (1933), a further selection of Middleton's work that contained "The Welcome Home", another supernatural story. Several more of Middleton's previously unpublished eerie tales were included in influential anthologies assembled by Gawsworth during the 1930s.

Despite the sad circumstances of his short life, there's a certain irony that his best-known story, "The Ghost Ship", is one of the genre's few classic humorous tales; many of the other stories in that first collection are bleaker in tone, however. "The Conjurer" is, on the face of things, quite a light affair—until you start to think through the consequences of its stark ending...

Certainly the audience was restive. In the first place it felt that it had been defrauded, seeing that Cissie Bradford, whose smiling face adorned the bills outside, had failed to appear, and secondly, it considered that the deputy for that famous lady was more than inadequate. To the little man who sweated in the glare of the limelight and juggled desperately with glass balls in a vain effort to steady his nerve it was apparent that his turn was a failure. And as he worked he could have cried with disappointment, for his was a trial performance, and a year's engagement in the Hennings' group of music-halls would have rewarded success. Yet his tricks, things that he had done with the utmost ease a thousand times, had been a succession of blunders, rather mirth-provoking than mystifying to the audience. Presently one of the glass balls fell crashing on the stage, and amidst the jeers of the gallery he turned to his wife, who served as his assistant.

"I've lost my chance," he said, with a sob; "I can't do it!"

"Never mind, dear," she whispered. "There's a nice steak and onions at home for supper."

"It's no use," he said despairingly. "I'll try the disappearing trick and then get off. I'm done here." He turned back to the audience.

"Ladies and gentlemen," he said to the mockers in a wavering voice, "I will now present to you the concluding item of my entertainment. I will cause this lady to disappear under your very eyes, without the aid of any mechanical contrivance or artificial device." This was the merest showman's patter, for, as a matter of fact, it was not a very wonderful illusion. But as he led his wife forward to present her to the audience the conjurer was wondering whether the mishaps that had ruined his chance would meet him even here. If something should go wrong—he felt his wife's hand tremble in his, and he pressed it tightly to reassure her. He must make an effort, an effort of will, and then no mistakes would happen. For a second the lights danced before his eyes, then he pulled himself together. If an earthquake should disturb the curtains and show Molly creeping ignominiously away behind he would still meet his fate like a man. He turned round to conduct his wife to the little alcove from which she should vanish. She was not on the stage!

For a minute he did not guess the greatness of the disaster. Then he realised that the theatre was intensely quiet, and that he would have to explain that the last item of his programme was even more of a fiasco than the rest. Owing to a sudden indisposition—his skin tingled at the thought of the hooting. His tongue rasped upon cracking lips as he braced himself and bowed to the audience.

Then came the applause. Again and again it broke out from all over the house, while the curtain rose and fell, and the conjurer stood on the stage, mute, uncomprehending. What had happened? At first he had thought they were mocking him, but it was impossible to misjudge the nature of the applause. Besides, the stage-manager was allowing him call after call, as if he were a star. When at length the curtain remained down, and the orchestra struck up the opening bars of the next song, he staggered off into the wings as if he were drunk. There he met Mr. James Hennings himself.

"You'll do," said the great man; "that last trick was neat. You ought to polish up the others though. I suppose you don't want to tell me how you did it? Well, well, come in the morning and we'll fix up a contract." And so, without having said a word, the conjurer found himself hustled off by the Vaudeville Napoleon. Mr. Hennings had something more to say to his manager.

"Bit rum," he said. "Did you see it?"

"Queerest thing we've struck."

"How was it done do you think?"

"Can't imagine. There one minute on his arm, gone the next, no trap, or curtain, or anything."

"Money in it, eh?"

"Biggest hit of the century, I should think."

"I'll go and fix up a contract and get him to sign it tonight. Get on with it." And Mr. James Hennings fled to his office.

Meanwhile the conjurer was wandering in the wings with the drooping heart of a lost child. What had happened? Why was he a success, and why did people stare so oddly, and what had become of his wife? When he asked them the stage hands laughed, and said they had not seen her. Why should they laugh? He wanted her to explain things, and hear their good luck. But she was not in her dressing-room, she was not anywhere. For a moment he felt like crying.

Then, for the second time that night, he pulled himself together. After all, there was no reason to be upset. He ought to feel very pleased about the contract, however it had happened. It seemed that his wife had left the stage in some queer way without being seen. Probably to increase the mystery she had gone straight home in her stage dress, and had succeeded in dodging the stage doorkeeper. It was all very strange; but, of course, there must be some simple explanation like that. He would take a cab home and find her there already. There was a steak and onions for supper.

As he drove along in the cab he became convinced that this theory was right. Molly had always been clever, and this time she had certainly succeeded in surprising everybody. At the door of his house he gave the cabman a shilling for himself with a light heart. He could afford it now. He ran up the steps cheerfully and opened the door. The passage was quite dark, and he wondered why his wife hadn't lit the gas.

"Molly!" he cried, "Molly!"

The small, weary-eyed servant came out of the kitchen on a savoury wind of onions.

"Hasn't missus come home with you, sir?" she said.

The conjurer thrust his hand against the wall to steady himself, and the pattern of the wall-paper seemed to burn his finger-tips.

"Not here!" he gasped at the frightened girl. "Then where is she? Where is she?"

"I don't know, sir," she began stuttering; but the conjurer turned quickly and ran out of the house. Of course, his wife must be at the theatre. It was absurd ever to have supposed that she could leave the theatre in her stage dress unnoticed; and now she was probably worrying because he had not waited for her. How foolish he had been.

It was a quarter of an hour before he found a cab, and the theatre was dark and empty when he got back to it. He knocked at the stage door, and the night watchman opened it.

"My wife?" he cried.

"There's no one here now, sir," the man answered respectfully, for he knew that a new star had risen that night.

The conjurer leant against the doorpost faintly.

"Take me up to the dressing-rooms," he said. "I want to see whether she has been there while I was away."

The watchman led the way along the dark passages. "I shouldn't worry if I were you, sir," he said. "She can't have gone far." He did not know anything about it, but he wanted to be sympathetic.

"God knows," the conjurer muttered, "I can't understand this at all."

In the dressing-room Molly's clothes still lay neatly folded as she had left them when they went on the stage that night, and when he saw them his last hope left the conjurer, and a strange thought came into his mind.

"I should like to go down on the stage," he said, "and see if there is anything to tell me of her."

The night watchman looked at the conjurer as if he thought he was mad, but he followed him down to the stage in silence. When he was there the conjurer leaned forward suddenly, and his face was filled with a wistful eagerness.

"Molly!" he called, "Molly!"

But the empty theatre gave him nothing but echoes in reply.

1931

THE VANISHING TRICK

Charles Davy

Charles Bertram Davy (1897–1985) was born in Exeter and educated at Rugby School. During the First World War he served as a driver in the French Red Cross, before returning to his studies, in 1919, at Corpus Christi College. He left without obtaining a degree, as he found academic life in Oxford artificial after the horrors he had witnessed during the war. Instead, he trained as a journalist, in the hope of being able to do some good in the world.

Davy went on to have a varied press career, working as the literary editor, film critic, and assistant editor of *The Yorkshire Post* throughout most of the 1930s and early 1940s, before becoming assistant editor of *The Observer* in 1944. He also edited a book on cinema (*Footnotes to the Film*, 1937) and the sociological *The Three Spheres of Society* (1946); the latter appeared under the pseudonym Charles Waterman, as he did not wish his personal views to compromise his journalistic integrity.

The excellent "The Vanishing Trick", which first appeared in the May 1931 edition of *The English Review* and was then included in *The Evening Standard Book of Strange Stories* (1934), appears to be Davy's only published short story; given its quality, this feels a real shame. However, in a minor feat of bookish conjuring, I'm delighted to be able to materialise its words here among the pages of this anthology, some 90 years after they last appeared in print.

I am a conjurer—out of work. I shall have to get back to it, because it's my living. But not at once. My hand isn't steady yet.

Most of my jobs are private—smoking concerts, bazaars, parties, and so on. I'm pretty good with cards and I don't mind working under people's noses. In the summer I generally fix up with a concert party, round the seaside towns. I can take a turn in a chorus—had to learn how, for that. It's a change from town work and keeps you going through August.

Well, I'm not working now because of a chance meeting and what happened afterwards. I know what I saw and I know I wasn't dreaming. Anyway, a conjurer doesn't believe in such things—much.

My bad luck started when I got a job at a church bazaar at Hastings. I was due at the hall early in the afternoon; so I went down in the morning and took a walk along the promenade—I'm fond of the sea. I knew I'd want a bit of food before the show; I looked out for a place, and presently I saw a little hotel—"open to non-residents." I thought that would suit me because I like my meals quiet, and sure enough there were only three other people there and they'd started ahead of me. A funny little waiter was running round, and as soon as I saw him, I knew I'd seen him before—where, I couldn't think. I fancied he knew me, too, but he didn't want to show it. So I sat wondering—and then I remembered.

It had been while I was up on the East Coast, the summer before. I was with a concert party, a good one. We had the pier pavilion at Birling for a fortnight, changing the programme, of course, a bit every day. I was working a vanishing trick, among others. Just the usual thing—vanishing a girl from a box and finding her in a cabinet. Vanishing tricks are always popular—I used to do it at almost every performance. I'd picked up the box second-hand. It was old-fashioned, but it was simple and fairly quick. It never let me down.

Well, one morning I'd gone to the pavilion for letters. Afterwards I was standing on the pier, watching some old fellows fishing, when a little middle-aged man came and stood beside me. I thought I'd seen him in the audience a few nights before, but I wasn't sure. After a bit he said: "You're the conjurer, aren't you? I saw your performance. I hope you don't mind my speaking to you?"

He seemed nervous, so I said no, I didn't mind; what did he want? Anything I could do for him?

"Yes," he said, "I had an idea. Now that box trick of yours—when you vanish the girl—that's a good one." He looked at me—a quick sort of anxious look. "But it's got a weak spot, hasn't it?"

I thought he was going to tell me how it was done. There's always someone in every audience who knows all the tricks better than you do. So to humour him I just said, "Oh, what's that?"

"You use a confederate," he said. "That spoils it. Now, this is my idea. Why don't you get someone from the audience and vanish *him*?"

This was a new one to me. I'd never thought of it—never heard of anyone trying it. How easy d'you think it'd be to get someone to step on the stage and lie down in a box? Besides, those boxes aren't automatic—only I wasn't going to say so, straight off.

"All right," I said, "but who'd come? No chance of it."

"I'd come," he said. "Why not take me on—show me how to do it? I don't look like a confederate, do I?"

He was right there. He was short, perhaps fifty, with a drooping moustache and blinking eyes—the kind of man you might find behind the counter of a little shop of his own. No one'd ever think he was part of the show.

"What's the idea?" I said. "Want to see how it's done?"

"No," he said. "Never mind that. I just want a chance to do it. I'm small—you want a small man, don't you?"

"He'd have to be pretty small," I said. I began to see points in the idea. A bit of novelty always goes down well. I knew there was nobody in the pavilion just then. "Look here," I said, "if you're serious, we'll have a rehearsal. I don't mind trying it—but you wouldn't get anything for it, you know. Wouldn't be worth my while."

He shook his head. I could see he was absolutely set on the idea. Probably hadn't ever thought I'd agree.

"I don't want anything," he said. "It's just my fancy. You show me now, can you? It won't take long, will it?"

Well, to cut the story short, I took him inside, got the box out and showed him how it worked. He just had to press a catch and slip down under the stage, through a trap. Then he had to go round and work the false door of the cabinet, from the back. It was simple enough, and he was quick at it, too.

"That's all right," he said, when he'd done it twice. "I'll be here on Tuesday. I've promised to bring the wife. I'll get a seat at the end of a row. You ask for someone to step up and then look at me, see? Make it easy for me."

I still didn't know what he was getting at, but I agreed. I thought very likely he wouldn't be there after all, when it came to the point. Anyway, I thought, I'd look out for him, and if he wasn't there, I'd do the trick in the ordinary way. I didn't see that much harm could come from trying it.

As soon as I'd agreed, he scuttled off. Seemed to be in a hurry. I stayed on the pier a bit, watching the fishing and wondering what he was up to. By the time I went home I was beginning to feel sorry I'd ever listened to him.

However, Tuesday night came and there he was in the front row with a big, powerful-looking woman, red-faced, next to him. He caught my eye but gave no sign. At length I brought out the box trick, almost meaning to do it in the usual way. But I'd promised him. So I went to the front of the stage and worked a bit of patter—about anyone who wanted to make himself scarce, and so on. I looked at my little man—he was out of his seat like a knife. I thought the woman next to him—his wife, I supposed—was mighty surprised, but she didn't say anything. Perhaps she was too surprised. She just stared, very red in the face.

Well, I could see there were people in the audience who knew my little man. That was good for me. Made it seem more natural. I put him in the box, waved the wand, opened the box—and he'd gone all right. The audience clapped, but the red-faced woman didn't clap. She'd shut her mouth very tight, and I thought the little man was going to catch it when he got home.

Still, that wasn't my affair. He'd asked for it. I did a little business—taking the sides out of the box, tapping them, and so on, to give him time. Then I went to open the cabinet. It was empty. The audience began to laugh—I had to think of something quickly. Fortunately I've learnt how to keep my head—you've got to in conjuring. I shut the cabinet, went to the front of the stage and began to talk about dematerialising—said my assistant had to dematerialise himself in the box and rematerialise in the cabinet, and that needed time. In a minute or two he'd be there all right, I said—not believing it, because

I thought he'd lost his nerve. Still, I had to say something. Then I got on quickly to another trick—just an easy one with coloured handkerchiefs—and while I worked I thought out what I should say if the cabinet was empty again.

Well, I had to open it again as soon as I'd finished with the handkerchiefs and, of course, it was still empty. So I signed for someone in the wings to fetch it off and went back to try and put over a yarn about vanishing people too thoroughly. I was just getting the audience to listen when out of the corner of my eye I saw the red-faced woman stand up. I knew she was going to shout at me, and she did—in a hoarse kind of voice, very unpleasant. Wanted to know what I'd done with her husband. Where'd he gone?

I said I wished I knew. Of course, the audience laughed, and when the woman came up and shook her umbrella at me over the footlights, they laughed all the more. Some one called out: "He's gone off with Elsie—oh, Ma!"—but the woman wasn't worrying. She was set on me. While we were arguing and the audience was laughing, the manager came on—told me to get off quick—send on the others for a chorus. I didn't wait. I roused up the others, and I was just going to look for my little man when I met the manager coming round to the back with the woman. She glared at me. The manager said, very sharply: "Where'd he be? Underneath somewhere?"

Well, we looked in every corner—under the stage, in the dressing-rooms—the woman snorting, probing with her umbrella, getting redder and redder. Fortunately the show had got started again all right and it was nearly over, anyway.

We went out on to the pier—it was a dark, windy night—and looked all round, but there was absolutely no sign of my little man. He really had vanished—clean gone. At last the woman turned on us like a fury—said she was going straight to the police, we'd all be arrested—I don't know what else. Seemed to think we'd done it on purpose. I was glad to see her go marching off down the pier, I can tell you, and just then the lights went on round the pavilion and the audience began to come out.

Next day we had the police, of course—a sergeant, but he didn't stay long, just looked at the trap and asked a few questions. We weren't to blame, really, and he seemed to know something about the woman. We had a couple of reporters, too—wonderful publicity it all was, in the end. The place was packed that afternoon and again at night. The manager wanted us to stay another week, but he couldn't get the bookings altered in time. We had to move on, up the coast to Hunstanton. Even there it did us good. The papers were still running the story; they published the little man's photograph—my photograph. But they didn't find the little man—never a word or a trace of him anywhere. Some people thought he'd jumped into the sea—temporarily insane, you know—only then his body would have been washed up sooner or later, and it never was.

And now, as I sat at lunch, I felt sure I'd found him at last. He was the waiter. He'd cut off his moustache, but I knew I wasn't wrong, particularly after I'd caught him looking at me, in a funny, frightened sort of way, once or twice.

I waited till I'd almost finished and the other people had gone. Then I beckoned to him and said, "Been doing any more vanishing tricks lately?"

He didn't try to deny it. He glanced quickly over his shoulder, then bent down, resting one hand on the table, and said anxiously, "You aren't going to give me away, are you?"

"No," I said, "why should I? What are you doing here?"

"I'm all right here," he said, "if I can stay. I only want to be left alone."

"What happened to you that night?" I asked. "You framed it, I suppose, didn't you, to get away?"

He nodded. "Yes, I got away. I'm grateful. It was just what I wanted."

"But why all that trouble?" I said. "Why did you have to vanish out of a box?"

He looked round again, to see if the room was empty, I suppose. Then he drew a chair up to my table.

"I couldn't stay with my wife any more," he said. "D'you understand that? Your trick gave me an idea."

"I still don't see it," I said. "Why not just walk out of the house?"

"Ah," he said, gazing at me very seriously, "you're not married, perhaps?"

I admitted that I was not.

"Then you won't know," he said. "My wife wasn't one to give a man much freedom. We had a little business—fancy goods and confectionery. I had to mind the shop and in the evenings I never went out except with her. She had a firm hand—fair got me under. After a time you can't break loose. I don't know why, but you can't. Then I couldn't just walk off in daylight. They all knew me in the town. She'd have been after me too quick. That meant after dark, only I was never out alone in the evening. I thought your trick'd be just right—give me a start. See what I mean?"

He looked up at me, a puzzled kind of look. Didn't seem quite to know what he meant himself, but wanted me to understand it.

"You see, it was that *vanishing*," he said. "That's what I liked—just what I'd wanted, time and again. Never saw how I could do it. Then, when I saw your trick, I thought—if I could do that I'd be all right, out of it, quickly. I'd be away by myself and no questions asked. No questions, that was it."

"Well," I said, to humour him, "what did you do? Slip out of the theatre and run away? You got me into a nice mess, you know."

He nodded, but he didn't seem to hear my last words. I don't suppose he'd ever thought of that side of it. He'd just had his one idea—nothing else.

"Yes," he said, "I knew there'd be no one about on the pier while the show was on. Just a turnstile to get out—they used to lock up the rest. I walked—walked to Yarmouth, all night. Came to London. No one had seen me. Got a waiter's job. I'd been a waiter before I was married. Everything was all right—ought to have stayed there."

"Why didn't you?" I said. "How long have you been down here?"

"Month," he said. "It's quiet, you see. I like a quiet place. Only I'm afraid—" He dropped his voice and leant forward over the table—"I'm afraid they're going to get on to me. I saw someone I knew the other day. I'm afraid I did."

Well, I suppose I'd have gone on listening to him, but just then I caught sight of the clock. In half an hour I was due to start my show. I pushed back my chair.

"Here, let's have the bill," I said. "I'm late, talking to you."

He got up but he didn't give me the bill at once. He stood fumbling with his napkin.

"I'd be better in London," he said. "I'm not going back, anyway—not for anything—not even if they find me."

"I don't want you to go back," I said. "What's it to me? I shan't go about saying I've seen you. Let's have the bill—that's what I want."

He glanced at me—he still didn't move.

"You won't?" he said. "No—I was scared when I saw you, but I don't much mind. Anyway, I—"

I interrupted him, made him fetch the bill—sent him running for it. I hadn't got time to waste. But in a way I was sorry when I'd gone and left him looking after me from the door. I didn't want to scare him. Perhaps if I hadn't been in such a hurry, I might have—but that can't be helped now.

Well, I did my show and a second show again a bit later and caught a train at seven. In the train I thought of my little man. My belief was that he'd be back at Birling soon. To stay hidden for ever—no one can do it, not in this country. Anyway, he wasn't the type. But I felt sorry for him. I remembered that woman.

In London, during the next week, I hadn't much to do—one evening job and one kids' party—it was near Christmas. For Boxing week I was booked—a music-hall down near Putney. I knew the place—always going to turn into a cinema, but never did, though they showed pictures on Sunday. It was twice nightly for me, but you have to take what you can get, nowadays.

It was on the Wednesday in that week that it happened—the first house. My act started at 6.50. I had a girl working with me, one I'd often had before—it's worth it, for a week. For the box trick she wore a special rig—used to go and put it on while I showed the box to the audience. On this Wednesday night she'd gone as usual, and when I'd finished showing the box I looked round to see if she was ready. She wasn't there—but in the wings I saw my little man, in his waiter's clothes. He was looking straight at me with a queer kind of intent expression—standing quite still.

I was scared. I couldn't think how he'd got there or what he was doing, particularly in those clothes. I wondered, too, all in the same moment, what had happened to my girl. I felt something had gone wrong and was going to go more wrong if I didn't stop it.

But before I could do anything my little man was walking on to the stage, still staring at me with the same expression. He walked a bit stiffly, somehow—mechanically, almost. I suppose I might have turned him round and pushed him off. But almost anything's better than a scene on the stage, and somehow I couldn't push him off—I don't know why. The way he was walking on made me feel queer. I thought he'd determined to vanish again through my box, and that it wouldn't be easy to stop him. I just felt I'd better be quick. I wanted to get him in and get him vanished before anything happened.

I introduced him to the audience—said what I was going to do and so on, the usual thing. While I was speaking, I felt the audience go quiet—a sort of hush—all of a sudden. I glanced over my shoulder—my little man was still there, but he wasn't looking at me now—he was looking at the box. Then he began to get in of his own accord. I hadn't time to wonder about the audience. I had to attend to the box. I wanted to be sure he got in the right way. He did, but he seemed to fall in, and for a moment I almost thought he really had fallen. It was queer, but I had to get the box shut. A kind of murmur had started in the audience, and I fumbled, trying to be quick. As soon as I stood up and turned round, the murmur stopped—dead silence.

I got off a bit of patter, then turned back to the box, and as I turned, I saw out of the corner of my eye my girl assistant standing in the wings—staring at me, pale, I thought. I just motioned to her to stay there. Then I threw the box open—and next moment I was trying to get it shut, as quick as I could. My little man was still there, but he was all crumpled and crushed, his head smashed in—blood dripping out of the box.

After that I don't know quite what happened, except that I was trying to get the box shut because I didn't want the audience to see. I got it shut—then I remember the curtain coming down. The manager of the hall was on the stage and two of the hands were picking up the box to carry it off. I started to say something—"Look out—put it down—" but they paid no attention, and I found myself in the wings, with the next turn starting and the manager telling me I was drunk. Of course, that was silly—you can't do conjuring on drink—but I didn't stop to listen. I wanted the box opened and that thing in it taken away. I went over to the box and opened the top quickly—not the sides. You can believe me or not, but it was empty—clean empty. Not even a spot of blood.

After that I remember sitting down and the manager shaking me by the shoulder. He told me to get out—I was fired. He said it several times, but I didn't care. I just sat there, and after a bit I saw there was quite a crowd staring at me. I looked at the box—it was still empty. How could you explain that? I knew it was no use trying.

I got up and went to my dressing-room and the manager followed me. I only wanted to get out of the theatre, but the manager—he was Jewish—kept saying: "Why you act like that? What you think you do—play the fool by yourself, eh? Spoil my show, eh? What's the big idea?"

Then I saw what he meant and I asked him if he hadn't seen anyone with me on the stage. He stared and began to look a bit frightened, I thought. He said he'd seen no one—absolutely no one—so I knew I'd seen a ghost. I didn't tell him—just went on dressing, and after a moment I heard the door shut. I think he'd decided I was mad and didn't like staying with me.

When I was dressed I went out. The manager was there and several others—stage hands and folk from other acts—but no one spoke. They just stared at me. Then I saw my assistant. She looked white. I asked her where she'd been. She said she'd just been coming on—just leaving her dressing-room—when she'd torn half her skirt off on a nail. She showed me the tear. It was a funny accident, but I didn't ask any more. I just told the manager I'd send for my stuff in the morning and went out. It was a fine night—early still. I found a pub and had a couple of brandies. Then I walked about the streets a bit and began to feel better. Only I didn't go home. I had a room in Kennington and I knew I should sit there thinking. I wanted company. So I went to a hotel and had another drink and took a room there and went to bed with the light on.

I suppose I slept because I found it was morning and the light still burning. Then I remembered—and I wondered if I really had been mad or dreaming the night before. In daylight you can't believe these things so easily. I was still wondering while I got dressed and had breakfast. Then I bought a paper, and on an inside page a paragraph jumped at me:

HOTEL TRAGEDY.
WAITER FALLS DOWN LIFT SHAFT.

> Albert Creasey, waiter at the Magnolia Hotel, Russell Square, was killed last night through falling down the lift shaft from the top floor, where he had his own room. The tragedy occurred just before seven o'clock, shortly after Creasey had been visited in his room by a plain clothes police officer. Creasey, who had been at the hotel only since Sunday, apparently stayed in his room for a few minutes after the officer had left and then opened the lift gate on the top landing and stepped into the shaft.
>
> It is understood that the visit of the police officer had no connection with any criminal proceedings. Inquiries were being made for Creasey on behalf of his wife, with whom he had not lived for several months.

The name was right and the time was right. I knew I'd seen my little man just as he was walking to the lift and after he'd fallen.

Anyway, I've sold my box. I can't face that trick again.

1912

THE LITTLE TOWN

J. D. Beresford

John Davys Beresford (1873–1947) was the son of the local vicar in the village of Castor, located just west of Peterborough. As a youngster he suffered from what he described as "a case of infant paralysis" that left him lame (this was probably polio)—an event that seems likely to have influenced the subject matter of two of his most well-known novels, *The Hampdenshire Wonder* (1911) and *The Camberwell Miracle* (1933), both of which are concerned with child protagonists affected by miraculous abilities. Beresford was an admirer of H. G. Wells, producing a volume of critical appreciation of his fellow author of science fiction in 1915. Like Wells, Beresford was prolific, producing almost fifty novels in his lifetime, several volumes of non-fiction and short stories, as well as numerous essays. He also happened to be the father of Elisabeth Beresford, creator of the Wombles.

"The Little Town" is a remarkable tale from Beresford's excellent first short-story collection, *Nineteen Impressions* (1918), though the story itself dates from 1912. I include it here as, to my mind, the strange setting of that odd show in the Kosmos theatre perfectly fits the bill for this anthology—and in any case it feels too good a tale not to share. But for those looking for a neat, allegorical explanation of the story, beware! Beresford himself, in the introduction to *Nineteen Impressions* dismisses the obvious solution to the question of the puppeteer's identity:

At the best I could only say that if the story meant anything at all—and I was not the least sure whether it did or not—it meant that under the stress of such an excitement as the discovery of an unknown town, a man might be moved to dream of the shadow of some relation between himself and the impersonal; that he might, in fact, achieve the moment's separation which reveals the apparently commonplace as a vision of wonder.

I

"It is quite a small place."

That was all the information I could obtain. I had been referred to the omniscient Joe Shepperton and this was all he could tell me. "St. Erth," he had said. "In Cornwall?" And when I had explained that this was another St. Erth, he had said, "Oh! quite a small place." Probably he had never before heard of it...

As I looked out into the darkness and tried to dodge the reflection of my own face in the window, it seemed that we were passing through country of a kind which was quite unfamiliar to me. I had a vision of mountains and the broad roll of great forests; an effect that may have been produced by clouds. The yellow-lighted reflection of the now familiar interior jutted out before me, its floor diaphanous and traversed by two streaks of shining metal. And my own white face peered in at me with strained, searching eyes, frowning at me when our glances met, trying to peer past me into the light and warmth of the railway carriage.

Once we crossed an interminable bridge that roared a sonorous resentment against our passage. I could not explain that bridge. We were not near the sea and no English river could surely have been so wide. Yet the bridge was not a viaduct, for I caught the gleam of water below, some reflection of paler shadows from the lift of the sky.

This adventure into unknown country was immensely exciting. It was discovery. I gave up my strained inquiry into the world beyond, and let my imagination wander out into mystery. I was in the midst of high romance when the magnificent energy of our triumphant speed was checked by the sickening grind of the brake...

The little station was a terminus; one forsaken, gloomy platform that stretched a grey finger into the night out of which we had come. I tried to see what was on the further side, across the metals, but beyond was a black void. I received the impression that I was on an immense height, that the dimly seen low stone wall was the parapet of some awful abyss.

I could form no idea of the town during my minute's walk from the station to the rooms I had engaged. The whole place seemed to be very ill-lighted. All I could see was that it hung on the side of a hill.

I went out when I had had something to eat. It was only a few minutes past eight, and I was eager for adventure. I told my landlady that I was going down into the town to explore.

"It's very dark," she said, with a note of warning in her voice.

The street in which I was staying dipped gently towards the town; but as I went on, the dip became more pronounced. I congratulated myself on the fact that there would be no difficulty in finding my way back. The lie of the land would direct me, I had merely to ascend again.

My street was longer than I had expected. At first there were houses on one side only, but further down the roadway narrowed and there were houses on each side. I classified my lodgings as being in a sort of suburb grown up round the railway station which was detached for obvious reasons—no railway but a funicular could have been carried down that hill.

I came to the bottom of the street at last and found another narrow street running across right and left. Opposite to me an alley continued the descent in nearly a straight line. Far below a dim lamp was burning. I decided to keep straight on and plunged down the alley.

It was interminably long. At the lamp it twisted suddenly but still descended the hill.

"The place is bigger than I thought," was my reflection. I saw, however, that as the road continually fell before me, I must be keeping a right line.

The town was not deserted. There were movements and the sound of voices all about me; figures loomed up out of the darkness to meet me and clattered past over the rough cobbles. I heard laughter, too, and whisperings in the dim black recesses of courts and doorways, and once or twice I caught the tinkle of some thin high music far away in the distance.

Everywhere I was conscious of the stir and struggle of life, of unseen creatures as careless of my presence as I of theirs.

And still I had not come as yet to the town itself. I had pictured to myself some wider streets, or open market, a place of lighted shops and visible life. I began to wonder if I had not passed by this imagined centre. I became a trifle impatient. I hurried on; down, always down, through the wriggling maze of tiny narrow alleys and passageways, lighted only by an occasional flickering lamp, bracketed out from some corner house.

"A small place, indeed," I said to myself. "It is an enormous place." I received the impression that I might walk on for ever through that tedious ravel of streets. Yet I knew that I could not be walking in a circle, for I was always descending.

I gave no thought now to the long toil of my return up the mountain—already I thought of it as a mountain—I felt that I must and would reach the bottom.

It was not what I had expected to find, yet the reality, when I came upon it, was so inevitable that I believed it to be the thing I had always anticipated.

I turned at last out of a passage so narrow that my body brushed the wall on either side, into a small square of low houses and the floor of the square was flat. On all sides it was entered by passages such as that from which I had just emerged, and all of them led upwards. About and above me I could vaguely distinguish an infinite slope of houses, ranging up tier above tier, lost at last in the black immensity. I appeared to be at the bottom of some Titanic basin among the mountains; at the centre of some inconceivably vast collection of mean houses that swarmed over the whole face of visible earth.

"There is surely no other place like it in the world," I said to myself in wonder.

II

There was light in the square; two lamps that flanked an open door. Above the door was a faded sign. I guessed the place to be a hall of entertainment, probably a "picture palace."

I walked over to it and read the sign; it bore the one word "Kosmos."

"Some charlatan," I decided.

No one was taking money at the door, and after a moment's hesitation I went in.

It was a queer little hall. The bareness of the walls was partly hidden by pathetic attempts at decoration; some red material was rudely draped over the raw brickwork; and a few unframed, dingy canvases—the subjects indistinguishable—were hung on this background.

At the end was a rough proscenium opening, and behind it a stage that appeared to me quite brilliantly lighted, after my long sojourn in the darkness.

In the body of the hall some twenty persons were seated on rough benches staring at the still unoccupied stage.

I found a seat near the door and waited. It came to me that the stage was disproportionately large for the size of the hall.

And then out of the wings came wobbling a tiny figure, and I realised that this great stage was set for a puppet-show. The whole thing was so impossibly grotesque, that I nearly laughed aloud...

Presently I turned my attention for a moment to the vague forms sitting round me, some of them silhouetted against the light of the stage. But none of them returned my stare. "Rustics!" I thought, with a touch of contempt. "Men and women of such small intelligence and narrow experience that even such an amateur show as this amuses them."

I turned back to the performance, though the foolishness of the dolls' actions was beneath criticism.

Nevertheless, after a time, a certain fascinated interest began to grow upon me, and I watched the performance, chafing at its slowness—with increasing attention. I tried to disentangle some meaning, some story, some purpose from the apparently aimless movements of these tiny dolls staggering about their gigantic setting. Every now and again I thought that I understood, that there was an indication of some sequence of action, some development of a theme. But always the leading figures wavered or fell at the actual moment, and chaos followed; a hopeless, maddening jumble.

One piece of management, however, deserved and received my approbation. I had never in any marionette show I have ever witnessed, seen the suspending wires so cleverly concealed. Stare and criticise as I would I could see no sign of any mechanism whereby the dolls were supported and animated. This did, indeed, give me a curious sense of reality, it made me feel that these poor ridiculous little figures had a sentient life of their own. Then some senseless action or helpless collapse reminded me of the invisible wires, and my pity for the feeble dolls was turned to contempt for the ineptitude of the operator.

Dwelling on that ineptitude, I began to lose my temper and I became conscious that other members of the audience were being similarly affected. I heard impatient sighs and half-suppressed groans of despair when some doll attempted to strut across the stage and collapsed half-way.

I looked round me again and saw that men were twitching their arms, hands and fingers; leaning this way and that as if to influence the movement of the dolls—just as a man will strain and grimace in order to influence the run of a ball over which he has no sort of control.

I discovered that I had been unconsciously making the same foolish movements, and, also, that our attempted directions were not concerted. There was no unison, no characteristic sway in this direction or that. It was plain that we wished to influence the dolls in contradictory ways.

But one feeling, I am convinced, animated us all; we were unanimously and angrily critical of the unseen operator; we were all convinced that we could work the unseen wires far more efficiently than that bungling performer. Indeed, the fact, so far as I was concerned, seemed clearly demonstrable. The actions of the dolls were so infantile, so contemptibly purposeless.

That obsession grew upon me. The mismanagement of the whole stupid affair began to appear of quite transcendent importance.

I could not watch without striving to help, and I was forced to watch...

III

The performance closed abruptly.

The curtain descended without notice, apparently in the middle of the play, unheralded by any grouping or arrangement which might suggest a finale.

The audience, almost in darkness, were left to stumble out as best they could.

I could not find the exit and when I did find a door it was not the right one. It opened on to a flight of steep narrow stairs.

It occurred to me that this must be the way up into the flies, to the place in which the operator sat and controlled his dolls. In a sudden mood of determination I decided to seek him out—I would give him some primitive instruction. He must be some ignorant countryman. I would give him a few useful hints in the conduct of his business; suggest a story for his dolls to act, some sequent, purposeful story moving towards a climax...

I stumbled upwards in the dark, one hand on the cold rough wall, the other stretched out before me to guard against any obstacle which might be in my path. It was a very long staircase, for the proscenium opening was a high one. When I was nearly at the top, the stairway twisted unexpectedly, and I found myself looking down on the still brilliantly lighted stage.

Before me in a great chair that was almost a throne, an old man sat gazing tenderly down upon the stage below him. There was a calm gentle wisdom upon his face and he moved his hands slowly this way and that.

I looked down and saw that although the curtain had fallen and the hall was empty, the performance was still going on in the same, aimless, inexplicable manner.

Perhaps the old man was practising his art, or perhaps he did not know that the curtain had fallen and the audience gone away—in any case he sat there with a sweet intent smile, passing his outspread hands slowly to and fro over the heads of those foolish, inept figures beneath.

And even then I could see no wires, no connection between those mesmeric hands and the tottering figures.

A strange diffidence had come over me. From where I stood it appeared an immensely difficult task to control and guide the movements of those below.

My anxiety to instruct died out of me. I began to marvel at the dexterity with which the old man would sometimes raise a falling doll by the lift of his little finger. And from my new point of view I thought I could at last discern some purpose in the play...

For a time I stood motionless, watching, and then I looked again at the operator seated in his great chair. He was quite unconscious of my presence. He wore always the same serene, gentle smile. He was in no way perturbed when his dolls stumbled and fell. He sat serene, intent; and his hand moved ceaselessly to and fro over the great stage.

I crept away softly and found my way out.

When I reached the square again the moon had risen.

I looked up and saw the little railway station a few hundred yards away.

It was a stiff climb, but I reached home in ten minutes.

The town was, after all, quite a small place...

In the morning I wondered whether the old man still sat in the same place manipulating his dolls.

I wondered whether he was a charlatan or only very old, and very, very foolish.

1939

THE EXTRAORDINARILY HORRIBLE DUMMY

Gerald Kersh

The life story of Gerald Kersh (1911–1968) reads like something out of a novel. Born into a large Jewish immigrant family in the southwest London suburb of Teddington, and dying, aged 57, in the hilltop New York State artist colony of Cragsmoor, the years between were more remarkable still.

Kersh was a physically imposing figure, capable of tearing telephone directories in half and bending coins between his teeth. He sported a goatee which, coupled with his dark eyes, gave him a menacing appearance that he seemed to enjoy. A wonderful teller of tall stories, his other occupations included bouncer, wrestler, and fish-and-chip shop fryer. In the Second World War, Kersh served in the Coldstream Guards, during which time he also penned the bestselling army novel *They Died with Their Boots Clean* (1941); he was discharged in 1943 after both of his legs were broken in a bombing raid.

Kersh's first novel, *Jews Without Jehovah* (1934), had only a brief time in print before defamation proceedings from three of his uncles and a cousin forced his publisher to pull the title—shortly afterwards, Kersh was run over by one of the same uncles in a car purchased using the proceeds of the libel action. It was, however, with his third novel, *Night and the City* (1938), that Kersh made his literary breakthrough; also partly autobiographical, Kersh utilised his pre-war experience of the seedier parts of London's Soho in the book, which was later adapted twice for the big screen (in 1950 and 1992). Similarly squalid London backstreets are depicted in the blackly comic *Fowlers End* (1957), regarded by many as Kersh's best novel.

Kersh was a prolific and successful writer of short fiction—including horror and sci-fi. Here I'm pleased to include "The Extraordinarily Horrible Dummy" (which first appeared in *Penguin Parade 6*, an anthology of new writing from 1939) for its wonderful portrayal of a troubled showman, and also for its role in one of the great pieces of horror cinema: the closing Michael Redgrave segment of the Ealing Studios portmanteau film *Dead of Night* (1945).

Long rumoured to be the inspiration behind the movie's ventriloquial vignette, Kersh authority Paul Duncan has settled the matter by unearthing correspondence between Kersh and the film's screenwriter, John Baines. Kersh had been working for the Ministry of Information, writing scenarios and commentaries for war films, and had previously contributed the story "Umpity Poo" to Ealing, which was made into the wartime propaganda piece *Nine Men* (1943). So when Baines contacted Kersh with his adaptation of "The Extraordinarily Horrible Dummy"—albeit claiming the script had been unrecognisably altered from the source—Kersh believed the film would be in the same vein as *Nine Men* and did not ask for payment. Although he refrained from pursuing the matter once he realised that *Dead of Night* was a commercial project, he felt misused by the experience—a feeling exacerbated by his lack of onscreen credit.

So, next time you're watching from behind the sofa as the dummy Hugo terrifyingly walks across the room at the conclusion of *Dead of Night*, spare a thought for Gerald Kersh and the horrible Micky.

An uneasy conviction tells me that this story is true, but I hate to believe it. It was told to me by Ecco, the ventriloquist, who occupied a room next to mine in Busto's apartment house. I hope he lied. Or perhaps he was mad? The world is so full of liars and lunatics that one never knows what is true and what is false.

All the same, if ever a man had a haunted look that man was Ecco. He was small and furtive. He had disturbing habits; five minutes of his company would have set your nerves on edge. For example, he would stop in the middle of a sentence, say *Ssh*! in a compelling whisper, look timorously over his shoulder and listen to something. The slightest noise made him jump. Like all Busto's tenants, he had come down in the world. There had been a time when he topped bills and drew fifty pounds a week. Now, he lived by performing to theatre queues.

And yet he was the best ventriloquist I have ever heard. His talent was uncanny. Repartee cracked back and forth without pause, and in two distinct voices. There were even people who swore that his dummy was no dummy, but a dwarf or a small boy with painted cheeks, trained in ventriloquial back-chat. But this was not true. No dummy was ever more palpably stuffed with sawdust. Ecco called it Micky; and his act, "Micky and Ecco."

All ventriloquists' dummies are ugly, but I have yet to see one uglier than Micky. It had a home-made look. There was something disgustingly avid in the stare of its bulging blue eyes, the lids of which clicked as it winked; and an extraordinarily horrible ghoulishness in the smacking of its great, grinning, red wooden lips. Ecco carried Micky with him wherever he went, and even slept with it. You would have felt cold at the sight of Ecco, walking upstairs, holding Micky at arm's length. The dummy was large and robust; the man was small and wraithlike; and in a bad light you would have thought: *The dummy is leading the man*!

I said he lived in the room next to mine. But in London you may live and die in a room, and the man next door may never know. I should never have spoken to Ecco but for his habit of practising ventriloquism by night. It was nerve-racking. At the best of times it was hard to find rest under Busto's roof; but Ecco made nights hideous, really hideous. You know the shrill, false voice of the ventriloquist's dummy? Micky's voice was not like that. It was shrill, but querulous; thin, but real—not Ecco's voice distorted, but a *different* voice. You would have sworn that there were two people quarrelling. *This man is good*, I thought. Then: *But this man is perfect*! And at last, there crept into my mind this sickening idea: *There are two men*!

In the dead of night, voices would break out:

"Come on, try again!"

"I can't!"

"You must—"

"I want to go to sleep."

"Not yet; try again!"

"I'm tired, I tell you; I can't!"

"And I say try again."

Then there would be peculiar singing noises, and at length Ecco's voice would cry:

"You devil! You devil! Let me alone, in the name of God!"

One night, when this had gone on for three hours I went to Ecco's door, and knocked. There was no answer. I opened the door. Ecco was sitting there, grey in the face, with Micky on his knee. "Yes?" he said. He did not look at me, but the great painted eyes of the dummy stared straight into mine.

I said, "I don't want to seem unreasonable, but this noise..."

Ecco turned to the dummy and said, "We're annoying the gentleman. Shall we stop?"

Micky's dead red lips snapped as he replied, "Yes. Put me to bed."

Ecco lifted him. The stuffed legs of the dummy flapped lifelessly as the man laid him on the divan and covered him with a blanket. He pressed a spring. *Snap*! the eyes closed. Ecco drew a deep breath and wiped sweat from his forehead.

"Curious bedfellow," I said.

"Yes," said Ecco. "But... please—" And he looked at Micky, frowned at me and laid a finger to his lips. "Ssh!" he whispered.

"How about some coffee?" I suggested.

He nodded. "Yes, my throat is very dry," he said. I beckoned. That disgusting stuffed dummy seemed to charge the atmosphere with tension. He followed me on tiptoe and closed his door silently. As I boiled water on my gas-ring I watched him. From time to time he hunched his shoulders, raised his eyebrows and listened. Then, after a few minutes of silence, he said suddenly, "You think I'm mad."

"No," I said, "not at all; only you seem remarkably devoted to that dummy of yours."

"I hate him," said Ecco; and listened again.

"Then why don't you burn the thing?"

"For God's sake!" cried Ecco, and clasped a hand over my mouth. I was uneasy—it was the presence of this terribly nervous man that made me so. We drank our coffee, while I tried to make conversation.

"You must be an extraordinarily fine ventriloquist," I said.

"Me? No, not very. My father, yes. He was great. You've heard of Professor Vox? Yes, well he was my father."

"Was he, indeed?"

"He taught me all I know; and even now... I mean... without him, you understand—nothing! He was a genius. Me, I could never control the nerves of my face and throat. So you see, I was a great disappointment to him. He... well, you know; he could eat a beefsteak, while Micky, sitting at the same table, sang *Je crois entendre encore*. That was genius. He used to make me practise, day in and day out—*Bee, Eff, Em, En, Pe, Ve, Doubleyou*, without moving the lips. But I was no good. I couldn't do it. I simply couldn't. He used to give me hell. When I was a child, yes, my mother used to protect me a little. But afterward! Bruises—I was black with them. He was a terrible man. Everybody was afraid of him. You're too young to remember: he looked like—well, look."

Ecco took out a wallet and extracted a photograph. It was brown and faded, but the features of the face were still vivid. Vox had a bad face; strong but evil—fat, swarthy, bearded and forbidding. His huge lips were pressed firmly together under a heavy black moustache, which grew right up to the sides of a massive flat nose. He had immense eyebrows, which ran together in the middle; and great, round, glittering eyes.

"You can't get the impression," said Ecco, "but when he came out to the stage in a black cloak lined with red silk, he looked just like the Devil. He took Micky with him wherever he went—they used to talk in public. But he was a great ventriloquist—the greatest ever. He used to say, 'I'll make a ventriloquist of you if it's the last thing, I ever do.' I had to go with him wherever he went, all over the world; and stand in the wings and watch him; and go home with him at night and practise again—*Bee, Eff, Em, En, Pe, Ve, Doubleyou*—over and over again, sometimes till dawn. You'll think I'm crazy."

"Why should I?"

"Well... This went on and on, until—*ssh*—did you hear something?"

"No, there was nothing. Go on."

"One night I... I mean, there was an accident. I—he fell down the elevator shaft in the Hotel Dordogne, in Marseilles. Somebody left the gate open. He was killed." Ecco wiped sweat from his face. "And that night I slept well, for the first time in my life. I was twenty years old then. I went to sleep, and slept well. And then I had a horrible dream. He was back again, see? Only not he, in the flesh; but only his voice. And he was saying: 'Get up, get up and try again, damn you; get up I say—I'll make a ventriloquist of you if it's the last thing I ever do. Wake up!'

"I woke up. You will think I'm mad.

"I swear. I still heard the voice; and it was coming from..."

Ecco paused and gulped.

I said, "Micky?" He nodded. There was a pause; then I said, "Well?"

"That's about all," he said. "It was coming from Micky. It has been going on ever since; day and night. He won't let me alone. It isn't I who makes Micky talk. Micky makes me talk. He makes me practise still... day and night. I daren't leave him. He might tell the... he might... oh God; anyway, I can't leave him... I can't."

I thought, *This poor man is undoubtedly mad. He has got the habit of talking to himself, and he thinks—*

At that moment I heard a voice; a little, thin, querulous, mocking voice, which seemed to come from Ecco's room. It said:

"Ecco!"

Ecco leaped up, gibbering with fright. "There!" he said. "There he is again. I must go. Forgive me. I'm not mad; not really mad. I must—"

He ran out. I heard his door open and close. Then there came again the sound of conversation, and once I thought I heard Ecco's voice, shaking with sobs, saying: *Bee, Eff, Em, En, Pe, Ve, Doubleyou...*

He is crazy, I thought; *yes, the man must be crazy... And before, he was throwing his voice... calling himself...*

But it took me two hours to convince myself of that; and I left the light burning all night, and I swear to you that I have never been more glad to see the dawn.

1975

(WRITTEN C.1947)

PUNCH AND JUDY

Frederick Cowles

Frederick Ignatius Cowles (1900–1948) was born in Cambridge, where he began his working career as a librarian at Trinity College—an ideal environment for a fledgling author of ghost stories.

Cowles went on to write several books and articles on travel and folklore before having two dedicated collections of supernatural tales published during his lifetime: *The Horror of Abbot's Grange* (1936) and *The Night Wind Howls* (1938). His final collection, *Fear Walks the Night*, remained unpublished for almost half a century, appearing in print for the first time in 1993 (though Hugh Lamb did include "Punch and Judy" in his 1975 anthology *The Star Book of Horror, No.1*). These latter stories, written not long before Cowles's premature death, are far more assured and varied than his earlier tales, which have a tendency to feature reworkings of ideas by other writers, including E. F. Benson, Bram Stoker, and, in particular, Cowles's fellow former Cambridge resident M. R. James.

No such accusations of unoriginality can be thrown at this wonderful, late Cowles effort, however, though the presence of the troubled travelling Punch and Judy showman is surely a nod to James's "The Story of a Disappearance and an Appearance". Despite both men's connections with Cambridge, their respective dates there don't neatly coincide and so it would seem unlikely (though not impossible) that they ever met in person; we do know, however, that Cowles did own an autographed copy of James's *Ghost Stories of an Antiquary*.

I came upon him in a green lane near Lewes. My attention was attracted by a long, oblong affair, covered with a shabby waterproof sheet and mounted on a kind of two-wheeled trolley. On one side of this contraption was some faded lettering which, as I drew nearer, I made out to be—*Prof. Jack Smith. The Oldest Show in the World.* A crude painting of Punch confirmed that this was the set-up of a travelling Punch and Judy showman. Snores from under the hedge revealed the presence of the Professor who was sprawled on the grass in a most inelegant attitude. An empty bottle by an outstretched hand indicated the source of the gentleman's profound slumber.

Something urged me to hurry on, for there was an indefinable unpleasantness about the sleeping man. I caught a glimpse of a cruel mouth, the bristly stubble of an unshaven chin, and dirty, greying hair under a dilapidated felt hat. There was even something sinister, I felt, about that oblong article on wheels. Yet there is always an attraction about a Punch and Judy show and I suppose the glamour is shared, in some measure, by the man who operates the puppets. I hesitated just a moment too long. The Professor awakened, struggled into a sitting posture, and regarded me through bleary, bloodshot eyes which were set so close in his head that they gave him a foxy appearance.

"Good-afternoon," I said, feeling that the conventions must at least be satisfied.

"Good-afternoon to you," he replied in a hoarse voice. "Are yer making for Lewes?"

I told him I had just left the town and was out for a country walk.

"Too bloody 'ot fer walkin'," he said. "I'm fagged out with wheelin' that there barrer. The blarsted thing gets 'eavier with every mile. I'm gettin' past this game."

He dragged himself to his feet, picked up the empty bottle, regarded it ruefully and threw it into the hedge. It was evident that he had once been a fine figure of a man. But the broad shoulders were stooped, there was an unhealthy look about his flabby limbs, and I fancied there was a hunted look in his eyes. He must have realised I was weighing him up for, as if following on his last remark, he shot out at me—"How old do yer think I am?"

I tried to be kind and hazarded a guess at fifty-six. "So that's what yer think," he said with a mirthless laugh. "Well you're a long way out. Knock orf ten an' you're still on the wrong side. I'm only forty-five, but I've 'ad enough worry these last few days to put me in me grave. It's a poor case when the only way of gettin' sleep is ter drink it out of a bottle. An' with whisky the price it is an' not so easy to git, there's too many hours to a day an' far too many to a night."

I made sympathetic noises and, to change the subject, said something about the show.

"Aye," he replied. "The oldest show on earth. All about a murder and a 'anging. It's queer 'ow folks likes a murder, even if it's only old Punch knockin' Judy's brains out with 'is stick." He looked towards the barrow and quickly turned back to me. It was then I knew for certain that he was afraid. Stark, naked fear lurked in those shifty, bloodshot eyes. His hand clutched my arm and he spoke in an urgent whisper. "Tell me, guv'ner. Tell me the truth as Gord's yer maker.

Can you see a little dorg—a little white dorg with a black marking on its left ear, a-sittin' on that barrer?"

I looked in the direction indicated and replied sharply. "There's no dog there. It must be the whisky making you see things."

"Not this time it ain't, guv'ner. It's bin there fer three days now." He began to babble something about a sailor, a dog and a newspaper. I couldn't make head or tail of what he was saying. Then, with a desperate effort, he seemed to pull himself together and spoke more rationally.

"They all likes the Punch and Judy show an' that means they likes a good murder. You likes it, mister, an' knows as it's true ter life. I'm frightened, guv'ner, an' that's Gord's truth. I've got ter tell someone about it else I shall go crackers." He began babbling again and, convinced I had a madman to deal with, I decided it safer to humour him.

"Tell me what you like," I said, "if it is going to help you at all. Only, for heaven's sake, pull yourself together man if you expect me to listen to you."

He sat down again and I perched myself on a handy tree stump, ready to make off if he showed any signs of becoming violent. It isn't an exactly pleasant sensation to know that you are alone in an unfrequented lane with a fellow who may be a dangerous maniac.

"Now all this 'appened over ten years ago," began the Professor. "I was a bit better lookin' in them days than wot I am now, an' there was a girl. Her name was Daisy—Daisy Greening—an' I met 'er at Maidstone. She liked the show an' she liked me, an' so we became friendly an' started walkin' out tergether. I was makin' good money an' it wasn't so long before we decided to get spliced. We got a cottage, at Detling fer five bob a week, an' furnished it with a few odds and ends as I picked up in me travels. It was to 'ave bin a proper little love nest. But things don't always turn out the way they are planned, an' Daisy as a sweetheart an' Daisy as a wife was two different things. I soon found out that she 'ad the temper of a bitch, an' I set meself out to cure it, for I always did 'old as a man should be master in 'is own 'ouse. Well, ter make a long story short, within twelve months she took out a summons agin me fer cruelty, an' the bleedin' magistrates made a separation order under which I was ter pay 'er ten bob a week.

"I wasn't the sort of chap to take all that lyin' down, mister. Most of the time I was away with me show. But in betweens I was in Maidstone an' I kept me eye on little Daisy who'd gorn back ter live with 'er dear mother. It wasn't so long before I found out there was another chap in the offing—a sailor, name of Ted Richards. When 'e was on leaf they'd go orf into the country tergether just like a couple of love-birds, an me 'aving ter pay me ten bob into the Court every week.

"Well, I bided me time. I took good care they never ran into me 'cause I didn't want 'im ter know what I looked like. I let it go on fer nearly a year, an' I might 'ave let 'em carry on even longer but for the fact I discovered by accident as they were plannin' ter set up 'ouse tergether when 'is next leaf come round. It didn't matter much for, by then, I was ready ter put an end ter their love dreams. Wouldn't you feel the same, guv'ner, if yer wife was carryin' on with another man an' you was still 'avin ter keep 'er out of yer 'ard-earned money?"

He gave me a nasty leer and I hurriedly agreed. I felt a physical repulsion for the man, but I dared not attempt to leave him.

"It was on a day in November when 'er precious Ted's ship docked at Sheerness. I knew which pub he'd make for as soon as 'e came ashore, an' I was there ready for 'im. It was easy enough ter get pally. A few drinks an' we was bosom friends. I 'ad a little shed down in Blue Town—a shack I rented fer storing me show. I told the sailor I'd some whisky there an' 'e didn't think twice about comin' along with me. He wasn't expecting a blow between the eyes with a lump of lead piping. But that's what 'e got an' it split 'is skull like an egg-shell. Later on I packed 'im all nice and comfortable into my little booth, covered it with the mackintosh sheet, an' left 'im fer the night.

"Perhaps yer knows the Isle of Sheppey an' perhaps yer don't. Sheerness is the only place of any size on the island, but there are a number of villages where a Punch and Judy man could always be certain of a few bob. I used ter work 'em pretty regular, an' I knew the whole island like the palm of me 'and. There is a part of the coast, between Minster and Leysdown, where the mud cliffs are always givin' way—or they used ter be always tumblin' down in them days. Usually only small falls took place, but sometimes a whole great chunk just toppled over into the sea. Once a blinkin' church disappeared in a night. I had explored those cliffs fer days on end an' knew all the most dangerous places.

"There was a light railway which ran to the different villages—a ragtime sort of affair where the driver 'ad ter get out at every level-crossin' to open the gates, an' then wait for the guard to shut 'em again after they 'ad driven through.

"The next morning I wheeled my show down to the railway station. I 'ad a little dorg then—a black and white terrier what took part in the show, an' I remember 'ow the animal whimpered at my 'eels as I pushed the barrer through the streets. The guard, who knew me quite well, passed the usual joke about the 'corfin on wheels', little thinkin' that this time he was nearer the truth then 'e guessed. I travelled in 'is van so as ter keep me eyes on the barrer an', all the way, that blarsted dorg whimpered and yapped, although I nearly kicked the guts out of it.

"It was barely eight o'clock when we got to Leysdown an' nobody seemed to take any interest in me or me barrer. I wheeled it out to the cliffs an' along the sea path until I reached the spot I 'ad chosen. It was a tiny bay where the waves 'ad smashed away the under part of the cliff, makin' a kind of cave. There was no one about an' it didn't take me long to unload the body, drop it to the beach, an' drag it into the 'ole. An' then that damned dorg started 'owling loud enough to be 'eard in Sheerness. I grabbed 'old of it, bashed it's 'ead against a rock, an' chucked it in to keep the sailor company. I'd brought a couple of crowbars with me an' stuck them into the top of the cliff. By using them as levers I soon managed to dislodge about ten tons of soil an' Daisy's lover was beneath it.

"I went back into Leysdown an' give a show for the kids at the school. I also gave shows that day at Eastchurch and Minster, an' only one person asked me where me little dorg 'ad gone." He glanced uneasily towards the barrow and started to his feet with a cry. "There 'e is, there 'e is," he whimpered, pointing with a shaking hand. "Can't you see 'im now, mister, sittin' on the barrer?"

I assured him that no dog was visible to me. But, I must confess, I was badly frightened and ready to take to my heels at any moment. The man seemed to gain control of himself again and came closer to me.

"It all 'appened ten years ago," he croaked, "'an now they've both got out. I daresn't set up me show 'cause, when I did it last Monday at Cranbrook, the sailor an' the dorg both got inside with me an' nearly sent me screamin' mad." He looked towards the barrow again and gripped my arm. "Tell me 'onest, guv'ner," he pleaded. "Can't yer see that bleedin' dorg sittin' there an' grinnin' at me?"

Once again I told him that no dog was to be seen and tried to soothe him.

"You bloody liar," the Professor yelled. "You can see the dorg all right an' yer think I don't know. It's bin there ever since I read that bit in the paper four days ago. An I'll tell yer somethin' else." He came closer and I recoiled from his foetid breath. "The sailor's inside the booth an' I daresn't open it. Now I've got to push them both around for the rest of my life." Wild bursts of hideous laughter broke from his throat. "It's a good joke, ain't it?" he screamed. "Ted Richards is livin' at Chatham with my wife. The sailor I killed wasn't 'im at all."

Still laughing wildly he rushed across to the barrow, seized the handles and went pelting off down the lane as if the Devil was after him.

Chief Inspector Stanton, of the Sussex Constabulary, is an old friend of mine and I suppose I should have gone to him at once with my story. But I hate to be laughed at and, on reflection, the tale seemed most improbable. The Professor was obviously the victim of delusions induced by alcoholic excesses.

More than twenty-four hours passed before I mentioned the business to Stanton and I only did so then because we happened to meet at the club. I could see a gleam of interest flicker in his eyes as soon as I began the tale of my encounter. He listened quietly while I described the ramblings of the Punch and Judy man, and then he said, "I suppose there was a name painted on the barrow and I dare wager it happened to be Jack Smith."

"True enough," I replied. "You don't mean to say you've nabbed him already."

"Not exactly. He hanged himself last night in an old barn on the Brighton road."

"Good Lord!" I exclaimed. "Then the man *was* mad and his delusions got the better of him."

"I'm not so certain about the delusions. We managed to trace his wife this afternoon and she is living at Chatham with a sailor called

Edward Richards. That part of the tale was true enough and so was the bit about the murder. We found this in Smith's pocket. It was evidently torn from one of the East Kent newspapers and is about five days old."

He extracted a dirty slip of printed paper from his notebook and handed it over to me. It was a short paragraph recording the fall of a portion of the cliffs near Leysdown, on Sheppey, and the subsequent discovery of the skeleton of a man with the bones of a dog at his side. "From an identity disc found near the remains," the report concluded, "there is reason to believe that the unfortunate person was a seaman. The police have the matter in hand and we are given to understand there is suspicion of foul play."

"Then he did get the wrong man?" I said, handing back the slip of paper.

"That's about the sum of it," replied Stanton in his laconic manner. "But there are a couple of points about the suicide which puzzles me. In the soft earth under the body were the marks of a dog's paws and, from the state of Smith's trousers and legs, it was obvious that the animal had been jumping up at him as he swung from the beam. The pawmarks were only in that one spot and we haven't found any traces of a stray dog. I suppose you are certain there wasn't a terrier with him yesterday afternoon."

"There was no dog there," I stated without hesitation. "Smith swore he could see one, but it wasn't visible to my eyes."

"Curious," said Stanton. "The other thing is even more mysterious. When we came to examine the booth it was saturated with water and mud, and a most unholy stench hung around it. The doctor says the dampness was undoubtedly caused by sea water, and maintains that the smell was that of a decomposing corpse."

1929

THE HAUNTED ROUNDABOUT

"Simplex"

"The Haunted Roundabout" appeared in society magazine *The Tatler* on 13 March 1929. Its author used the pseudonym "Simplex"—and this is the only story I have managed to find from someone using that name. At the time *The Tatler* (which still exists in glossier form today, though it has dropped the definite article from its title) regularly featured short stories, and for a period from October 1926 offered readers a £50 prize to share their weird experiences and have their "queer stories" published in the magazine. "The Haunted Roundabout", however, seems to post-date those tales that purportedly portray real experiences.

Despite the word's meaning, "Simplex" is by no means a simple figure to identify. Even with assistance from the inimitable Johnny Mains*—if anyone can uncover the identity of a mystery ghost story writer then that person is surely him!—the only real clue seems to be that of a serial letter writer who used the same moniker in the mid-1920s to the *Hinckley Guardian*, a Leicestershire newspaper. Which, assuming both figures are one and the same, would imply that he (or she) lived somewhere local to there in the East Midlands.

In any case, the author's identity does not really matter. What

* Johnny is the editor of various volumes of classic stories published by the British Library.

does matter is that "The Haunted Roundabout" is an effective, spooky tale that captures a particular and very English snapshot of village greens and travelling funfairs during the first half of the twentieth century. Later, in Robert Aickman's "The Swords", we will visit a less bucolic scene…

The Reverend Mr. Perkins, who is vicar of a large parish in the eastern counties, and who is a chaplain to a society of which I have the honour to be a member, once, while I was on a visit to his town, invited me to tea at the vicarage.

The conversation drifted at last on to ghosts, and when asked if he believed in such things, to my surprise he readily replied, "Yes, I have had one most uncanny experience which has left no doubt in my mind that such things actually do exist."

"Some years ago," he continued, "the local flower show, which is always held in August; took place in a field near my church, owing to the fact that the meadow in which it was usually held had been sold for building, and the day before the event was to open a number of steam tractors arrived, pulling Gypsy caravans and wagons containing the dismantled roundabouts, swing-boats, and other amusements.

"I have always felt that these poor wandering Gypsies are usually not very kindly received, and as they were temporarily my parishioners, I decided to go down and welcome them, and let them know that if I could assist them in any way during their stay I was prepared to do so. These sort of jobs are always rather uncomfortable—one always feels that one may be intruding, or worse still, unwelcome.

"However, these people seemed delighted to see me, and I was soon on the best of terms with them. The show, of course, only lasted one day, but the roundabouts, etc., were to remain for five days before they moved on to another fête at a town lying fourteen odd miles away. I was particularly busy that week, but made a special point of calling again to see how my Gypsy friends were. I found one family in great distress. The son, a lad of seventeen, had, it appeared, been the victim of a nasty accident while engaged in taking the fares on the roundabout cars during the flower-show day. The lad had slipped, and falling heavily inside the track—which was a drop of considerable height at that point—had broken his right arm and had been conveyed to the hospital.

"I was very sorry to hear this bad news, and at once volunteered to go and visit the lad at that institution, which offer they gladly accepted. I found that the boy was a bright young fellow, and we had a long chat, during which he told me the reason of his fall.

"'Excuse me, sir,' he remarked in introducing the subject, but do you believe in ghosts?'

"I was forced to confess that I did not, for at that time nothing of an occult nature had ever come my way.

"'Well,' he said earnestly, 'maybe we Gypsies can see more than you who live in towns, but it was a ghost that caused all this trouble.'

"I smiled rather broadly at this; it seemed so absurd to think a ghost could be responsible for so serious an accident, but the lad wasn't going to be laughed out of his theory, and continued—

"'It was as I was taking fares just before we were closing down about half-past eleven on Tuesday, sir, that it happened. Most of the people had gone home, and several of my cars were empty. Well, sir, I'd taken the fares of the people on my four, and was going to hand over the coppers to Mrs. Smith, who sits in the cash desk just under the organ in front of the machine. Being on the further side of track, I jumped on to a passing car, which was empty, in order to ride round and drop off in front of Mrs. Smith's desk. I jumped on all right and sat down in the car, when all of a sudden I noticed a man's body lying huddled on the floor of the front seat; his head was resting on the cushions, and to my horror I saw that he had a great wound in his forehead. I was so startled, sir, that in my hurry to get off the car I slipped and fell, and that's how I come to be here.'

"I must confess that I laughed inwardly at this recital, but the fellow seemed such a decent, sober lad that I determined to make a few judicious inquiries. Of course they all knew the lad's story; he had told them when he was picked up; the roundabout had been stopped at once and the cars had been thoroughly examined. Nothing was found.

"I was now more than ever inclined to taboo the whole story, when upon the Friday morning my bell was rung violently, and shortly afterwards the proprietor of the roundabout, Mr. Smith, was shown into my study, very red in the face, and clutching a very dirty panama hat. Having shaken hands, I asked him what I could do for him.

"'You'll pardon me for worrying you,' he broke out, 'but I'm in a great worry, sir. The roundabout is haunted. That dead man was seen in the car again last night. A young courtin' couple saw it, and the girl let out such a yell that we pulled up the engine sharp. But when we got up there, there was nothing to be seen saving the empty seat. I'd have thought they were trying to have us on, but you see, sir, our Tom saw the same thing when he broke his arm. It was the same car, too, No. 19.'

"I was deeply interested—obviously the man was in earnest.

"'At what time did this happen?' I inquired after a moment's pause.

"'I was too worried to think of that, sir,' replied the distressed showman, mopping the moisture from his head with a gaudy cotton handkerchief, 'but I suppose it must have been round eleven—say, quarter to twenty past the hour.'

"Although I believed these people (in fact, why should they make up such a tale), I still thought that there must be some mistake.

"'I tell you what, Mr. Smith,' I said, after a moment's reflection, 'I'll come over about eleven tonight and see if I can see anything myself.'

"So with this arrangement we parted, and having spent a rather busy day, I had supper, and about ten to eleven walked down to the show ground. There was the roundabout, a mass of coloured lights whirling round at a great speed to the accompaniment of some popular ragtime which was being 'churned out' by the steam organ. Over the hills and down the valleys the cars followed each other in an unending stream, while in the centre the little Italian figures on the organ drubbed away at their tiny drums in a truly life-like manner, while in a sort of ornate cockleshell desk sat Mrs. Smith at the seat of custom.

"It all seemed so absolutely material that one could not for a moment associate it with the occult. However, I'd given my promise, and accordingly, as the cars slowed down, I walked up the side of the track until I came to car No. 19 and took a seat in the second partition. The proprietor at once saw me, and swinging himself up as the machine started, sat down beside me. I'm afraid we didn't say much to each other, the noise of the organ was too deafening for that. The people had mostly gone home now, and the cars were only occupied here and there by a couple or so. We practically had the roundabout to ourselves.

"The sensation of rushing swiftly up and down the little hills was delightful in the cool, balmy air of a summer evening, and I was beginning to enjoy it immensely. We had been travelling in this way for perhaps five minutes, when Mr. Smith suddenly gripped my arm and pointed over the seat with his other hand. I at once leaned forward, and imagine my horror when I saw the body of a young man lying, or rather kneeling on the floor, with his head resting on the front seat and a ghastly wound in the centre of his forehead. We both leaned forward, impotently gazing at the apparition for some seconds in mute astonishment. It was so absolutely real, with its bloodless face and the great bleeding hole in its forehead, thrown into strong contrast by the dark hair and moustache, that I should have stopped the roundabout myself at once and reported the awful tragedy to the proprietor, had I not known that this thing was the body of no earthly being. Gradually it faded away, slowly—like a rainbow melts—and vanished.

"It was apparently an inexplicable mystery. The phenomenon had never occurred before that week. Certainly no tragedy had happened during the time Smith had owned the machine, and as he bought it straight from the makers it seemed impossible to give any reason for the ghastly spectre which haunted car No. 19. But only the week after, happening to pick up the morning paper, I read that a strange man had committed suicide by shooting himself in a roundabout car at the place where the Gypsies had gone to after leaving our town. It appeared that about 11.25 on the fourth night of their stay a man rather the worse for drink had entered the ground and insisted upon boarding a car on the roundabout, and having sat there for some time, he suddenly, to every one's horror, stood up, and placing a revolver to his head, pressed the trigger. By the time the attendants stopped the machine and rushed to his assistance life was extinct, and the corpse was conveyed to the local mortuary for identification by the police.

"I had the final details from Smith, jun., who had been left behind in hospital, when I next visited him. He had a letter from his father which he read to me. The man's body had been found just as we all saw it kneeling on the floor with its mutilated head resting on the seat in car No. 19. A photo of the deceased, cut from the local paper, was enclosed and had I needed further proof that this was indeed the same man, I saw at a glance that the face was identical with that of the spectre that I had seen on the haunted roundabout."

1948

THE BLACK FERRIS

Ray Bradbury

Ray Douglas Bradbury (1920–2012) was one of the great figures of American twentieth-century science fiction and fantasy, whose work also veered off into mystery and the macabre. In addition, he also wrote the screenplay for John Huston's 1956 version of *Moby Dick*, with many of his own works making it onto the small and big screens, notably François Truffaut's stylised 1966 adaptation of Bradbury's most famous novel, the book-burning dystopia *Fahrenheit 451* (1953).

Bradbury was born in Waukegan, Illinois, growing up here and in Tucson, Arizona, before moving permanently to Los Angeles when he was fourteen. Two years later in a second-hand Hollywood bookstore, he saw an advert for the Los Angeles Science Fiction Society and his future direction of travel was settled. Bradbury's first professional fiction sale came in 1941, preceding a run of 25 stories in *Weird Tales* magazine that established him as a writer, including "The Jar"(1944), the tale of a cursed curio picked up at a sideshow. His place in the literary scene was cemented soon after by the success of the hybrid novel/story collection *The Martian Chronicles* (1950).

Bradbury is the ultimate chronicler of the American fairground and sideshow experience, which is reflected in the title of his first story collection, *Dark Carnival* (1947), as well as parts of *The Illustrated Man* (1951). This love of carnivals stemmed from his childhood, in particular an event that took place in Waukegan in 1932, when he was transfixed by an encounter with a circus act known as Mr. Electrico, a meeting which spurred him on to become a writer.

> He was a performer sitting in an electric chair and a stagehand pulled a switch and he was charged with fifty thousand volts of pure electricity. Lightning flashed in his eyes and his hair stood on end. I sat below, in the front row, and he reached down with a flaming sword full of electricity and he tapped me on both shoulders and then the tip of my nose and he cried, "Live, forever!" And I thought, "God, that's wonderful. How do you do that?"

"The Black Ferris" was first published in the May 1948 edition of *Weird Tales*. With its boy protagonists, from whose naïve perspective we view the strange events, it has the feel of a children's story—a mode Bradbury excelled at, particularly in *The Halloween Tree* (1972), a classic childhood contemplation of mortality. However, his trademark dark lyricism remains on display at the story's heart. The hunchback Ferris wheel operator is a problematic stereotype for modern readers, though perhaps this is a nod from Bradbury to classic genre henchmen, such as Fritz (played by Dwight Frye), Dr. Frankenstein's assistant in Universal's classic 1931 movie *Frankenstein*—the first incarnation of what was to become the now-familiar "Igor" horror trope.

"The Black Ferris" is most notable for being the inspiration behind Bradbury's classic carnival novel *Something Wicked this Way Comes* (1962), with which it shares some key characters and plot moments. The novel also features versions of the real performers that Mr. Electrico introduced the young Bradbury to on that momentous circus visit. These include The Skeleton, The Dwarf and, of course, The Tattooed/Illustrated Man, who in the later novel becomes the malevolent Mr. Dark.

The carnival had come to town like an October wind, like a dark bat flying over the cold lake, bones rattling in the night, mourning, sighing, whispering up the tents in the dark rain. It stayed on for a month by the grey, restless lake of October, in the black weather and increasing storms and leaden skies.

During the third week, at twilight, on a Thursday, the two small boys walked along the lake shore in the cold wind.

"Aw, I don't believe you," said Peter.

"Come on, and I'll show you," said Hank.

They left wads of spit behind them all along the moist brown sand of the crashing shore. They ran to the lonely carnival grounds. It had been raining. The carnival lay by the sounding lake with nobody buying tickets from the flaky black booths, nobody hoping to get the salted hams from the whining roulette wheels, and none of the thin-fat freaks on the big platforms. The midway was silent; all the grey tents hissing on the wind like gigantic prehistoric wings. At eight o'clock perhaps, ghastly lights would flash on, voices would shout, music would go out over the lake. Now there was only a blind hunchback sitting on a black booth, feeling of the cracked china cup from which he was drinking some perfumed brew.

"There," said Hank, pointing.

The black Ferris wheel rose like an immense light-bulbed constellation against the cloudy sky, silent.

"I still don't believe what you said about it," said Peter.

"You wait, I saw it happen. I don't know how, but it did. You know how carnivals are; all funny. Okay; this one's even *funnier*."

Peter let himself be led to the high green hiding place of a tree.

Suddenly, Hank stiffened. "*Hist!* There's Mr. Cooger, the carnival man, now!" Hidden, they watched.

Mr. Cooger, a man of some thirty-five years, dressed in sharp bright clothes, a lapel carnation, hair greased with oil, drifted under the tree, a brown derby hat on his head. He had arrived in town three weeks before, shaking his brown derby hat at people on the street from inside his shiny red Ford, tooting the horn.

Now Mr. Cooger nodded at the little blind hunchback, spoke a word. The hunchback blindly, fumbling, locked Mr. Cooger into a black seat and sent him whirling up into the ominous twilight sky. Machinery hummed.

"See!" whispered Hank. "The Ferris wheel's going the wrong way. Backwards instead of forwards!"

"So what?" said Peter.

"Watch!"

The black Ferris wheel whirled twenty-five times around. Then the blind hunchback put out his pale hands and halted the machinery. The Ferris wheel stopped, gently swaying, at a certain black seat.

A ten-year-old boy stepped out. He walked off across the whispering carnival ground, in the shadows.

Peter almost fell from his limb. He searched the Ferris wheel with his eyes. "Where's Mr. Cooger!"

Hank poked him. "You wouldn't believe! Now *see*!"

"Where's Mr. Cooger at!"

"Come on, quick, run!" Hank dropped and was sprinting before he hit the ground.

*

Under giant chestnut trees, next to the ravine, the lights were burning in Mrs. Foley's white mansion. Piano music tinkled. Within the warm windows, people moved. Outside, it began to rain, despondently, irrevocably, forever and ever.

"I'm *so* wet," grieved Peter, crouching in the bushes. "Like someone squirted me with a hose. How much longer do we wait?"

"Sh!" said Hank, cloaked in wet mystery.

They had followed the little boy from the Ferris wheel, up through town, down dark streets to Mrs. Foley's ravine house. Now, inside the warm dining room of the house the strange little boy sat at dinner, forking and spooning rich lamb chops and mashed potatoes.

"I know his name," whispered Hank, quickly. "My Mom told me about him the other day. She said, 'Hank, you hear about the li'l orphan boy moved in Mrs. Foley's? Well, his name is Joseph Pikes and he just came to Mrs. Foley's one day about two weeks ago and said how he was an orphan run away and could he have something to eat, and him and Mrs. Foley been getting on like hot apple pie ever since.' That's what my Mom said," finished Hank, peering through the steamy Foley window. Water dripped from his nose. He held onto Peter who was twitching with cold. "Pete, I didn't like his looks from the first, I didn't. He looked—mean."

"I'm scared," said Peter, frankly wailing. "I'm cold and hungry and I don't know what this's all about."

"Gosh; you're dumb!" Hank shook his head, eyes shut in disgust. "Don't you see, three weeks ago the carnival came. And about the same time this little ole orphan shows up at Mrs. Foley's. And Mrs. Foley's son died a long time ago one night one winter, and she's never been the same, so here's this little ole orphan boy who butters her all around."

"Oh," said Peter, shaking.

"Come on," said Hank. They marched to the front door and banged the lion knocker.

After awhile the door opened and Mrs. Foley looked out.

"You're all wet, come in," she said. "My land," she herded them into the hall. "What do you want?" she said, bending over them, a tall lady with lace on her full bosom, and a pale thin face with white hair over it. "You're Henry Walterson, aren't you?"

Hank nodded, glancing fearfully at the dining room where the strange little boy looked up from his eating. "Can we see you alone, ma'm?" And when the old lady looked palely surprised, Hank crept over and shut the hall door and whispered at her. "We got to warn you about something, it's about that boy come to live with you, that orphan?"

The hall grew suddenly cold. Mrs. Foley drew herself high and stiff. "Well?"

"He's from the carnival, and he ain't a boy, he's a man, and he's planning on living here with you until he finds where your money is and then run off with it some night, and people will look for him but because they'll be looking for a little ten-year-old boy they won't recognise him when he walks by a thirty-five year man, named Mr. Cooger!" cried Hank.

"What *are* you talking about?" declared Mrs. Foley.

"The carnival and the Ferris wheel and this strange man Mr. Cooger, the Ferris wheel going backward and making him younger, I don't know how, and him coming here as a boy, and you can't trust him, because when he has your money he'll get on the Ferris wheel and it'll go *forward*, and he'll be thirty-five years old again, and the boy'll be gone forever!"

"Goodnight, Henry Walterson, don't *ever* come back!" shouted Mrs. Foley.

The door slammed. Peter and Hank found themselves in the rain once more. It soaked into and into them, cold and complete.

"Smart guy," snorted Peter. "Now you fixed it. Suppose he heard us, suppose he comes and *kills* us in our beds tonight, to shut us all up for keeps!"

"He wouldn't do that," said Hank.

"Wouldn't he?" Peter seized Hanks arm. "Look."

In the big bay window of the dining room now the mesh curtain pulled aside. Standing there in the pink light, his hand made into a menacing fist, was the little orphan boy. His face was horrible to see, the teeth bared, the eyes hateful, the lips mouthing out terrible words. That was all. The orphan boy was there only a second, then gone. The curtain fell into place. The rain poured down upon the house. Hank and Peter walked slowly home in the storm.

During supper, Father looked at Hank and said, "If you don't catch pneumonia, I'll be surprised. Soaked, you were, by God! What's this about the carnival?"

Hank fussed at his mashed potatoes, occasionally looking at the rattling windows. "You know Mr. Cooger, the carnival man, Dad?"

"The one with the pink carnation in his lapel?" asked Father.

"Yes!" Hank sat up. "You've seen him around?"

"He stays down the street at Mrs. O'Leary's boarding house, got a room in back. Why?"

"Nothing," said Hank, his face glowing.

After supper Hank put through a call to Peter on the phone. At the other end of the line, Peter sounded miserable with coughing.

"Listen, Pete!" said Hank. "I see it all now. When that li'l ole orphan boy, Joseph Pikes, gets Mrs. Foley's money, he's got a good plan."

"What?"

"He'll stick around town as the carnival man, living in a room at Mrs. O'Leary's. That way nobody'll get suspicious of him. Everybody'll be looking for that nasty little boy and he'll be gone. And he'll be walking around, all disguised as the carnival man. That way, nobody'll suspect the carnival at all. It would look funny if the carnival suddenly pulled up stakes."

"Oh," said Peter, sniffling.

"So we got to act fast," said Hank.

"Nobody'll believe us, I tried to tell my folks but they said hogwash!" moaned Peter.

"We got to act tonight, anyway. Because why? Because he's gonna try to kill us! We're the only ones that know and if we tell the police to keep an eye on him, he's the one who stole Mrs. Foley's money in cahoots with the orphan boy, he won't live peaceful. I bet he just tries something tonight. So, I tell you, meet me at Mrs. Foley's in half-an-hour."

"Aw," said Peter.

"You wanna die?"

"No." Thoughtfully.

"Well, then. Meet me there and I bet we see that orphan boy sneaking out with the money, tonight, and running back down to the carnival grounds with it, when Mrs. Foley's asleep. I'll see you there. So long, Pete!"

"Young man," said Father, standing behind him as he hung up the phone. "You're not going anywhere. You're going straight up to bed. Here." He marched Hank upstairs. "Now, hand me out every thing you got on." Hank undressed. "There're no other clothes in your room are there?" asked Father. "No, sir, they're all in the hall closet," said Hank, disconsolately.

"Good," said Dad and shut and locked the door.

Hank stood there, naked. "Holy Cow," he said.

"Go to bed," said Father.

Peter arrived at Mrs. Foley's house at about nine-thirty, sneezing, lost in a vast raincoat and mariner's cap. He stood like a small water hydrant on the street, mourning softly over his fate. The lights in the Foley house were warmly on upstairs. Peter waited for half-an-hour, looking at the rain-drenched slick streets of night.

Finally there was a darting paleness, a rustle in wet bushes.

"Hank?" Peter questioned the bushes.

"Yeah." Hank stepped out.

"Gosh," said Peter, staring. "You're—you're *naked*!"

"I ran all the way," said Hank. "Dad wouldn't let me out."

"You'll get pneumonia," said Peter.

The lights in the house went out.

"Duck," cried Hank, bounding behind some bushes. They waited. "Pete," said Hank. "You're wearing pants, aren't you?"

"Sure," said Pete.

"Well, you're wearing a raincoat, and nobody'll know, so lend me your pants," asked Hank.

A reluctant transaction was made. Hank pulled the pants on.

The rain let up. The clouds began to break apart.

In about ten minutes a small figure emerged from the house; bearing a large paper sack filled with some enormous loot or other.

"There he is," whispered Hank.

"There he goes!" cried Peter.

The orphan boy ran swiftly.

"Get after him!" cried Hank.

They gave chase through the chestnut trees, but the orphan boy was swift, up the hill, through the night streets of town, down past the rail yards, past the factories, to the midway of the deserted carnival. Hank and Peter were poor seconds, Peter weighted as he was with the heavy raincoat, and Hank frozen with cold. The thumping of Hank's bare feet sounded through the town.

"Hurry, Pete! We can't let him get to that Ferris wheel before we do, if he changes back into a man we'll never prove anything!"

"I'm hurrying!" But Pete was left behind as Hank thudded on alone in the clearing weather.

"Yah!" mocked the orphan boy, darting away, no more than a shadow ahead, now. Now vanishing into the carnival yard.

Hank stopped at the edge of the carnival lot. The Ferris wheel was going up and up into the sky, a big nebula of stars caught on the dark earth and turning forward and forward, instead of backward, and there sat Joseph Pikes in a green painted bucket-seat, laughing up and around and down and up and around and down at little old Hank standing there, and the little blind hunchback had his hand on the roaring, oily black machine that made the Ferris wheel go ahead and ahead. The midway was deserted because of the rain. The-merry-go-round was still, but its music played and crashed in the open spaces. And Joseph Pikes rode up into the cloudy sky and came down and each time he went around he was a year older, his laughing changed, grew deep, his face changed, the bones of it, the mean eyes of it, the wild hair of it, sitting there is the green bucket seat whirling, whirling swiftly, laughing into the bleak heavens where now and again a last split of lightning showed itself.

Hank ran forward at the hunchback by the machine. On the way he picked up a tent spike. "Here now!" yelled the hunchback. The black Ferris wheel whirled around. "You!" stormed the hunchback, fumbling out. Hank hit him in the kneecap and danced away. "Ouch!" screamed the man, falling forward. He tried to reach the machine brake to stop the Ferris wheel. When he put his hand on the brake, Hank ran in and slammed the tent spike against the fingers, mashing them. He hit them twice. The man held his hand in his other hand, howling. He kicked at Hank. Hank grabbed the foot, pulled, the man slipped in the mud and fell. Hank hit him on the other knee, hard. Hank hit him on the head, shouting.

The Ferris wheel went around and around and around.

"Stop, stop the wheel!" cried Joseph Pikes–Mr. Cooger, flung up in a stormy cold sky in the bubbled constellation of whirl and rush and wind.

"I can't move," groaned the hunchback. Hank jumped on his chest and they thrashed, biting, kicking.

"Stop, stop the wheel!" cried Mr. Cooger, a man, a different man and voice this time, coming around in panic, going up into the roaring hissing sky of the Ferris wheel. The wind blew through the high dark wheel spokes. "Stop, stop, oh please stop the wheel!"

Hank leaped up from the sprawled hunchback. He started in on the brake mechanism, hitting it, jamming it, putting hunks of metal in it, tying it with rope, now and again hitting at the crawling weeping dwarf.

"Stop, stop, stop the wheel!" wailed a voice high in the night where the windy moon was coming out of the vaporous white clouds now. "Stop..." The voice faded.

Now the carnival was ablaze with sudden light. Men sprang out of tents, came running. Hank felt himself jerked into the air with oaths and beatings rained on him. Terrible faces leered and gaped at him.

From a distance there was a sound of Peter's voice and behind Peter, at full tilt, a police officer with pistol drawn.

"Stop, stop the wheel!" In the wind the voice sighed away.

The voice repeated and repeated.

The dark carnival men tried to apply the brake. Nothing happened. The machine hummed and turned the wheel around and around. The mechanism was jammed.

"Stop!" cried the voice one last time.

Silence.

Without a word the Ferris wheel flew in a circle, a high system of electric stars and metal and seats. There was no sound now but the sound of the motor which died and stopped. The Ferris wheel coasted for a minute, all the carnival people looking up at it, the policeman looking up at it, Hank and Peter looking up at it.

The Ferris wheel stopped. A crowd had gathered at the noise. A few fishermen from the wharfhouse, a few switchmen from the rail yards. The Ferris wheel stood whining and stretching in the wind.

"Look," everybody said.

The policeman turned and the carnival people turned and the fishermen turned and they all looked at the occupant in the black painted seat at the bottom of the ride. The wind touched and moved the black wooden seat in a gentle rocking rhythm, crooning over the occupant in the dim carnival light.

A skeleton sat there, a paper bag of money in its hands, a brown derby hat on its head.

1969

THE SWORDS

Robert Aickman

Robert Aickman (1914–1981) was the grandson of the writer Richard Marsh, whose 1897 horror novel *The Beetle* enjoyed great contemporary success; when Aickman set up his own literary agency, around 1941, he named it after his grandfather. A fascinating figure, Aickman is certainly one of the twentieth-century's greatest practitioners of what he referred to as "strange tales". Although married, Aickman began a complicated affair with the novelist Elizabeth Jane Howard in 1945, and she left her husband, the conservationist Peter Scott, for Aickman two years later. Before they too separated, the pair collaborated on the 1951 collection *We Are for the Dark*, each contributing three stories that form a template for the enigmatic "Aickman-esque" tale. The 48 short works he produced over the next 30 years can be as elusive as their author—much more mysterious and obtuse than the majority of supernatural stories that stem from the Victorian tradition. But they are also, on the whole, quite brilliant.

Although it's one of Aickman's grimmest works—a seedy exposition of the physically dilapidated post-war English heartlands (with their dilapidated social attitudes on full display), and of the skewed sexual power dynamic between men and women—"The Swords" happens to be among my favourites of his oeuvre. Its first appearance was in *The Fifth Fontana Book of Great Ghost Stories* (1969), the anthology series that Aickman edited, later featuring in his own 1975 collection *Cold Hand in Mine*; the story was also filmed, somewhat improbably, as the first episode of a US 1997 television horror series titled *The Hunger*.

I think I'm partly drawn to "The Swords" from a vague personal connection to the tale's setting: the West Midlands conurbation of Wolverhampton, where my older brother attended polytechnic at the end of the 1980s. I went to stay with Chris just once in the three years he was there, when I was sixteen; I remember little except drinking Diamond White and eating kebabs—and his housemate's oversized poster of the German rock band Scorpions that leered from the wall of the lounge as I slept on the sofa. The highlight for me though, as a budding birdwatcher, was going to see a night heron—a rare, half-size version of our familiar long-necked waterbird, which had overshot from southern Europe and somehow found itself roosting in a small copse just outside Walsall; the pair of us glimpsed its fruit-bat-like approach in the dusk half-light, and then saw it again briefly as it rose from an insignificant area of marsh the following dawn. The whole episode now takes on a something of a fictional quality for me that wouldn't seem out of place in an Aickman story—though things would surely have taken a much darker or stranger turn had he have written it...

Fleeting glimpses of waterbirds would have not been unfamiliar to Aickman either, via his work and travels with the Inland Waterways Association (the organisation he co-founded with another writer of ghost stories, L. T. C. Rolt). In *Know Your Waterways* (1955), a guide for British boating holidays, Aickman describes the so-called Birmingham Canal Navigations as "dreary", stating that "in the Black Country (which lies between Birmingham and Wolverhampton) even dreariness can have a forlorn, romantic quality"—a twisted sense of which most certainly imbues "The Swords".

Corazón malherido
Por cinco espadas

—FEDERICO GARCIA LORCA

My first experience?

My first experience was far more of a test than anything that has ever happened to me since in that line. Not more agreeable, but certainly more testing. I have noticed several times that it is to beginners that strange things happen, and often, I think, to beginners only. When you know about a thing, there's just nothing to it. This kind of thing included—anyway, in most cases. After the first six women, say, or seven, or eight, the rest come much of a muchness.

I was a beginner all right; raw as a spring onion. What's more, I was a real mother's boy: scared stiff of life, and crass ignorant. Not that I want to sound disrespectful to my old mother. She's as good as they come, and I still hit it off better with her than with most other females.

She had a brother, my uncle Elias, I should have said that we're all supposed to be descended from one of the big pottery families, but I don't know how true it is. My gran had little bits of pot to prove it, but it's always hard to be sure. After my dad was killed in an accident, my mother asked my uncle Elias to take me into his business. He was a grocery wholesaler in a moderate way—and nothing but cheap lines. He said I must first learn the ropes by going out on the road.

My mother was thoroughly upset because of my dad having died in a smash, and because she thought I was bound to be in moral danger, but there was nothing she could do about it, and on the road I went.

It was true enough about the moral danger, but I was too simple and too scared to involve myself. As far as I could, I steered clear even of the other chaps I met who were on the road with me, I was pretty certain they would be bad influences, and I was always bound to be the baby of the party anyway. I was dead rotten at selling and I was utterly lonely—not just in a manner of speaking, but truly lonely. I hated the life but Uncle Elias had promised to see me all right and I couldn't think of what else to do. I stuck it on the road for more than two years, and then I heard of my present job with the building society—read about it, actually, in the local paper—so that I was able to tell Uncle Elias what he could do with his cheap groceries.

For most of the time we stopped in small hotels—some of them weren't bad either, both the room and the grub—but in a few towns there were special lodgings known to Uncle Elias, where I and Uncle Elias's regular traveller, a sad chap called Bantock, were ordered by Uncle Elias to go. To this day I don't know exactly why. At the time I was quite sure that there was some kick-back for my uncle in it, which was the obvious thing to suppose, but I've come since to wonder if the old girls who kept the lodgings might not have been my uncle's fancy women in the more or less distant past. At least once, I got as far as asking Bantock about it, but he merely said he didn't know what the answer was. There was very little that Bantock admitted to knowing about anything beyond the current prices of soapflakes and Scotch. He had been forty-two years on the road for my uncle when one day he dropped dead of a thrombosis in Rochdale. Mrs. Bantock, at least, had been one of my uncle's women off and on for years. That was something everyone knew.

These women who kept the lodgings certainly behaved as if what I've said was true. You've never seen or heard such dives. Noises all night so that it was impossible to sleep properly, and often half-dressed tarts beating on your door and screaming that they'd been swindled or strangled. Some of the travellers even brought in boys, which is something I have never been able to understand. You read about it and hear about it, and I've often seen it happen, as I say, but I still don't understand it. And there was I in the middle of it all, pure and unspotted. The woman who kept the place often cheeked me for it. I don't know how old Bantock got on. I never found myself in one of these places at the same time as he was there. But the funny part was that my mother thought I was extra safe in one of these special lodgings, because they were all particularly guaranteed by her brother, who made Bantock and me go to them for our own good.

Of course it was only on *some* of the nights on the road. But always it was when I was quite alone. I noticed that at the time when Bantock was providing me with a few introductions and openings, they were always in towns where we could stay in commercial hotels. All the same, Bantock had to go to these special places when the need arose, just as much as I did, even though he never would talk about them.

One of the towns where there was a place on Uncle Elias's list, was Wolverhampton. I fetched up there for the first time, after I had been on the job for perhaps four or five months. It was by no means my first of these lodgings, but for that very reason my heart sank all the more as I set eyes on the place and was let in by the usual bleary-eyed cow in curlers and a dirty overall.

There was absolutely nothing to do. Nowhere even to sit and watch the telly. All you could think of was to go out and get drunk, or bring someone in with you from the pictures. Neither idea appealed very much to me, and I found myself just wandering about the town. It must have been late spring or early summer, because it was pleasantly warm, though not too hot, and still only dusk when I had finished my tea, which I had to find in a café, because the lodging did not even provide tea.

I was strolling about the streets of Wolverhampton, with all the girls giggling at me, or so it seemed, when I came upon a sort of small fair. Not knowing the town at all, I had drifted into the run-down area up by the old canal. The main streets were quite wide, but they had been laid out for daytime traffic to the different works and railway yards, and were now quiet and empty, except for the occasional lorry and the boys and girls playing around at some of the corners. The narrow streets running off contained lines of small houses, but a lot of the houses were empty, with windows broken or boarded up, and holes in the roof. I should have turned back, but for the sound made by the fair; not pop songs on the amplifiers, and not the pounding of the old steam organs, but more a sort of high tinkling, which somehow fitted in with the warm evening and the rosy twilight. I couldn't at first make out what the noise was, but I had nothing else to do, very much not, and I looked around the empty back streets, until I could find what was going on.

It proved to be a very small fair indeed; just half a dozen stalls, where a few kids were throwing rings or shooting off toy rifles, two or three covered booths, and, in the middle, one very small roundabout. It was this that made the tinkling music. The roundabout *looked* pretty too; with snow-queen and icing sugar effects in the centre, and different coloured sleighs going round, each just big enough for two, and each, as I remember, with a coloured light high up at the peak. And in the middle was a very pretty, blonde girl dressed as some kind of pierrette. Anyway she seemed very pretty at that time to me. Her job was to collect the money from the people riding in the sleighs, but the trouble was that there weren't any. Not a single one. There weren't many people about at all, and inevitably the girl caught my eye. I felt I looked a charley as I had no one to ride with, and I just turned away. I shouldn't have dared to ask the girl herself to ride with me, and I imagine she wouldn't have been allowed to in any case. Unless, perhaps, it was her roundabout.

The fair had been set up on a plot of land which was empty simply because the houses which had stood on it had been demolished or just fallen down. Tall, blank factory walls towered up on two sides of it, and the ground was so rough and uneven that it was like walking on lumpy rocks at the seaside. There was nothing in the least permanent about the fair. It was very much here today and gone tomorrow. I should not have wondered if it had had no real business to have set up there at all. I doubted very much if it had come to any kind of agreement for the use of the land. I thought at once that the life must be a hard one for those who owned the fair. You could see why fairs like that have so largely died out from what things used to be in my gran's day, who was always talking about the wonderful fairs and circuses when she was a girl. Such customers as there were, were almost all mere kids, even though kids do nowadays have most of the money. These kids were doing a lot of their spending at a tiny stall where a drab-looking woman was selling ice-cream and toffee-apples. I thought it would have been much simpler and more profitable to concentrate on that, and enter the catering business rather than trying to provide entertainment for people who prefer to get it in their houses. But very probably I was in a gloomy frame of mind that evening. The fair was pretty and old-fashioned, but no one could say it cheered you up.

The girl on the roundabout could still see me, and I was sure was looking at me reproachfully—and probably contemptuously as well. With that layout, she was in the middle of things and impossible to get away from. I should just have mooched off, especially since the people running the different stalls were all beginning to shout at me, as pretty well the only full adult in sight, when, going round, I saw a booth in more or less the farthest corner, where the high factory walls made an angle. It was a square tent of very dirty red and white striped canvas, and over the crumpled entrance flap was a rough-edged, dark painted, horizontal board, with written on it in faint gold capital letters THE SWORDS. That was all there was. Night was coming on fast, but there was no light outside the tent and none shining through from inside. You might have thought it was a store of some kind.

For some reason, I put out my hand and touched the hanging flap. I am sure I should never have dared actually to draw it aside and peep in. But a touch was enough. The flap was pulled back at once, and a young man stood there, sloping his head to one side so as to draw me in. I could see at once that some kind of show was going on. I did not really want to watch it, but felt that I should look a complete imbecile if I just ran away across the fairground, small though it was.

"Two bob," said the young man, dropping the dirty flap, and sticking out his other hand, which was equally dirty. He wore a green sweater, mended but still with holes, grimy grey trousers, and grimier sandshoes. Sheer dirt was so much my first impression of the place that I might well have fled after all, had I felt it possible. I had not noticed this kind of griminess about the rest of the fair.

Running away, however, wasn't on. There were so few people inside. Dotted about the bare, bumpy ground, with bricks and broken glass sticking out from the hard earth, were twenty or thirty wooden chairs, none of them seeming to match, most of them broken or defective in one way or another, all of them chipped and off-colour. Scattered among these hard chairs was an audience of seven. I know it was seven, because I had no difficulty in counting, and because soon it mattered. I made the eighth. All of them were in single units and all were men: this time men and not boys. I think that I was the youngest among them, by quite a long way.

And the show was something I have never seen or heard of since. Nor even read of. Not exactly.

There was a sort of low platform of dark and discoloured wood up against the back of the tent—probably right on to the factory walls outside. There was a burly chap standing on it, giving the spiel, in a pretty rough delivery. He had tight yellow curls, the colour of cheap lemonade but turning grey, and a big red face, with a splay nose, and very dark red lips. He also had small eyes and ears. The ears didn't seem exactly opposite one another, if you know what I mean. He wasn't much to look at, though I felt he was very strong, and could probably have taken on all of us in the tent single-handed and come out well on top. I couldn't decide how old he was—either then or later. (Yes, I did see him again—twice.) I should imagine he was nearing fifty, and he didn't look in particularly good condition, but it seemed as though he had just been made with more thew and muscle than most people are. He was dressed like the youth at the door, except that the sweater of the chap on the platform was not green but dark blue, as if he were a seaman, or perhaps acting one. He wore the same dirty grey trousers and sandshoes as the other man. You might almost have thought the place was some kind of boxing booth.

But it wasn't. On the chap's left (and straight ahead of where I sat at the edge of things and in the back row) a girl lay sprawled out facing us in an upright canvas chair, as faded and battered as everything else in the outfit. She was dressed up like a French chorus, in a tight and shiny black thing, cut low, and black fishnet stockings, and those shiny black shoes with super high heels that many men go for in such a big way. But the total effect was not particularly sexy, all the same. The different bits of costume had all seen better days, like everything else, and the girl herself looked more sick than spicy. Under other conditions, I thought to begin with, she might have been pretty enough, but she had made herself up with green powder, actually choosing it apparently, or having it chosen for her, and her hair, done in a tight bun, like a ballet dancer's, was not so much mousy as plain colourless. On top of all this, she was lying over the chair, rather than sitting in it, just as if she was feeling faint or about to be ill. Certainly she was doing nothing at all to lead the chaps on. Not that I myself should have wanted to be led. Or so I thought at the start.

And in front of her, at the angle of the platform, was this pile of swords. They were stacked criss-cross, like cheese-straws, on top of a low stool, square and black, the sort of thing they make in Sedgeley and Wednesfield and sell as Japanese, though this specimen was quite plain and undecorated, even though more than a bit chipped. There must have been thirty or forty swords, as the pile had four corners to it, where the hilts of the swords were set diagonally above one another. It struck me later that perhaps there was one sword for each seat, in case there was ever a full house in the tent.

If I had not seen the notice outside, I might not have realised they *were* swords, or not at first. There was nothing gleaming about them, and nothing decorative. The blades were a dull grey, and the hilts were made of some black stuff, possibly even plastic. They looked thoroughly mass-produced and industrial, and I could not think where they might have been got. They were not fencing foils but something much solider, and the demand for real swords nowadays must be mainly ceremonial, and less and less even of that. Possibly these swords came from suppliers for the stage, though I doubt that too. Anyway, they were thoroughly dingy swords, not a credit at all to the regiment.

I do not know how long the show had been going on before I arrived, or if the man in the seaman's sweater had offered any explanations. Almost the first thing I heard was him saying "And now, gentlemen, which of you is going to be the first?"

There was no movement or response of any kind. Of course there never is.

"Come *on*," said the seaman, not very politely. I felt that he was so accustomed to the backwardness of his audiences that he was no longer prepared to pander to it. He did not strike me as a man of many words, even though speaking appeared to be his job. He had a strong accent, which I took to be Black Country, though I wasn't in a position properly to be sure at that time of my life, and being myself a Londoner.

Nothing happened.

"What you think you've paid your money for?" cried the seaman, more truculent, I thought, than sarcastic.

"You tell us," said one of the men on the chairs. He happened to be the man nearest to me, though in front of me.

It was not a very clever thing to say, and the seaman turned it to account.

"You," he shouted, sticking out his thick, red forefinger at the man who had cheeked him. "Come along up, We've got to start somewhere."

The man did not move. I became frightened by my own nearness to him. I might be picked on next, and I did not even know what was expected of me, if I responded.

The situation was saved by the appearance of a volunteer. At the other side of the tent, a man stood up and said, "I'll do it."

The only light in the tent came from a single Tilley lamp hissing away (none too safely, I thought) from the crosspiece of the roof, but the volunteer looked to me exactly like everyone else.

"*At* last," said the seaman, still rather rudely. "Come on then."

The volunteer stumbled across the rough ground, stepped on to my side of the small platform, and stood right in front of the girl. The girl seemed to make no movement. Her head was thrown so far back that, as she was some distance in front of me, I could not see her eyes at all clearly. I could not even be certain whether they were open or closed.

"Pick up a sword," said the seaman sharply.

The volunteer did so, in a rather gingerly way. It looked like the first time he had ever had his hand on such a thing, and, of course, I never had either. The volunteer stood there with the sword in his hand, looking an utter fool. His skin looked grey by the light of the Tilley, he was very thin, and his hair was failing badly.

The seaman seemed to let him stand there for quite a while, as if out of devilry, or perhaps resentment at the way he had to make a living. To me the atmosphere in the dirty tent seemed full of tension and unpleasantness, but the other men in the audience were still lying about on their hard chairs looking merely bored.

After quite a while, the seaman, who had been facing the audience, and speaking to the volunteer out of the corner of his mouth, half-turned on his heel, and still not looking right at the volunteer, snapped out: "What are you waiting for? There are others to come, though we could do with more."

At this, another member of the audience began to whistle "Why are we waiting?" I felt he was getting at the seaman or showman, or whatever he should be called, rather than at the volunteer.

"Go on," shouted the seaman, almost in the tone of a drill instructor. "Stick it in."

And then it happened, this extraordinary thing.

The volunteer seemed to me to tremble for a moment, and then plunged the sword right into the girl on the chair. As he was standing between me and her, I could not see where the sword entered, but I could see that the man seemed to press it right in, because almost the whole length of it seemed to disappear. What I could have no doubt about at all was the noise the sword made. A curious thing was that we are so used to at least the idea of people being stuck through with swords, that, even though, naturally, I had never before seen anything of the kind, I had no doubt at all of what the man had done. The noise of the sword tearing through the flesh was only what I should have expected. But it was quite distinct even above the hissing of the Tilley. And quite long drawn out too. And horrible.

I could sense the other men in the audience gathering themselves together on the instant and suddenly coming to life. I could still see little of what precisely had happened.

"Pull it out," said the seaman, quite casually, but as if speaking to a moron. He was still only half-turned towards the volunteer, and still looking straight in front of him. He was not looking at anything; just holding himself in control while getting through a familiar routine.

The volunteer pulled out the sword. I could again hear that unmistakable sound.

The volunteer still stood facing the girl, but with the tip of the sword resting on the platform. I could see no blood. Of course I thought I had made some complete misinterpretation, been fooled like a kid. Obviously it was some kind of conjuring.

"Kiss her if you want to," said the seaman. "It's included in what you've paid."

And the man did, even though I could only see his back. With the sword drooping from his hand, he leaned forwards and downwards. I think it was a slow and loving kiss, not a smacking and public kiss, because this time I could hear nothing.

The seaman gave the volunteer all the time in the world for it, and, for some odd reason, there was no whistling or catcalling from the rest of us; but, in the end, the volunteer slowly straightened up.

"Please put back the sword," said the seaman, sarcastically polite.

The volunteer carefully returned it to the heap, going to some trouble to make it lie as before.

I could now see the girl. She was sitting up. Her hands were pressed together against her left side, where, presumably, the sword had gone in. But there was still no sign of blood, though it was hard to be certain in the bad light. And the strangest thing was that she now looked not only happy, with her eyes very wide open and a little smile on her lips, but, in, spite of that green powder, beautiful too, which I was far from having thought in the first place.

The volunteer passed between the girl and me in order to get back to his seat. Even though the tent was almost empty, he returned to his original place religiously. I got a slightly better look at him. He still looked just like everyone else.

"Next," said the seaman, again like a sergeant numbering off.

This time there was no hanging back. Three men rose to their feet immediately, and the seaman had to make a choice.

"You then," he said, jabbing out his thick finger towards the centre of the tent.

The man picked was elderly, bald, plump, respectable-looking, and wearing a dark suit. He might have been a retired railway foreman or electricity inspector. He had a slight limp, probably taken in the way of his work.

The course of events was very much the same, but the second comer was readier and in less need of prompting, including about the kiss. His kiss was as slow and quiet as the first man's had been: paternal perhaps. When the elderly man stepped away, I saw that the girl was holding her two hands against the centre of her stomach. It made me squirm to look.

And then came the third man. When he went back to his seat, the girl's hands were to her throat.

The fourth man, on the face of it a rougher type, with a cloth cap (which, while on the platform, he never took off) and a sports jacket as filthy and worn out as the tent, apparently drove the sword into the girl's left thigh, straight through the fishnet stocking. When he stepped off the platform, she was clasping her leg, but looking so pleased that you'd have thought a great favour had been done her. And still I could see no blood.

I did not really know whether or not I wanted to see more of the details. Raw as I was, it would have been difficult for me to decide.

I didn't have to decide, because I dared not shift in any case to a seat with a better view. I considered that a move like that would quite probably result in my being the next man the seaman called up. And one thing I knew for certain was that whatever exactly was being done, I was not going to be one who did it. Whether it was conjuring, or something different that I knew nothing about, I was not going to get involved.

And, of course, if I stayed, my turn must be coming close in any case.

Still, the fifth man called was not me. He was a tall, lanky, perfectly black man. I had not especially spotted him as such before. He appeared to drive the sword in with all the force you might expect of a black man, even though he was so slight, then threw it on the floor of the platform with a clatter, which no one else had done before him, and actually drew the girl to her feet when kissing her. When he stepped back, his foot struck the sword. He paused for a second, gazing at the girl, then carefully put the sword back on the heap.

The girl was still standing, and it passed across my mind that the man might try to kiss her again. But he didn't. He went quietly back to his place. Behind the scenes of it all, there appeared to be some rules, which all the other men knew about. They behaved almost as though they came quite often to the show, if a show was what it was.

Sinking down once more into her dilapidated canvas chair, the girl kept her eyes fixed on mine. I could not even tell what colour her eyes were, but the fact of the matter is that they turned my heart right over. I was so simple and inexperienced that nothing like that had ever happened to me before in my whole life. The incredible green powder made no difference. Nothing that had just been happening made any difference. I wanted that girl more than I had ever wanted anything. And I don't mean I just wanted her body. That comes later in life. I wanted to love her and tousle her and all the other, better things we want before the time comes when we know that however much we want them, we're not going to get them.

But, in justice to myself, I must say that I did *not* want to take my place in a queue for her.

That was about the last thing I wanted. And it was one chance in three that I should be next to be called. I drew a deep breath and managed to scuttle out. I can't pretend it was difficult. I was sitting near the back of the tent, as I've said, and no one tried to stop me. The lad at the entrance merely gaped at me like a fish. No doubt he was quite accustomed to the occasional patron leaving early. I fancied that the bruiser on the platform was in the act of turning to me at the very instant I got up, but I knew it was probably imagination on my part. I don't think he spoke, nor did any of the other men react. Most men at shows of that kind prefer to behave as if they were invisible. I did get mixed up in the greasy tent flap, and the lad in the green sweater did nothing to help, but that was all. I streaked across the fairground, still almost deserted, and still with the roundabout tinkling away, all for nothing, but very prettily. I tore back to my nasty bedroom, and locked myself in.

On and off, there was the usual fuss and schemozzle in the house, and right through the hours of darkness. I know; because I couldn't sleep. I couldn't have slept that night if I'd been lying between damask sheets in the Hilton Hotel. The girl on the platform had got deep under my skin, green face and all: the girl and the show too, of course. I think I can truly say that what I experienced that night altered my whole angle on life, and it had nothing to do with the rows that broke out in the other bedrooms, or the cackling and bashing on the staircase, or the constant pulling the plug, which must have been the noisiest in the Midlands, especially as it took six or seven pulls or more for each flush. That night I really grasped the fact that most of the time we have no notion of what we really want, or we lose sight of it. And the even more important fact that what we really want, just doesn't fit in with life as a whole, or very seldom. Most folk learn slowly, and never altogether learn at all. I seemed to learn all at once.

Or perhaps not quite, because there was very much more to come.

The next morning I had calls to make, but well before the time arrived for the first of them I had sneaked back to that tiny, battered, little fairground. I even skipped breakfast, but breakfast in Uncle Elias's special lodging was very poor anyway, though a surprising number turned up for it each day. You wondered where so many had been hiding away all night. I don't know what I expected to find at the fair. Perhaps I wasn't sure I should find the fair there at all.

But I did. In full daylight, it looked smaller, sadder, and more utterly hopeless for making a living even than the night before. The weather was absolutely beautiful, and so many of the houses in the immediate area were empty, to say nothing of the factories, that there were very few people around. The fair itself was completely empty, which took me by surprise. I had expected some sort of Gypsy scene and had failed to realise that there was nowhere on the lot for even Gypsies to sleep. The people who worked the fair must have gone to bed at home, like the rest of the world. The plot of land was surrounded by a wire-mesh fence, put up by the owner to keep out tramps and meth-drinkers, but by now the fence wasn't up to much, as you would expect, and, after looking round, I had no difficulty in scrambling through a hole in it, which the lads of the village had carved out for fun and from having nothing better to do. I walked over to the dingy booth in the far corner, and tried to lift the flap.

It proved to have been tied up at several places and apparently from the inside. I could not see how the person doing the tying had got out of the tent when he had finished, but that was the sort of trick of the trade you would expect of fairground folk. I found it impossible to see inside the tent at all without using my pocket-knife, which I should have hesitated to do at the best of times, but while I was fiddling around, I heard a voice just behind me.

"What's up with *you*?"

There was a very small, old man standing at my back. I had certainly not heard him come up, even though the ground was so rough and lumpy. He was hardly more than a dwarf, he was as brown as a horse-chestnut or very nearly, and there was not a hair on his head.

"I wondered what was inside," I said feebly.

"A great big python, two miles long, that don't even pay its rent," said the little man.

"How's that?" I asked. "Hasn't it a following?"

"Old-fashioned," said the little man. "Old-fashioned and out of date. Doesn't appeal to the women. The women don't like the big snakes. But the women have the money these times, *and* the power and the glory too." He changed his tone, "You're trespassing."

"Sorry, old man," I said. "I couldn't hold myself back on a lovely morning like this."

"I'm the watchman," said the little man. "I used to have snakes too. Little ones, dozens and dozens of them. All over me, and every one more poisonous than the next. Eyes darting, tongues flicking, scales shimmering: then *in*, right home, then back, then in again, then back. Still in the end, it wasn't a go. There's a time and a span for all things. But I like to keep around. So now I'm the watchman. While the job lasts. While anything lasts. Move on then. Move on."

I hesitated.

"This big snake you talk of," I began, "this python—"

But he interrupted quite shrilly.

"There's no more to be said. Not to the likes of you, any road. Off the ground you go, and sharply. Or I'll call the police constable. He and I work hand in glove. I take care to keep it that way. You may not have heard that trespass is a breach of the peace. Stay here and you'll be sorry for the rest of your life."

The little man was actually squaring up to me, even though the top of his brown skull (not shiny, by the way, but matt and patchy, as if he had some trouble with it) rose hardly above my waist. Clearly, he was daft.

As I had every kind of reason for going, I went. I did not even ask the little man about the times of performances that evening, or if there were any. Inside myself, I had no idea whether I should be back, even if there were performances, as there probably were.

I set about my calls. I'd had no sleep, and, since last night's tea, no food, and my head was spinning like a top, but I won't say I did my business any worse than usual. I probably felt at the time that I did, but now I doubt it. Private troubles, I have since noticed, make very little difference to the way most of us meet the outside world, and as for food and sleep, they don't matter at all until weeks and months have passed.

I pushed on then, more or less in the customary way (though, in my case, the customary way, at that job, wasn't up to very much at the best of times), and all the while mulling over and around what had happened to me, until the time came for dinner. I had planned to eat in the café where I had eaten the night before, but I found myself in a different part of the city, which, of course, I didn't know at all, and, feeling rather faint and queer, fell instead into the first place there was.

And there, in the middle of the floor, believe it or not, sitting at a Formica-topped table, was my girl with the green powder, and, beside her, the seaman or showman, looking more than ever like a run-down boxer.

I had not seriously expected ever to set eyes on the girl again. It was not, I thought, the kind of thing that happens. At the very most, I might have gone again to the queer show, but I don't think I really would have done, when I came to think out what it involved.

The girl had wiped off the green powder, and was wearing a black coat and skirt and a white blouse, a costume you might perhaps have thought rather too old for her, and the same fishnet stockings. The man was dressed exactly as he had been the night before, except that he wore heavy boots instead of dirty sandshoes, heavy and mud-caked, as if he had been walking through fields.

Although it was the dinner-hour, the place was almost empty, with a dozen unoccupied tables, and these two sitting in the centre. I must almost have passed out.

But I wasn't really given time. The man in the jersey recognised me at once. He stood up and beckoned to me with his thick arm, "Come and join us." The girl had stood up too.

There was nothing else I could do but what he said.

The man actually drew back a chair for me (they were all painted in different, bright colours, and had been reseated in new leatherette), and even the girl waited until I had sat down before sitting down herself.

"Sorry you missed the end of last night's show," said the man.

"I had to get back to my lodgings. I suddenly realised." I made it up quite swiftly. "I'm new to the town," I added.

"It can be difficult when you're new," said the man, "What'll you have?"

He spoke as if we were on licensed premises, but it was pretty obvious we weren't, and I hesitated.

"Tea or coffee?"

"Tea, please," I said.

"Another tea, Berth," called out the man. I saw that the two of them were both drinking coffee, but I didn't like the look of it, any more than I usually do.

"I'd like something to eat as well," I said, when the waitress brought the tea. "Thank you very much," I said to the man.

"Sandwiches: York ham, salt beef, or luncheon meat. Pies. Sausage rolls," said the waitress. She had a very bad stye on her left lower eyelid.

"I'll have a pie," I said, and, in due course, she brought one, with some salad on the plate, and the bottle of sauce. I really required something hot, but there it was.

"Come again tonight," said the man.

"I'm not sure I'll be able to."

I was finding it difficult even to drink my tea properly, as my hands were shaking so badly, and I couldn't think how I should cope with a cold pie.

"Come on the house, if you like. As you missed your turn last night."

The girl, who had so far left the talking to the other, smiled at me very sweetly and personally, as if there was something quite particular between us. Her white blouse was open very low, so that I saw more than I really should, even though things are quite different today from what they once were. Even without the green powder, she was a very pale girl, and her body looked as if it might be even whiter than her face, almost as white as her blouse. Also I could now see the colour of her eyes. They were green. Somehow I had known it all along.

"In any case," went on the man, "it won't make much difference with business like it is now."

The girl glanced at him as if she was surprised at his letting out something private, then looked at me again and said, "Do come." She said it in the friendliest, meltingest way, as if she really cared. What's more, she seemed to have some kind of a foreign accent, which made her even more fascinating, if that was possible. She took a small sip of coffee.

"It's only that I might have another engagement that I couldn't get out of. I don't know right now."

"We mustn't make you break another engagement," said the girl, in her foreign accent, but sounding as if she meant just the opposite.

I managed a bit more candour. "I might get out of my engagement," I said, "but the truth is, if you don't mind my saying so, that I didn't greatly care for some of the others in the audience last night."

"I don't blame you," said the man very dryly, and rather to my relief, as you can imagine. "What would you say to a private show? A show just for you?" He spoke quite quietly, suggesting it as if it had been the most normal thing in the world, or as if I had been Charles Clore.

I was so taken by surprise that I blurted out, "What! Just me in the tent?"

"In your own home, I meant," said the man, still absolutely casually, and taking a noisy pull on his pink earthenware cup. As the man spoke, the girl shot a quick, devastating glance. It was exactly as if she softened everything inside me to water. And, absurdly enough, it was then that my silly pie arrived, with the bit of green salad, and the sauce. I had been a fool to ask for anything at all to eat, however much I might have needed it in theory.

"With or without the swords," continued the man, lighting a cheap looking cigarette, "Madonna has been trained to do anything else you want. Anything you may happen to think of." The girl was gazing into her teacup.

I dared to speak directly to her, "Is your name really Madonna? It's nice."

"No," she said, speaking rather low. "Not really. It's my working name," She turned her head for a moment, and again our eyes met.

"There's no harm in it. We're not Catholics," said the man, "though Madonna was once."

"I like it," I said. I was wondering what to do about the pie I could not possibly eat.

"Of course a private show would cost a bit more than two bob," said the man. "But it would be all to yourself, and, under those conditions, Madonna will do anything you feel like." I noticed that he was speaking just as he had spoken in the tent: looking not at me or at anyone else, but straight ahead into the distance, and as if he were repeating words he had used again and again and was fed up with but compelled to make use of.

I was about to tell him that I had no money, which was more or less the case, but didn't.

"When could it be?" I said.

"Tonight, if you like," said the man. "Immediately after the regular show, and that won't be very late, as we don't do a ten or eleven o'clock house at a date like this. Madonna could be with you at a quarter to ten, easy. And she wouldn't necessarily have to hurry away either, not when there's no late-night matinée. There'd be time for her to do a lot of her novelties if you'd care to see them. Items from her repertoire, as we call them. Got a good place for it, by the way? Madonna doesn't need much. Just a room with a lock on the door to keep out the non-paying patrons, and somewhere to wash her hands."

"Yes," I said. "As a matter of fact, the place I'm stopping at should be quite suitable, though I wish it was brighter, and a bit quieter too."

Madonna flashed another of her indescribably sweet glances at me. "I shan't mind," she said softly.

I wrote down the address on the corner of a paper I had found on my seat, and tore it off.

"Shall we call it ten pounds?" said the man, turning to look at me with his small eyes. "I usually ask twenty and sometimes fifty, but this is Wolverhampton not the Costa Brava, and you belong to the refined type."

"What makes you say that?" I asked; mainly in order to gain time for thinking what I could do about the money.

"I could tell by where you sat last night. At pretty well every show there's someone who picks that seat. It's a special seat for the refined types. I've learnt better now than to call them up, because it's not what they want. They're too refined to be called up, and I respect them for it. They often leave before the end, as you did. But I'm glad to have them in at any time. They raise the standard. Besides, they're the ones who are often interested in a private show, as you are, and willing to pay for it. I have to watch the business of the thing too."

"I haven't got ten pounds ready in spare cash," I said, "but I expect I can find it, even if I have to fiddle it."

"It's what you often have to do in this world," said the man. "Leastways if you like nice things."

"You've still got most of the day," said the girl, smiling encouragingly.

"Have another cup of tea?" said the man.

"No thanks very much."

"Sure?"

"Sure."

"Then we must move. We've an afternoon show, though it'll probably be only for a few kids. I'll tell Madonna to save herself as much as she can until the private affair tonight."

As they were going through the door on to the street, the girl looked back to throw me a glance over her shoulder, warm and secret. But when she was moving about, her clothes looked much too big for her, the skirt too long, the jacket and blouse too loose and droopy, as if they were not really her clothes at all. On top of everything else, I felt sorry for her. Whatever the explanation of last night, her life could not be an easy one.

They'd both been too polite to mention my pie. I stuffed it into my attaché case, of course without the salad, paid for it, and dragged off to my next call, which proved to be right across the town once more.

I didn't have to do anything dishonest to get the money.

It was hardly to be expected that my mind would be much on my work that afternoon, but I stuck to it as best I could, feeling that my life was getting into deep waters and that I had better keep land of some kind within sight, while it was still possible. It was as well that I did continue on my proper round of calls, because at one of the shops my immediate problem was solved for me without my having to lift a finger. The owner of the shop was a nice old gentleman with white hair, named Mr. Edis, who seemed to take to me immediately I went through the door. He said at one point that I made a change from old Bantock with his attacks of asthma (I don't think I've so far mentioned Bantock's asthma, but I knew all about it), and that I seemed a good lad, with a light in my eyes. Those were his words, and I'm not likely to make a mistake about them just yet, seeing what he went on to. He asked me if I had anything to do that evening. Rather pleased with myself, because it was not an answer I should have been able to make often before, not if I had been speaking the truth, I told him that Yes, I had a date with a girl.

"Do you mean with a Wolverhampton girl?" asked Mr. Edis.

"Yes. I've only met her since I've been in the town." I shouldn't have admitted that to most people, but there was something about Mr. Edis that led me on and made me want to justify his good opinion of me.

"What's she like?" asked Mr. Edis, half-closing his eyes, so that I could see the red all round the edges of them.

"Gorgeous." It was the sort of thing people said, and my real feelings couldn't possibly have been put into words.

"Got enough small change to treat her properly?"

I had to think quickly, being taken so much by surprise, but Mr. Edis went on before I had time to speak.

"So that you can cuddle her as you want?"

I could see that he was getting more and more excited.

"Well, Mr. Edis," I said, "as a matter of fact, not quite enough. I'm still a beginner in my job, as you know."

I thought I might get a pound out of him, and quite likely only as a loan, the Midlands people being what we all know they are.

But on the instant he produced a whole fiver. He flapped it in front of my nose like a kipper.

"It's yours on one condition."

"I'll fit in if I can, Mr. Edis."

"Come back tomorrow morning after my wife's gone out—she works as a traffic warden, and can't hardly get enough of it—come back here and tell me all about what happens."

I didn't care for the idea at all, but I supposed that I could make up some lies, or even break my word and not go back at all, and I didn't seem to have much alternative.

"Why, of course, Mr. Edis. Nothing to it."

He handed over the fiver at once.

"Good boy," he said. "Get what you're paying for out of her, and think of me while you're doing it, though I don't expect you will."

As for the other five pounds, I could probably manage to wangle it out of what I had, by scraping a bit over the next week or two, and cooking the cash book a trifle if necessary, as we all do. Anyway, and being the age I was, I hated all this talk about money. I hated the talk about it much more than I hated the job of having to find it. I did not see Madonna in that sort of way at all, and I should have despised myself if I had. Nor, to judge by how she spoke, did it seem the way in which she saw me. I could not really think of any other way in which she would be likely to see me, but I settled that one by trying not to think about the question at all.

My uncle Elias's special lodging in Wolverhampton was not the kind of place where visitors just rang the bell and waited to be admitted by the footman. You had to know the form a bit, if you were to get in at all, not being a resident, and still more if, once inside, you were going to find the exact person you were looking for. At about half past nine, I thought it best to start lounging around in the street outside. Not right on top of the house door, because that might have led to misunderstanding and trouble of some kind, but moving up and down the street, keeping both eyes open and an ear cocked for the patter of tiny feet on the pavement. It was almost dark, of course, but not quite. There weren't many people about but that was partly because it was raining gently, as it does in the Midlands: a soft, slow rain that you can hardly see, but extra wetting, or so it always feels. I am quite sure I should have taken up my position earlier if it hadn't been for the rain. Needless to say, I was like a cat on hot bricks. I had managed to get the pie inside me between calls during the afternoon. I struggled through it on a bench just as the rain was beginning. And at about half past six I'd had a cup of tea and some beans in the café I'd been to the night before. I didn't want any of it. I just felt that I ought to eat something in view of what lay ahead of me. Though, of course, I had precious little idea of what that was. When it's truly your first experience, you haven't; no matter how much you've been told and managed to pick up. I'd have been in a bad state if it had been any woman that was supposed to be coming, let alone my lovely Madonna.

And there she was, on the dot, or even a little early. She was dressed in the same clothes as she had worn that morning. Too big for her and too old for her; and she had no umbrella and no raincoat and no hat.

"You'll be wet," I said.

She didn't speak, but her eyes looked, I fancied, as if she was glad to see me. If she had set out in that green powder of hers, it had all washed off.

I thought she might be carrying something, but she wasn't, not even a handbag.

"Come in," I said.

Those staying in the house were lent a key (with a deposit to pay on it), and, thank God, we got through the hall and up the stairs without meeting anyone, or hearing anything out of the way, even though my room was at the top of the building.

She sat down on my bed and looked at the door. After what had been said, I knew what to do and turned the key. It came quite naturally. It was the sort of place where you turned the key as a matter of course. I took off my raincoat and let it lie in a corner. I had not turned on the light. I was not proud of my room.

"You must be soaked through," I said. The distance from the fairground was not all that great, but the rain was of the specially wetting kind, as I've remarked.

She got up and took off her outsize black jacket. She stood there holding it until I took it and hung it on the door. I can't say it actually dripped, but it was saturated, and I could see a wet patch on the eiderdown where she had been sitting. She had still not spoken a word. I had to admit that there seemed to have been no call for her to do so.

The rain had soaked through to her white blouse. Even with almost no light in the room I could see that. The shoulders were sodden and clinging to her, one more than the other. Without the jacket, the blouse looked quainter than ever. Not only was it loose and shapeless, but it had sleeves that were so long as to droop down beyond her hands when her jacket was off. In my mind I had a glimpse of the sort of woman the blouse was made for, big and stout, not my type at all.

"Better take that off too," I said, though I don't now know how I got the words out. I imagine that instinct looks after you even the first time, provided it is given a chance. Madonna did give me a chance, or I felt that she did. Life was sweeter for a minute or two than I had ever thought possible.

Without a word, she took off her blouse and I hung it over the back of the single bedroom chair.

I had seen in the café that under it she had been wearing something black, but I had not realised until now that it was the same tight, shiny sheath that she wore in the show, and that made her look so French.

She took off her wet skirt. The best I could do was to drape it over the seat of the chair. And there she was, super high heels and all. She looked ready to go on stage right away, but that I found rather disappointing.

She stood waiting, as if for me to tell her what to do.

I could see that the black sheath was soaking wet, anyway in patches, but this time I didn't dare to suggest that she took it off.

At last Madonna opened her mouth, "What would you like me to begin with?"

Her voice was so beautiful, and the question she asked so tempting, that something got hold of me and, before I could stop myself, I had put my arms round her. I had never done anything like it before in my whole life, whatever I might have felt.

She made no movement, so that I supposed at once I had done

the wrong thing. After all, it was scarcely surprising, considering how inexperienced I was.

But I thought too that something else was wrong. As I say, I wasn't exactly accustomed to the feel of a half-naked woman, and I myself was still more or less fully dressed, but all the same I thought at once that the feel of her was disappointing. It came as a bit of a shock. Quite a bad one, in fact. As often, when facts replace fancies. Suddenly it had all become rather like a nightmare.

I stepped back.

"I'm sorry," I said.

She smiled in her same sweet way. "I don't mind," she said.

It was nice of her, but I no longer felt quite the same about her. You know how, at the best, a tiny thing can make all the difference in your feeling about a woman, and I was far from sure that this thing was tiny at all. What I was wondering was whether I wasn't proving not to be properly equipped for life. I had been called backward before now, and perhaps here was the reason.

Then I realised that it might all be something to do with the act she put on, the swords. She might be some kind of freak, or possibly the man in the blue jersey did something funny to her, hypnotised her, in some way.

"Tell me what you'd like," she said, looking down at the scruffy bit of rug on the floor.

I was a fool, I thought, and merely showing my ignorance.

"Take that thing off," I replied. "It's wet. Get into bed. You'll be warmer there."

I began taking off my own clothes.

She did what I said, squirmed out of the black sheath, took her feet gently out of the sexy shoes, rolled off her long stockings. Before me for a moment was my first woman, even though I could hardly see her. I was still unable to face the idea of love by that single, dim electric light, which only made the draggled room look more draggled.

Obediently, Madonna climbed into my bed and I joined here there as quickly as I could.

Obediently, she did everything I asked, just as the man in the blue sweater had promised. To me she still felt queer and disappointing—flabby might almost be the word—and certainly quite different from what I had always fancied a woman's body would feel like if ever I found myself close enough to it. But she gave me my first experience none the less, the thing we're concerned with now. I will say one thing for her: from first to last she never spoke an unnecessary word. It's not always like that, of course.

But everything had gone wrong. For example, we had not even started by kissing. I had been cram full of romantic ideas about Madonna, but I felt that she was not being much help in that direction, for all her sweet and beautiful smiles and her soft voice and the gentle things she said. She was making herself almost too available, and not bringing out the best in me. It was as if I had simply acquired new information, however important, but without any exertion of my feelings. You often feel like that, of course, about one thing or another, but it seemed dreadful to feel it about this particular thing, especially when I had felt so differently about it only a little while before.

"Come on," I said to her. "Wake up."

It wasn't fair, but I was bitterly disappointed, and all the more because I couldn't properly make out why, I only felt that everything in my life might be at stake.

She moaned a little.

I heaved up from on top of her in the bed and threw back the bedclothes behind me. She lay there flat in front of me, all grey—anyway in the dim twilight. Even her hair was colourless, in fact pretty well invisible.

I did what I suppose was rather a wretched thing. I caught hold of her left arm by putting both my hands round her wrist, and tried to lug her up towards me, so that I could feel her thrown against me, and could cover her neck and front with kisses, if only she would make me want to. I suppose I might under any circumstances have hurt her by dragging at her like that, and that I shouldn't have done it. Still no one could have said it was very terrible. It was quite a usual sort of thing to do, I should say.

But what actually happened was very terrible indeed. So simple and so terrible that people won't always believe me. I gave this great, bad-tempered, disappointed pull at Madonna. She came up towards me and then fell back again with a sort of wail. I was still holding on to her hand and wrist with my two hands, and it took me quite some time to realise what had happened. What had happened was that I had pulled her left hand and wrist right off.

On the instant, she twisted out of the bed and began to wriggle back into her clothes. I was aware that even in the almost non-existent light she was somehow managing to move very swiftly. I had a frightful sensation of her beating round in my room with only one hand, and wondered in terror how she could possibly manage. All the time, she was weeping to herself, or wailing might be the word. The noise she made was very soft, so soft that but for what was happening, I might have thought it was inside my own head.

I got my feet on to the floor with the notion of turning on the light. The only switch was of course by the door. I had the idea that with some light on the scene, there might be certain explanations. But I found that I couldn't get to the switch. In the first place, I couldn't bear the thought of touching Madonna, even accidentally. In the second place, I discovered that my legs would go no farther. I was too utterly scared to move at all. Scared, repelled, and that mixed-up something else connected with disappointed sex for which there is no exact word.

So I just sat there, on the edge of the bed, while Madonna got back into her things, crying all the while, in that awful, heart-breaking way which I shall never forget. Not that it went on for long. As I've said, Madonna was amazingly quick. I couldn't think of anything to say or do. Especially with so little time for it.

When she had put on her clothes, she made a single appallingly significant snatch in my direction, caught something up, almost as if she, at least, could see in the dark. Then she had unlocked the door and bolted.

She had left the door flapping open off the dark landing (we had time-switches, of course), and I could hear her pat-patting down the staircase, and so easily and quietly through the front door that you might have thought she lived in the place. It was still a little too early for the regulars to be much in evidence.

What I felt now was physically sick. But I had the use of my legs once more. I got off the bed, shut and locked the door, and turned on the light.

There was nothing in particular to be seen. Nothing but my own clothes lying about, my sodden-looking raincoat in the corner, and the upheaved bed. The bed looked as if some huge monster had risen through it, but nowhere in the room was there blood. It was all just like the swords.

As I thought about it, and about what I had done, I suddenly vomited. They were not rooms with hot and cold running water, and I half-filled the old-fashioned washbowl, with its faded flowers at the bottom and big thumbnail chippings round the rim, before I had finished.

I lay down on the crumpled bed, too fagged to empty the basin, to put out the light, even to draw something over me, though I was still naked and the night getting colder.

I heard the usual sounds beginning on the stairs and in the other rooms. Then, there was an unexpected, businesslike rapping at my own door.

It was not the sort of house where it was much use first asking who was there. I got to my feet again, this time frozen stiff, and, not having a dressing-gown with me, put on my wet raincoat, as I had to put on something and get the door open, or there would be more knocking, and then complaints, which could be most unpleasant.

It was the chap in the blue sweater; the seaman or showman or whatever he was. Somehow I had known it might be.

I can't have looked up to much, as I stood there shaking, in only the wet raincoat, especially as all the time you could hear people yelling and beating it up generally in the other rooms. And of course I hadn't the slightest idea what line the chap might choose to take.

I needn't have worried. Not at least about that.

"Show pass off all right?" was all he asked; and looking straight into the distance as if he were on his platform, not at anyone or anything in particular, but sounding quite friendly notwithstanding, provided everyone responded in the right kind of way.

"I think so," I replied.

I daresay I didn't appear very cordial, but he seemed not to mind much.

"In that case, could I have the fee? I'm sorry to disturb your beauty sleep, but we're moving on early."

I had not known in what way I should be expected to pay, so had carefully got the ten pounds into a pile, Mr. Edis's fiver and five single pounds of my own, and put it into the corner of a drawer, before I had gone out into the rain to meet Madonna.

I gave it to him.

"Thanks," he said, counting it, and putting it into his trousers pocket. I noticed that even his trousers seemed to be seaman's trousers, now that I could see them close to, with him standing just in front of me. "Everything all right then?"

"I think so," I said again. I was taking care not to commit myself too far in any direction I could think of.

I saw that now he was looking at me, his small eyes deep-sunk.

At that exact moment, there was a wild shriek from one of the floors below. It was about the loudest human cry I had heard until then, even in one of those lodgings.

But the man took no notice.

"All right then," he said.

For some reason, he hesitated a moment, then he held out his hand. I took it. He was very strong, but there was nothing else remarkable about his hand.

"We'll meet again," he said. "Don't worry."

Then he turned away and pressed the black time-switch for the staircase light. I did not stop to watch him go. I was sick and freezing.

And so far, despite what he said, our paths have not recrossed.

For more Tales of the Weird titles
visit the British Library Shop (shop.bl.uk)

We welcome any suggestions, corrections or feedback you may have,
and will aim to respond to all items addressed to the following:

The Editor (Tales of the Weird), British Library Publishing,
The British Library, 96 Euston Road, London NW1 2DB

We also welcome enquiries through our social media accounts, @BL_Publishing.